DEAD ON MY FEET

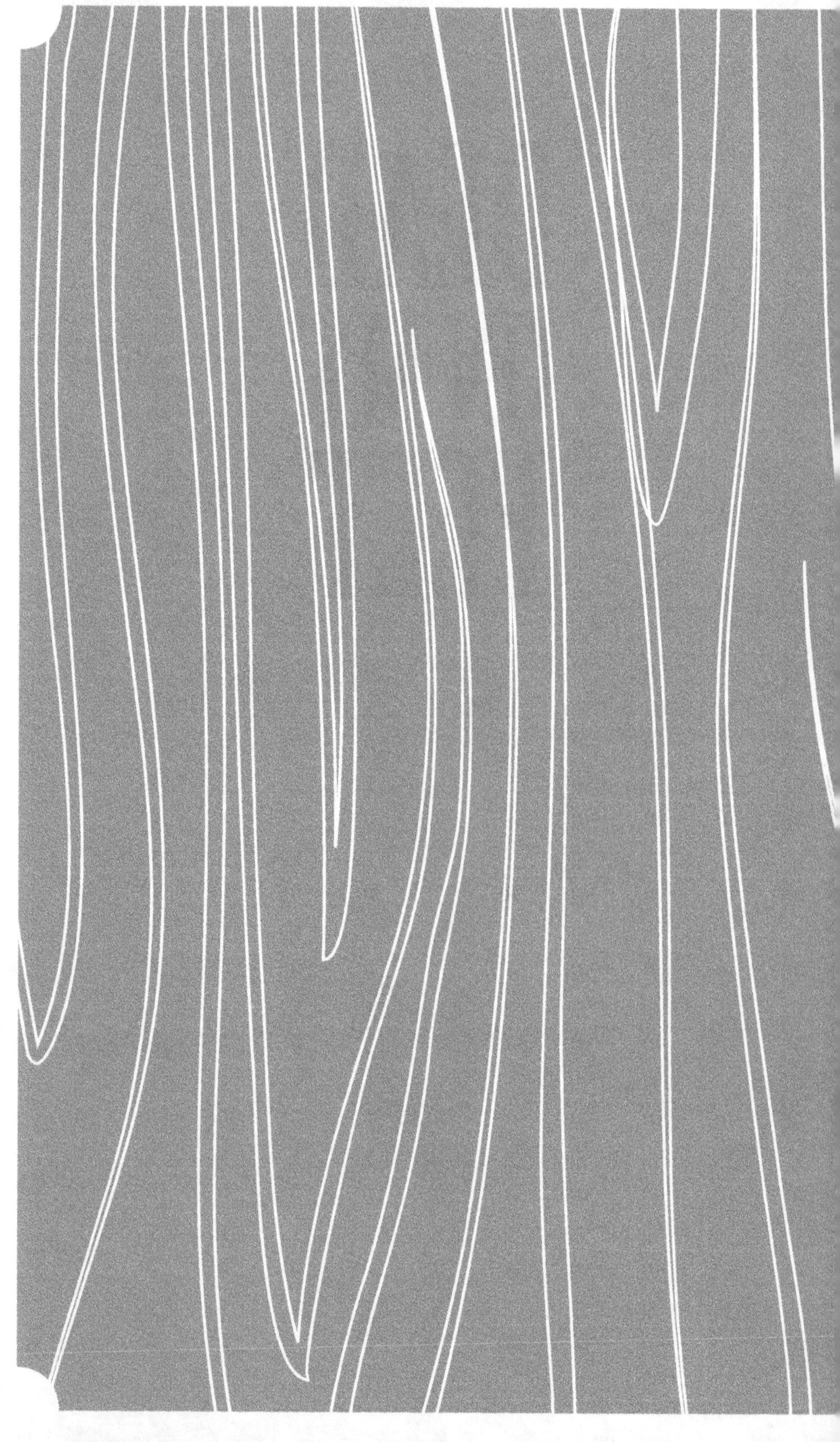

DEAD ON MY FEET

PATRICIA BRODERICK

CamCat Publishing, LLC
Brentwood, Tennessee 37027
camcatpublishing.com

Hardcover ISBN 9780744304800
Paperback ISBN 9780744301724
Large-Print Paperback ISBN 9780744302080
eBook ISBN 9780744302295
Audiobook ISBN 9780744302264

Library of Congress Control Number: 2021931138

Cover and book design by Maryann Appel

5 3 1 2 4

To my mother, Eleanor, with love.

CHAPTER ONE

Milo is dead. Milo has died. Milo's body was found.

How was it possible that I was suffering from writer's block? This had everything—a glamorous, mysterious man, sudden death, the rich and famous. This obit should write itself. I looked at the clock on the wall, ticking out the minutes and seconds to my deadline—*dead* being the operative part of that word.

I looked over at Finn O'Connor. Milo had been on ice for a few hours before Finn got the news from his source at the cop shop. Since then, I had been scrambling through our puny archives and the internet to dredge what I could about the creative genius who had shod the carefully tended feet of the elite, from coast to coast and across the globe.

Simultaneously, I had been trying to nail a few quotes from the swells who populated La Joya society. Fortunately, my pal and society writer, Priscilla Potter, had come to my rescue by mining her contacts and supplying a few gems.

"Nooo!" one of Milo's circle commented. "That's not possible. Only last night, we attended an amazing dinner party on his boat. He couldn't have been more alive!"

Yes, dead people are usually alive before they're, well, dead, but I had to use what Cilla was sending my way. On the other hand, it was interesting that the designer to the stars and shipping magnate was still alive and kicking only a few hours before his untimely demise. But at this point, the cops weren't sharing any details about the shoe mogul's actual cause of death, just that a couple of kayakers had discovered his body in the cove around sunrise.

"Hey, Nell! Howzit going over there? We need a few minutes to coordinate the copy, so what's your ETA?"

Oh, shut up, Finnian.

"Give me fifteen . . ."

"I'll give you ten . . ."

"Who died and made you Ben Bradlee?"

That's when we heard the booming voice of Captain Jack Cobb, the editor in chief of the *Coastal Crier*, who had apparently just woken up from his afternoon snooze on the hammock outside, sleeping off his liquid lunch at O'Toole's Irish pub.

"Will you two shuddup and get back to work? We got lots of folks out there waiting to get the lowdown on the stiff."

Sure, what would the denizens of La Joya, California, the jewel by the sea, do without their community rag? Well, they did have access to the internet and social media, not to mention other local media outlets. But we had lots of awesome ads all geared to keeping the rich folks shelling out their megabucks, so who cared about breaking news? Cap'n Jack was a former commercial fisherman, not a newsman, and lived in his own little bubble. I sure didn't want to be sticking any pins in it today.

By midafternoon, Finn, Cilla, and I were huddled together, trying to make a coherent package, considering we had so little info and so far had been unable to find the kayakers/witnesses. So Finn did his best to set the scene, while Cilla and I handled the background on Milo, an enigmatic figure, and salted the obit with the aforementioned gems, such as they were. Ticktock.

"What about Dame Cavendish?" I asked Cilla, referring to the dotty dowager who was letting me stay in her guesthouse in exchange for ghostwriting her memoir. "Could you reach her?"

Cilla shook her head, making her shiny mane of red curls shimmy.

"Dame C has no cell and she is unlisted. No way will she give out the number for her landline, not even to an influential society scribe like me."

Finn and I exchanged a look, but we let that go.

"Okay, you two, enough with the eye rolls," Cilla growled. "That was said with irony. And besides, why don't *you* try and get her digits?"

Well, I had no time left to drive up scenic La Joya Shores Road, but I made a mental note to wrestle a phone number out of Dame C. "Okay, I'll talk to her tonight for the follow-up, assuming she has anything juicy to convey."

"Are you kidding?" Cilla said. "That dame dishes on everybody in the village, especially around cocktail hour. Haven't you started chatting with her about the memoir yet?"

Actually, it would be easier to try to pin down her squawky parrot, Robespierre. Dame C was continually flitting around her manse and gardens, tending to her aviary and her exotic plants while treating me to stream-of-consciousness declarations about her colorful life. I had yet to start transcribing the notes from the recorder I always kept handy, and I wasn't looking forward to it.

"In a manner of speaking," I said. "But I don't recall hearing her mention Milo."

At that point, Finn butted in and pointed at the clock.

"We done here, ladies?"

We were. It was time to put this baby to bed.

When I arrived in tony La Joya six months ago, at Cilla's invitation, I had already zigged and zagged my way through a hodgepodge of media outlets, broadcast and print, pushing for my big break. While I was tucked away in the basement of a cable TV station in Kansas, tracking twisters and putting out alerts . . . "Get thee to your storm cellars! Now!" . . . an epiphany occurred.

Cilla to the rescue. She and I had attended the University of New Hampshire and coedited the student newspaper with dreams of winning the Pulitzer before we turned thirty. That ship had sailed by a few years. Cilla was always more politically astute in handling her career and, unlike me, kept her head down and her opinions to herself. This didn't land her at *The*

New York Times, but she was more than content carving out a nice little niche for herself, ingratiating herself into La Joya society and the party circuit. Life was good. So, when I told her that I desperately needed to get out of Kansas, she offered me this gig on the *Crier*, a creaky shopper that had taken over a vacated Jack in the Box, complete with the lingering scent of fried onions and rancid oil.

So I packed up my cats, Prudence and Patience, and the rest of my meager stuff in my 2003 Mustang and hit the yellow-brick road, otherwise known as I-70, for a rollicking ride for miles and miles, my mewling kitties stuck in their carriers, in a sweltering summer with a busted air-conditioner. With a few stays at Motel 6s, I managed to survive the twenty-three-hour trek with my sanity. My cats have never been sane.

I was so eager to take this job that it didn't occur to me to ask Cilla about housing, a mistake, given I was moving to one of the most expensive seaside enclaves on the West Coast. As she is allergic to cats and has an affinity for rich guys, young and old, sharing an apartment was not an option. But she had that all figured out. That's how I met Dame C, a former chorus girl who turned B-movie femme fatale a lot of years ago. Word has it that she started out as a butcher's daughter from Queens. But she had married well, apparently more than once, and reinvented herself as the grand dame of La Joya. She lived in a mansion by the sea and just happened to have a granny flat available.

"Are you kidding?" I had told Cilla. "I can't afford an outhouse in La Joya on my salary."

She just rolled her eyes, telling me, "It's not an outhouse, it's a granny flat outside her house, and I brokered a deal for you. All you have to do is help her write her memoir and the place is "yours."

Sounded okay. But as the butler ushered me into the main house, it was like walking into a Hitchcock movie. The living room was an aviary where birds of every species perched, cooing and cackling and pooping.

Then . . . gaaaa! This feathered falcon of fury swooped down, wings thrashing, and I shrieked, covered my head with my arms, and ducked for cover.

When I looked up, there was Dame Cavendish, descending the spiral staircase, seemingly oblivious to my terror. She was decked out in a vivid green gown trimmed with feathers and was sporting a feather boa, her head crowned with what resembled a delicately sculptured miniature bird cage.

She swept her arm above her head, and the birdies were silenced. Impressive. Gliding over to me, and checking me out from head to foot, she frowned.

"Miss Bly, Priscilla informs me that you are a cat person." She grimaced as though I was actually a rat person. "I'm afraid that won't do. If you wish to stay here, you will have to dispose of the felines."

Dispose of? Like put them in a sack and weigh them down with stones? But I'm not one to miss an opportunity, so I gave it my best shot.

"Oh, you don't have to worry about Patience and Prudence, Dame Cavendish. You see, both of my felines are strict vegans. They'd never touch a mouse, let alone a bird."

I offered her my most sincere smile.

She considered this and nodded. "Well, that's different and most commendable."

Little did she know that my kitties would consider her aviary an all-you-can-eat buffet. Dame C then turned on her heel, which was, surprisingly, shod in a sensible-looking gardening shoe, as was the other heel.

"Follow me and I'll show you to your new quarters."

On our way to the outhouse, I mean the granny flat, she stopped and turned to me.

"Is Nellie Bly a pen name?" Before letting me answer, she added, "You must be aware that Nellie Bly is the nom de plume of a nineteenth-century journalist . . . a muckraker?"

Sob sister was a popular term for female journalists back then, but I didn't correct her.

"I come by the name honestly, Dame Cavendish. Bly is my mother's birth name. She's a journalist herself, and hoped I'd follow in her footsteps. Hence the name Nellie." I didn't mention that my mother chased down real stories all over the world, while I merely . . . dabbled. "She considered her a fine role model for me."

Back at the office, we filed the story and I headed home, that is, to Dame C's estate. I was eager to hear her thoughts on Milo and her reaction to his untimely demise.

I wasn't even certain my landlady had heard about Milo. From what I have been able to determine, she has no cable, only a small fifties-era TV set tucked away in a back room and a matching radio, circa midcentury. Maybe earlier. Whether they worked or not, who knew? Her landline was one of those outsized phones, ornate and lacquered white, the sort that Bette Davis or Joan Crawford would scream into hysterically.

She also lived up a twisty, turny road, overlooking the sea and isolated. It's not as though a neighbor could pop over anytime to chat about what's new in the village, as the hub of La Joya was known as. She did receive the daily paper along with the *Crier*, but her copies wouldn't arrive until tomorrow. Still, as Cilla informed me, Dame C always seemed to have an endless stream of gossip, so she had a pipeline somewhere. Maybe a ham radio?

Well, I was about to find out and wasn't crazy about being the bearer of bad news if it turned out that Milo had been a close friend.

I had taken to calling my new home Birdland, as those squawky seed bags were everywhere. Quigley, a stoic older gentleman with steel-gray hair and a military bearing who was employed as her butler, retainer, and aide-de-camp, seemed oblivious to the din. I rapped the ornate bronze knocker carved in the shape of some winged creature, and he answered.

"Hi, Quigley." I saluted, only because he inspired that kind of greeting. "Is she in?"

He nodded and waved me in. As usual, I found myself ducking and weaving to avoid her feathered friends as they swooped and shrieked. The poop smells were not a treat either, and I avoided this place as much as possible.

"Madam is in her craft room, putting the finishing touches on a feeder for the garden." He gave me a sharp look and added, "You know that she does not like to be disturbed while she is working."

Quigley's voice was deep and sonorous, reminding me of one of those old-time radio announcers . . . "Who knows? The Shadow knows!"

"I understand, but a body's been found down in the cove, and I need to chat with Dame C about it. I think she'd want to know, because it will be all over the news tomorrow."

Quigley sighed and told me to head over to the granny flat and she'd join me there if she had the time. Dame C seemed to prefer tête-à-têtes there, probably because she got a tad cranky seeing me diving under furniture to fend off her demon birds.

I trekked across the cobblestones that cut through an emerald-green lawn and sloped down to my wee cozy cottage. From the outside it looked like a gingerbread house, and inside that theme continued with a tasteful collection of quaint furnishings. It was the sort of place a family of gnomes would call home, and there was not one single image of a feathered fiend. I didn't know whether this pleased or dismayed my kitties, who were now snoozing in matching window boxes between the kitchen and living area. My sleeping quarters were in a loft up a short flight of stairs.

I had just finished changing out of my work togs into a T-shirt and clam diggers when I heard the rap on my door, and there stood Dame Cavendish, looking regal despite being dressed in paint-splattered overalls and a matching hat, apparently no longer feeling the need to put on airs for the likes of me. She was holding a martini in each hand. Before I could greet her, she handed me a drink and brushed past me, giving my dozing cats the stink eye.

"Milo is dead," she informed me, settling down on the comfy chair and taking a sip of her drink. "I assume you know this, Nellie?"

So much for breaking news.

"How did you find out so fast?"

She waved this off, took another sip, and said, "I have my sources. Now, tell me what you know."

I sat down on the settee and took a generous gulp of the martini, not a beverage I normally imbibe, but what the heck. It had been a long day.

"We spent the afternoon pulling the story together," I said, nibbling on an olive. "The cops didn't share much with us, just that a couple of kayakers found Milo's body in the cove and they didn't say if it was an accident or—"

"His feet."

I almost choked on the olive. "His feet?"

"Milo's feet were encased in very expensive hand-tooled leather boots, trimmed with the hide of an alligator," she said, and all I could do was sputter.

"Boots . . ."

"Stuffed with cement—what do they call it in those gangster movies I used to make? Cement shoes, that's it. Anyway, he didn't sink. Apparently, he got caught up in some flotsam and jetsam and ended up on a sandbar with his head exposed above the water."

My head was swimming, trying to process all of this. Maybe it was the martini, which tasted like a double.

"Well, I guess that rules out Milo falling out of his yacht. I was told that he was hosting a party last night, so he must have been murdered after everyone left. John Jeffers went on and on about how alive Milo was . . ."

Dame C put forth a very loud and wet raspberry. "John Jeffers is a fool. In any event, Milo had his enemies, you know, Nellie."

My antennae went up.

"The kind that would send him to sleep with the fishes? Well, I guess dead men tell no tales."

Dame C took another slug. "Oh, Milo won't be telling any more tales, dear. It would be difficult when one has a hunk of ivory jammed down one's throat."

CHAPTER TWO

My head was spinning even faster, so I put the martini glass down and took a deep breath.

"A hunk of ivory—down his throat—"

Dame C cut me off and stood. "Must I repeat myself? And why aren't you taking notes?"

"You want to be quoted for my story?"

She lifted her hands to the heavens and bellowed, "Of course not! Why would I give up these juicy tidbits? You will be recording this for my memoir."

Moving into the granny flat had seemed like a perfect alternative to bunking down in my Mustang with two cranky cats. Who knew I'd be pitting Dame C's largesse against my duty to report the news?

"Dame C—"

"Cate, with a C, and *never* Cat!" Again she turned her death stare on my snoozing kitties. "You will be chronicling my fascinating life . . . much as James Boswell did for Samuel Johnson . . . so we will need to bond. Therefore, you may call me—"

"Sam?"

I regretted that, even as it escaped my lips.

"Must I keep repeating myself, Nellie?" She sighed, sat, and took another swallow. "You may call me Cate, but only in private. Otherwise, I will remain Dame Cavendish. Understood?"

I shrugged. "Works for me. But I am working on a follow-up to Milo's . . . well, murder. That is my day job, Cate."

"By the time your little sheet comes out next week, the story of his grisly demise will be all over the news, so my quotes will mean nothing."

"But you implied that Milo was a tad shady . . ."

"A tad? Ha! That's an understatement." She stood again, with the agility of a woman half her age. "Come up to the house with me and I'll share a few nuggets." Dame C, aka Cate, strode to the door, then turned and glared at me. "And for goodness sake, bring a tape recorder or a notebook or whatever modern contraptions you people use nowadays."

My landlady, or land dame as it were, had required me to sign a nondisclosure agreement prohibiting me from breathing a word about her confidences to anyone until the memoir was signed, sealed, and delivered to the publisher and she was making the rounds of the talk shows. Yes, she had a publishing contract with a major imprint, and no, I would not be receiving an "as told to Nellie Bly" credit. The glory, such as it was, would be hers alone. But given that her tidbits and nuggets would no doubt be salacious and possibly libelous, I'd just as soon stay below the radar.

I fished my microrecorder out of my handbag, just as Prudence and Patience, my short-haired progeny, stirred and meowed and started to sidle to their feeding bowls in the kitchen.

Cats can be a pain, but at least I don't have to walk them twice a day and pick up their poop. Meanwhile, Cate, with a C, folded her arms and tapped her toe as I opened a can of pussy paté and filled their bowls. When I straightened, Dame C plucked the can out of my hand and read the label, frowning.

"I thought you said that your cats were vegan?" She shoved the can a few inches from my face. "It says 'contains meat by-products.'"

Oops.

"Maybe I misspoke, uh, Cate, but I really needed this place, and they're house cats, so you don't really have to worry about Pru and Pat breaching your aviary."

She slammed the can on the counter, causing the cats to skitter, and stormed out of the house, gesturing at me to follow.

Back to Birdland.

Dame C led me up a spiral staircase, tossing her painter's cap over the bannister, narrowly missing the macaw, or whatever bird it was, and stirring up a new round of squawking and furious flapping, feathers flying hither and thither.

On the second floor, she strode down the hall and stopped at one of the rooms. At least, I thought it was a room until she led me inside. There before me was a vast array of shoes—

in every color, fabric, and style, arranged on floor-to-ceiling shelves.

Dame C waved, telling me, "There are many more, of course, in other rooms, but this should give you a feel for my collection."

I strolled through the giant walk-in closet, turned on the recorder, and started narrating what lay before me.

"These are Milo's creations?"

"This is the Milo room, Nellie. I have other rooms devoted to various designers—shoes, bags, dresses, jewels and the like, but these are his. Cost me a bloody fortune."

I noted the British affectation. Maybe the queen had knighted her, or whatever they do when they bestow one of those dame titles.

"You know, I haven't known you all that long, Cate, but I've only seen you wearing sensible shoes, not stuff like this."

She snorted.

"Indeed. Sensible. And that's because Milo destroyed my feet—pair after painful pair, year after year, at soiree after soiree. He deserved to die for that alone, and I'm not his only victim. He's made the podiatrists wealthy. They adore him."

I was trying to process this last bit, making sure the tape was still rolling.

"Are you implying that Milo was killed by a woman with sore feet?"

Dame C reached out and grabbed a diamond-and-sapphire-encrusted stiletto from the shelf and shook it at me.

"No, dear, I very much doubt that Milo met his end by inflicting La Joya matrons with bunions and hammertoes."

"What, then?"

She stroked the stiletto and lowered her voice, whispering into the tape recorder.

"Follow the ivory. And remember, Nellie, an elephant never forgets."

With that, Dame C replaced the stiletto on the shelf and walked out of the closet, leaving me to trail behind sputtering, "Elephants? What elephants?"

But she was halfway down the stairs, waving me off.

"That's enough for tonight, Nellie, dear. I've got to tend to my flock. See yourself out." She turned and started walking away.

"Dame Cav—uh, Cate, any chance you could give me your number?"

She whirled around, glaring at me as if I'd asked her for the nuclear codes.

"I give that out to nobody, Nellie. Why do you think it's unlisted?" She turned away, but I persisted.

"Wouldn't Johnson give Boswell his phone number?"

Did they even have phones back then? She faced me again and let out a dramatic sigh.

"Oh, very well," she said, while drawing her arm up and pointing a fiery red-enamel-tipped finger at me. "But you must guard it with your life."

She then pointed down at my still-whirring recorder. "Turn that thing off." As she started enumerating her phone number to me, I grabbed my pen and notebook. "No notes!" she hissed. "I will recite the number and you will memorize it, understand?"

"How about I just write it down and then swallow the paper?"

She was not amused.

Then she disappeared into the shadows. The second I heard the click of a door closing, I scribbled down the number before my memory faded.

It was dark in the living room and as smelly as ever, but the birds seemed becalmed, or asleep. I walked softly through the hall and out the back door, carefully navigating down the cobblestone path to my place, all the while trying to figure out what Dame Samuel Johnson was talking about.

CHAPTER THREE

It was sunset. Finn had called one of his sources, Detective Wendy Nakamura, to join us at "Starbucks by the Sea," which I much preferred to the "Starbucks by the Stalks" I had frequented during my Kansas gig. Sitting on the deck, we watched as the now off-duty detective stowed her surfboard in her SUV and waved to us, flashing the one-minute sign. Clad in a wetsuit, she disappeared into a changing room off the boardwalk, quickly emerged dressed in jeans and a tank top, and strolled over to us as gracefully as a panther.

"Here goes nothing, Finnian," I whispered, but he just shrugged and slurped his grande mocha Frappuccino.

"We'll see, Nell," he said, watching her approach. "She's cool."

Finn was a good-looking guy, in a film noirish short of way, equal parts Alan Ladd and Robert Mitchum with a little Bogie thrown in. He would have been at home in a fedora with his press card sticking up. I had never met the detective, but she cut a fine figure, toned and lithe, with sleek black hair. Was I jealous?

Maybe a little.

She dumped her shoulder bag on the ground, took a seat, raised the drink that Finn had ordered for her and removed the lid, releasing the steam.

"You like chai tea, right, Wendy?" Finn said. "Hope it didn't get cold."

"Nah," she said, blowing on the beverage. "By tomorrow, it will be cool enough to actually drink.

Finn sighed and stood up.

"I'll grab a cup of ice. You ladies get acquainted."

Detective Nakamura peered at me through the rising steam and I felt like raising my hands and proclaiming, "Okay, you got me! I did it!" Instead, I do what I always do when snared in an awkward silence. I babbled.

"So you're a surfer? Out there catching waves. But isn't this feeding time for those sharks? All those seals and sea lions perched on the rocks—a real buffet, right?" I caught my breath and slurped my grande black tea lemonade.

"I get out here when I can, but not often enough," Wendy said, still blowing on the hot chai. "Sunrise, sunset, whatever. I don't worry about that. I get in my zone. What about you?"

"Surfing? Nope. I don't catch any waves. I'm more worried about the waves catching me."

More gazing through the steam. Why was I feeling guilty?

"Finn said you came here from Kansas. Is that why you're sea shy?"

Sea shy?

"No, Kansas was my last pit stop. Actually, I grew up in New Hampshire and I loved going to the beach and jumping into the waves. Until, one day, when I was about eight, I got caught in a riptide. I was scared to death. My mother ran into the water and a lifeguard grabbed me and pulled me out. I still love the beach, but I'm more of a wader now."

Wendy took a tentative sip and winced, probably wondering why Finn was taking so long with her ice. Knowing him he was working the tables and chatting up the locals for newsy bits.

"You know what they say, Nellie. Confront your fears. You're missing out."

I just met this woman and she was lecturing me? Fortunately, before I said anything I'd regret, Wendy changed the subject.

"So you work with Finn at the *Crier.*"

"Yup, I'm on the dead beat."

Okay, probably not the smartest thing to say to a police detective, but she just smiled. "So you write the obits?"

Well, that hadn't been the original plan, but neither was being a weather girl in Kansas. I launched into defensive mode: "Well, in this town, writing obits is more glam than you'd think, Wendy, and they rake in buckets of bucks for the paper, so I spend a lot of time polishing these rags-to-riches stories. Fascinating stuff, some of them. It's really an art form, telling their stories."

Wendy took another sip and gave me a look. "Warts and all, Nellie?"

Before I had a chance to answer, Finn sauntered over, a cup of ice in hand, and plunked it down on the table. His ever-present reporter's notebook was tucked into the back pocket of his jeans, and he pulled it out before he sat down. He then fished a pen out of another pocket, and I knew that Finn had shifted into his "let's get down to business" mode.

Wendy must have sensed this too, as she carefully dropped ice cubes into her cup. "You're planning to take notes, Finn? I told you, whatever I tell you is on deep background. No notes. Agreed?"

Finn didn't look happy, but he shoved the pen and notebook to the side. "Fine, Wendy, for now. But this story is breaking, and we need to be ahead of the wave, you get that, right?"

She shrugged. I didn't know the details, but I suspected that the two of them, over time, had developed a mutually beneficial quid pro quo arrangement. Why she decided to throw in with a community weekly and not the big guns, I had no idea. On the other hand, the *Crier* was in the hub of the rich and famous, so we might be worth it. In the case of the late Milo, I figured that was true.

"Okay, then, let me turn the program over to Nellie and she'll share what she knows about Milo from a well-connected source." Finn turned to me. "I told her about that piece of ivory, but that's all."

I guess that was the lure to get Wendy's attention.

Without naming Dame C, I regaled Wendy with the few nuggets that I'd compiled in my notebook, which I had retrieved from my bag. Since I didn't want to identify Cate, I couldn't play my recording, especially after I'd signed the

NDA. I had to tread carefully between my role as Dame C's Boswell and my feverish desire for a scoop that could get me off obits and back with the majors. Okay, I had never actually made it to the majors, but I wasn't done trying.

When I finished, we were all quiet and Wendy seemed to be digesting all of this and wondering how much she could share without getting busted down to meter maid. I figured her long-term goal was becoming chief of detectives. We were all on thin ice.

"Here's the deal," she said, looking at us in turn with that steely gaze of hers. "I can't confirm or deny what your source said to you, Nellie, but I will tell you, in general terms, the significance of a hypothetical tusk that may or may not have been lodged in the deceased's throat."

We waited.

Wendy fished out a folder from her bag and put it on the table in front of her. "About forty thousand elephants, give or take, are killed every year for their tusks, and that's very bad news for conservationists, not to mention the elephants. According to a recent NPR report, that leaves about four hundred thousand pachyderms in Africa. Now, that may sound like a lot, but it's not. That's a tenth of the population wiped out in one year."

Finn and I exchanged a look and he asked, "Are you saying that Milo, the shoe mogul, was killed because he had something to do with killing elephants? Was he smuggling contraband?"

Wendy didn't get her gold shield for being stupid. She leaned forward. "Did I say anything about Milo and smuggling? No, Finn, I am merely educating you on the significance of a hypothetical tusk. Shall I continue?"

Looking sheepish, Finn shrugged and sipped his Frappuccino, better to keep his mouth shut.

"Anyway, the cartels that run the ivory trade know every trick in the book to stay below the radar," Wendy said, turning a page in the folder. "They use fake documents and hide the ivory with the legitimate products being shipped."

Always quick in putting two and two together, I remembered that Milo was a shipping magnate as well. Wendy took a sip of her chai tea and continued.

"This can involve a variety of ports before the booty gets to its final destination. Sometimes they separate the two tusks from an elephant and ship them at different times, and that makes them harder to track. When authorities do make busts, it's usually the small fry that get caught. It's been hard to nail the big fish, so the beat goes on. Asia is the big market, but it's a problem around the globe, including the US." Wendy looked up from her notes. "The good news is, a few years back, a biologist found a way to use the DNA in the tusks to find out where the elephants lived. Now, they're trying to use the science to track how the ivory is moved to its final stop."

Wendy closed the folder and returned it to her bag.

Finn tried again. "Okay, so, hypothetically, if, say, a sliver of ivory was shoved down Milo's throat, that might indicate that he had pissed off the cartel, right? Maybe double-dealing or—how about this? Milo got turned and was snitching."

"Well, Finn, anything is possible—hypothetically speaking."

"What if a conservationist is sending a message?" I wondered out loud. "Let the elephants live or else . . ."

Wendy turned to me. "Take my advice, Nellie. No wild accusations. Be cool until we get more evidence. I'm not the lead on this, but I am involved in the investigation. I can't promise you anything, but I'll give you what I can when I can. Agreed?"

Before I could answer, Finn said, "When will that be, Wendy? We're up against not only the local and national stations, cable and the daily, the goddamned internet and social media, and we don't even have an online edition yet, because our fearless leader is a freaking dinosaur."

Wendy held up her hand like a traffic cop.

"I know all that, Finn, but I can't risk my job, and right now, all Nellie has are rumors, so give us a day or two, and I should have something for you. Okay?"

Finn and I again exchanged looks and then he nodded. "Fine, Wendy, but I want to break this story. Nell has a good source; a source that promised more goodies tomorrow."

Wendy stood up, hoisted her bag over her shoulder, picked up her cup, and said, over her shoulder, as she strode away, "All for one and one for all."

I cocked an eyebrow. "I'm getting goodies tomorrow?" I asked Finn the moment Wendy was out of earshot.

He lifted his empty cup and hurled it into a nearby trash can. "All you have to do, Nell, is convince Dame Cavendish that if she helps break the case, her memoir will soon be a major motion picture, and she will be immortalized. Play on her ego. That should work, right?"

Hmmm. What would Boswell do?

CHAPTER FOUR

"What fascinated me most about Milo was his organ," Dame C told me during an early-evening session. Cate, martini in hand, had commandeered the comfy chair, leaving me with the settee.

The tape recorder was running, but I had learned from experience not to trust anything that plugs in or has batteries, so I also was taking notes. I wrote ORGAN in caps, accompanied by a few question marks.

"He had an organ?" I had declined the martini in favor of an iced tea to keep my wits sharp, but I was having second thoughts. "Milo was a musician?"

Cate stared at me and I felt a chill, even though it was a balmy night.

"Naturally, Milo had an organ, a very unusual one, Nellie. It was shaped like a corkscrew. I must say, he was a virtuoso with it, one of his only saving graces."

I wrote VIRTUOSO and more question marks.

"Uh, are we talking about a pipe organ?"

Dame C was nibbling on an olive, which I was sure she was about to hurl in my direction.

"Nellie, I do wish you'd try to keep pace with me. No, I'm not talking about a pipe organ. Do I have to spell it out?"

Well, the cats were snoozing up in the loft, but I doubt they'd be shocked. As for me, this revelation opened a whole new line of inquiry—not only for the memoir, but for Wendy's investigation and the scoop that Finn and I hoped to land.

"You and Milo were lovers?"

Cate was dressed in a canary-yellow hostess gown and matching slippers, her long legs tucked under her. She made a face.

"Love, my dear, had nothing to do with it. It was pure animal lust and it was a long time ago, somewhere between my third and fourth husbands, if I recall correctly."

Samuel "Cate" Johnson was not given to a chronological approach to her memoir. She used stream of consciousness, bouncing from midlife to her teen years, then back to her forties, then to one wacky recollection of being in her mother's womb. Oddly, she wouldn't tell me her age and, looking at her, it was hard to tell.

She'd had a lot of work done—good work too, not like those grotesque pictures you see in the tabloids. So, who knew? She could have been seventy or one hundred. What I had observed was an underlying athleticism, reminding me of Kate with a K, Miss Hepburn. Anyway, Cate with a C was all over the place and this did not make my job any easier.

"Look, Cate, I need to be straight with you. Finn and I are trying to figure out the motive for Milo's murder, and the cops won't even tell us if he was murdered. You told me that he was dumped in the cove wearing a set of cement designer shoes, accessorized by a chunk of elephant tusk stuck in his craw, right?"

She frowned and waved her toothpick at me. "That was off-the-record, Nellie. It's up to you and that dashing reporter to dig up the dirt, and believe me, there is plenty to be dug."

Play to her ego, that was Finn's advice.

"Fine, then feed me more tidbits. If you, Finn, and I can crack this case, think of the publicity you'll get. Your memoir will fly off the shelves, there will be long lines waiting for you to sign your books—and then, the brass ring—the movie, starring Dame Helen Mirren!"

I watched as Cate's green eyes widened and then narrowed.

"That won't do, Nellie." My heart sank, but then she added, "Helena Bonham Carter. I will accept nothing less."

"It's a deal!" I was on a roll. "So, if you two were getting it on, you must have noticed something a little sketchy about his business? Maybe there was some pillow talk? Shadowy figures, people lurking around that didn't fit his social circles?"

She sipped her martini. "Such as?"

Cate was back to being coy, and I knew that she wasn't going to make this easy.

It was a game for her.

"Such as a murderous cartel smuggling elephant tusks and God knows what else into La Joya, via Milo's ships."

Cate nearly dumped her martini as she sat straight up, and I noticed her hand trembling. "Who told you that?"

"What, that he had an import/export business? It came up in my res—"

"No, that he was involved with a smuggling ring, Nellie. Do keep up!"

"Oh, well, Finn and I met with a detective he kn—"

"You didn't mention my name?"

"No, of course not, and the detective didn't—"

"This detective, she suspects Milo smuggled ivory?"

"How did you know it's a woman?"

Dame C's stare told me she wouldn't answer that one, so I just continued. "She didn't exactly say that she suspected Milo of smuggling, but she did brief us on the smuggling that's going on around the world, including in the US, if not La Joya. She's willing to share what she knows, but we have to give her something in return. If you know anything about Milo's business or his partners, whatever, we might be able to solve this—you, me, and Finn. A scoop for Finn and me, a movie for you, and a big promotion for Detective Nakamura. What do you say?"

Cate thought about this and took a bigger sip of her drink. "And what happens to me, Nellie? Will they find me floating in the cove with a canary stuffed down my throat?"

Well, she probably wouldn't be floating, not with those cement slippers she'd be wearing, but I didn't tell her that. She made a good point.

"So he was part of a smuggling ring, indeed?" I knew she wasn't going to answer this one either, but a girl had to try. " Cate, if you're afraid, why did you tell me about the tusk in the first place? I mean, the news would have come out soon enough."

Cate sighed and put her glass down.

"I suppose that I was a bit bored and wanted to impress you, I don't know. It didn't seem like a big deal at the time, but now that you're talking about cartels and smuggling—well, it's become so real now."

For a brief moment the veil had dropped, and I could see the vulnerability that Dame C tried so hard to mask. But then she was back to her old self, no doubt dusting off the B-movie chops that had rescued her from the chorus line.

"Please, shut off that recorder," Cate commanded. "I want you to understand that I am not afraid of them—any of them."

Them? I swallowed hard, shut the recorder off, and put my pen down. Maybe we were entering Wendy's world of deep background.

"Them?" I prompted. "Who?"

Cate didn't answer right away; she just kept sliding the remaining olive back and forth along the toothpick. I waited.

"Milo had his dark side, you know."

"No, Cate, I didn't know. I never met him. I don't even know his last name. Does anyone?"

She waved her toothpick at me dismissively. "He's had many over the years, most of them fake, I'm sure, and I never believed a word he said to me. Milo was a genius at reinventing himself, but I only got to personally experience his metamorphosis from a roué to a raconteur and darling of the jet set way back when. It was all very heady and glamorous, and I was young and naïve. But I have no regrets."

I waited. She twiddled.

"I wouldn't dare judge you, Cate." Truer words were never spoken. "I just want to figure out what happened to Milo. If he was mixed up with cartels, other people in his circle could be in danger too. If you know something—"

Then she shut down. I was pushing too hard.

Rising gracefully, she tossed the toothpick into her now empty martini glass and headed for the door.

"That's all for tonight, Nellie," she said as she opened the door. "I'll sleep on this and we'll chat another time. Good night."

Exit stage left, fade to black.

CHAPTER FIVE

Social media was having a field day speculating about Milo's mysterious demise. The mainstream media had mostly stuck to the facts they had, saying that the designer had died under suspicious circumstances and details would be forthcoming pending an autopsy. But the popular websites had been sharing tantalizing tidbits, absent of any credible sources.

Some said a drunken Milo had fallen overboard following his glittering yacht party, others that he had jumped over the rail in a fit of despair, and yet others claimed that perhaps a jealous husband might have given old Milo a little push. But none of them had mentioned anything about a chunk of ivory shoved down Milo's throat, or the fact that he had been fitted with a pair of cement designer booties. That gave our gang a little time to poke around, and we had at least two advantages over everyone else: Dame C and Detective Nakamura. At least for now.

Then Cilla, my *Crier* colleague and lifelong buddy, came up with a plan. From experience, I knew this would be either brilliant or bonkers.

"Mitzi and Milt Morrison are hosting a fundraiser for Save the Shore, supposedly a drive to clean up the beach, but, if you want my opinion, it's really a slush fund to pay for their various NIMBY crusades. But you didn't hear that from me, Nellie."

With Cilla, I knew that I had to be patient and that she'd eventually get to the point. On this day, we were taking a break out back on the deck of the *Crier* and sharing a jar of sun tea she had brewed.

A few feet away, tucked into his hammock hung between two aging palm trees, Cap'n Jack was sleeping off his lunch, his snores punctuating our conversation.

"Anyway, I'll be attending, of course, but you can bet that this not-in-my-backyard crowd will have a lot more on their minds then shoveling sand. Milo will be the topic du jour."

I took a sip and watched as Cilla poured herself another glass. I was getting antsy, and in a few minutes I had to return to the dead beat.

"You're burying the lede, Cill. What does this have to do with me?"

She made a face, the one that said, "I'm getting there."

"What if you and Finn crash the party?" she said finally.

"Crash?"

"Yeah, you know, go undercover—pretend that you're part of the waitstaff. You carry those little trays of canapes and Finn hands out the bubbly. No one pays you any attention, so you get to sop up all the gossip—about Milo. Brilliant, am I right?"

Where to start.

"First of all, how are we supposed to infiltrate the help? I'm assuming the caterers know who they hired? Supplied them with uniforms, stuff like that?"

She flapped her hand. "They'll be too busy tending to the caviar, crudités, and crustaceans to notice who's doing the actual serving as long as everyone's getting fed and watered. As for the uniforms, they always keep a few spares tucked away in the kitchen. No problem."

"How do you know all this, Cilla?"

She gave me her megawatt grin. "I know 'cause that's how I got this gig, Nellie. Cap'n Jack told me I'd get the society slot if I delivered a big juicy scoop. You know, I've always been resourceful, so I sprang into action, found a bash to crash, slipped in, and—voilà!—before anyone even noticed, I was suited up and working the crowd. You wouldn't believe the dirt they dished. Nobody paid any attention to me. Of course, I had to drab down, not easy for me to do. But it was worth it."

None of this should have surprised me, knowing Cilla, who used to supplement her allowance by liberating items from her favorite stores. She never got caught.

"So, you delivered a nice, big juicy scoop to Jack and got the job?"

Cilla frowned. "Well, as it turned out, Jack didn't really care anything about who was getting a face-lift or who was insider trading. He likes to keep the society folks happy so they buy ads and pay for those obits. But he admired my pluck—that's the word he used: *pluck*. Also, I was able to smuggle out a basket of gourmet goodies and some primo booze, so Cap'n Jack was happy as a clam."

I stared into my sun tea as though it would infuse me with wisdom, but no such luck. "Getting back to your plan, Cill, why are you so sure that nobody at the party would recognize us?"

She gave me a pitiful look. How could I be so dense?

"No offense, Nellie, but you're not on TV anymore and that was back East. A small market too. The obits don't carry a byline or your photo, unlike "Partying with Priscilla." Not to brag about my column. It's not like you make the rounds of mortuaries and crematoriums to do your job, so even those rich undertakers wouldn't notice you."

Point taken.

"Okay, that's true for me, but what about Finn? He covers the town council meetings, which are presided over by the very same rich dudes and dames that attend those parties. And, as you well know, Finn has been a thorn in their patrician posteriors since he arrived in town. Are you telling me that he could stroll into the kitchen, swipe a uniform and parade around with a tray full of champagne flutes and not be recognized? Is he supposed to don a Groucho Marx disguise?"

Cilla thought about that, staring into her glass, but her sun tea didn't seem to offer any more enlightenment than mine. Then she brightened and I was almost certain that a virtual lightbulb had switched on.

"How about this then? Finn loves to gamble. Five-card stud, Texas Hold 'em, strip poker, not so sure. Anyway, most of these soirees have a game going on in some smoke-filled room—usually the man cave—you know, with lots of leather furniture, and framed fish and dead things with antlers. That would be his ticket. Imagine what he might hear at one of those tables."

Deep breath.

"Why would they invite Finn? He's been a pain—"

Eye roll.

"I know, I know, in their patrician posteriors. That's the point, Nellie. Don't you see? They hate Finn, so they would love to fleece him and send him home naked in a barrel." Cilla paused and seemed to be conjuring this image.

"But if Finn has a reputation as a card sharp—"

"Did I say that, Nellie? What I said was, Finn loves to play poker, but he plays it with his pals at the pub, including Cap'n Jack. Those guys and gals are fishermen and waitresses and landscapers—you know, the help. So, the society folks wouldn't be wise to how well Finn plays."

"But, Cill, you'd still have to get him invited, right?"

Her violet eyes sparkled.

"No problem there. Milt, who's hosting this NIMBY party with Mitzi, is kind of sweet on me." She shrugged as if to say, "Need I even say?" No, she needn't say. "He's also a serious gambler."

Cilla leaned in and lowered her voice. "I know all about that, the debts, the collectors coming around. Scary stuff. No broken kneecaps that I know of, but still. Anyway, all I've got to do is ring him up and say, 'Hi, Milty, it's Cilla. A favor? Could my pal, Finn O'Connor, come to the party and play a few hands with you and the gang?'"

She had placed her cell phone up to her ear to paint the picture. She even paused, as though she were waiting for Milty's response.

"He can? Oh, you are the best!" Another pause. "I should tell you, Milty, poor Finn loves to play, but he's really not very good and has lost a pile. I hate to encourage him, but, you know, he asked me to put in a word. How could I say no?"

Cilla then signed off and placed her cell on the table.

"You see, Nellie, easy peasy. He's in like Finn."

I vaguely remembered that the phrase was "in like Flynn" and had something to do with an old Hollywood scandal involving swashbuckler Errol Flynn. My mother was a vintage film buff and she stuffed my young head with lots of movie trivia.

Not always helpful.

"And why would these high rollers be dishing the dirt in front of Finn, even if he's not wearing a fedora with a press card tucked in the band? They know he's a reporter."

Cilla gave me another eye roll. "Do you know how hammered those guys get? Their man cave should have bourbon stalactites hanging from the ceiling. I don't know how they keep their cards straight."

"And you know this how?"

Cilla gave me another shrug. "I might have sat in on a hand or two."

I started to wonder how much she knew about strip poker. And how much I knew about my friend. But I let both pass.

It was time to get back to work.

"Okay, Cill, I'll run all this by Finn. But I can't promise anything."

"Finn's in!" Cap'n Jack snorted, swung his stubby legs over the hammock, and jumped down to the deck.

"How do you—" I sputtered.

"Who can snooze with you two magpies flapping your beaks? Anyway, it's a damn fine plan and I know Finn. He'll love it."

"He will?" I asked, but Jack was already stomping across the deck to the back door, tossing off his parting line.

"Cilla's got a good nose for news, Nellie. Scruples are optional. I like that. Plus, she's got—"

I know.

"Pluck."

CHAPTER SIX

Cap'n Jack was right about Finn. He was all in, so to speak, about his turn as a gullible gambler, just ripe to be plucked. But he did have one question.

"Please tell me I don't have to wear a tux."

I'd seldom seen the guy in anything but cargo pants, jeans, and T-shirts. A polo was about as fancy as he got.

Cilla sighed. "Would that be a deal breaker?"

This time Cilla had joined our confab at Starbucks, seated at our usual table out on the deck, under the twinkly lights, as the sun set and the sky shimmered in shades of pink and orange.

Finn scooped the whipped cream off his Frappuccino with the edge of the lid, licking it off. "Guess I'll have to take one for the team." He then tossed the lid into the trash, Frisbee style. "Are we all set to go, Cill?"

"Milty was all for it. Knowing him, he's already sized you up for a sucker and plans to relieve you of everything you've got, including your skivvies."

"Let's leave my skivvies out of this." Finn grinned. "You want me to do the hustler bit, ask them if an ace is higher than a king? What are these little shovels on the cards called? Like that? Or do I do what I do best?"

"What's that, Finnian?" I asked.

"Win, of course."

Cilla mulled that one over. "Just read the room and follow your gut, I guess. We've all got our parts to play. The goal is to dig up as much dirt as we can about Milo."

"You really think someone at the party knows who killed him?" I bit into a dark-chocolate peanut butter cup. "Drunk or not, is anyone likely to be gossiping about the cartel, after what happened to Milo?"

Cilla shrugged. "Nellie, these folks are not like us. Who knows how they think? Besides, we don't know for sure there is a cartel lurking around, do we? Maybe he was into something else."

Finn wiped a dollop of cream off his chin. "Wendy thinks so, even if she was only speaking 'hypothetically.' I figure the feds are probably all over this investigation, maybe with a little help from the local cops. Wendy does not like to be upstaged by anyone, and that's why she's willing to trade intel with us. She wants to crack this and get the glory."

When he said "glory," I was thinking "gory."

"What if gangsters are involved in Milo's death? I've been reading up on smugglers and they are serious sickos."

Cilla looked surprised. "Nellie, are you having second thoughts about this?"

Cilla had been to Mitzi and Milty's McMansion before and knew the layout of the kitchen, pantry, and mudroom, where the caterer stowed the fresh uniforms. Smooth as she was, Cilla had my part all figured out. She'd get there early with a hostess gift and, while the Morrisons were getting ready, wander out to the kitchen, chat up the waitstaff. While they bustled around, she'd saunter over to the back door and open it for a breath of fresh air, while I'd slip into the mudroom and get suited up. Easy peasy, as Cilla was fond of saying. But since we had hatched our undercover plot, a flock of butterflies had taken up residence in my tummy.

"Did you know that these monsters dismember people?" I asked.

Cilla and Finn gawked at me.

"Are you just finding out that cartels do bad things, Nell? How long have you been a reporter?" Finn asked.

"I know, I've read the stories, seen the movies. But I never covered any of that stuff. Now it seems awfully close to home."

No one spoke for a while. Finn slugged down his drink, Cilla sipped her latte, and I nibbled my chocolate, hoping that it would calm my nerves.

"We don't have much time, Nell," Finn said. "It would be nice to have something to report before we go to press. The party's tomorrow night. Among the three of us, we should be able to come up with something by Monday."

"Besides, as much as I hate to admit it," Cilla added, "we're small potatoes, Nellie. Nobody's going to be worrying about us."

Sure, and up to now I'd been nothing but a half-baked potato to boot, despite my best efforts. What was the worst that could happen? I didn't really need to ask, because the answer was clear. Who was I kidding? Milo had not put on his cement booties willingly. But I was in my prime and if I was ever going to make it as a journalist, this was the time. Maybe I could embroider that ditty on a pillow.

I took a deep breath and nodded. Then we all bumped fists. My mother would be proud.

"Okay, then, any questions?" Cilla asked.

"Yeah." Finn wiped his mouth with the back of his hand. "Where do I rent a tux and who's going to pay for it?"

Once again, I found myself wondering about Finnian O'Connor. Who was he? Where had he come from? And why, if he was such a hotshot, at least locally, was he spinning his wheels at a minor-league community newspaper, even in the rarified realm of La Joya?

Cap'n Jack must have known the answers to these questions, because he had hired him. But Cilla and I didn't have a clue, not for lack of trying.

Cilla was especially good at drawing people out, but even she got only vague answers when she asked Finn about his background.

"So, Finn, where are you from?"

Shrug. "Here and there. I've moved around a lot."

"Where did you work before?"

Steely stare. "I freelanced. I like being my own boss."

"But Cap'n Jack's your boss now, Finn. Why—"

Stands up, grabs his notebook, and heads to the door. "Gotta go, Cill. See ya."

If Jack wanted to enlighten us, he would have, but he didn't, so neither of us bothered to ask. Finn had been on the job before either of us had arrived, but not by much. He probably was a rolling stone who freelanced stories while he was on the road. Maybe Finn had run into hard times and needed a steady source of income. Gambling debts maybe? A past he was trying to escape? Or maybe this whole Milo melodrama had made me suspicious of everything and everybody. Maybe a cigar was just a cigar.

The following night, our tuxedoed ace reporter was seated at the card table in a back room of Milt Morrison's place as expensive cigar smoke rose into the air. I knew this because Cilla, who wasn't undercover and was actually working her beat, had poked her well-coifed head into the room, chirping, "Hi guys! Who's winning?"

In addition to Finn and Milt, the other poker players were the usual assortment of wealthy white males with money to lose and that's what most of them were probably doing, at least from what Cilla had observed. I watched her click-clacking her stilettos over the highly polished floor, waving and air kissing her way to the invisible waitperson—me—carrying a tray of exotic nibbles.

"Finn's in the chips and the other gents do not look happy," Cilla whispered as she plucked a caviar-encrusted cracker from my tray. "You can bet—so to speak—that they're not too happy with Milty for inviting him."

Of course, the big question was what, if anything, Finn was finding out about Milo, but that intel would have to wait until after the party was over. I'd only been on the job for an hour and my feet were killing me, even with sensible shoes. How did Cilla manage to glide through the evening as though she were walking on a cloud?

I looked down at Cilla's feet.

"Are those Milo shoes?"

Looking around at the crowd beaming that megawatt smile, Cilla nodded.

"Cate lent me a pair," she whispered. "I'm hoping they'll be a conversation piece, you know? Get someone talking about Milo." Her smile turned into a wince. "They're a little tight, but I'm working through the pain. Tomorrow I'll need bed rest."

A voice from across the room ended my briefing.

"Cilla! Come here. There's someone you must meet."

My pal squinted across the room and waved, whispering to me, "Mitzi wants some ink for her new best friend who, no doubt, just cut a huge check for the NIMBY fund—I mean the Save Our Shore stash. Well, I better get my phone out for a glam society pic. Good luck with the recon."

What I needed at that point, besides a nice warm footbath, was the loo, so I returned my platter to the kitchen. So far I hadn't collected any relevant intel about Milo. In fact, from what I had overheard, the guests were as curious about his demise as we were, and some of them wondered who would likely inherit the rich bachelor/playboy's empire. Good question. I'd file that away for later.

In the meantime it was time to do some snooping, and being an invisible waitperson, how hard could that be? Plus I really needed to pee. The help's bathroom was in the mudroom, better that we don't muck up the posh lounge, which Cilla told me was located upstairs at the end of the hall. All I needed to do was act as though I had a perfectly good reason to go upstairs, sort of like carrying a clipboard when you case a neighborhood.

I glanced around and no one seemed to be watching me, so I sauntered over to the majestic staircase and started wending my way up the marble steps on sore feet and a full bladder. On the landing I looked up and down the hall; all was quiet—although you never knew what was going on beyond closed doors. I kept walking until I spotted a door with a sign that read *Mesdames*, so this had to be the place. Maybe the *Messieurs* loo was at the other end of the hall. It occurred to me that the Morrisons' home might be a renovated boutique hotel, given the commercial restrooms.

I went into the gilded lounge, which was bathed in the sort of soft lighting that every fitting room should use. Potpourri scented the air, and flickering LED lights accented the vanity tables. Elegant chairs covered in rose-colored velvet were arranged in one corner. All that was missing was a crystal chandelier.

I heard a flush and quickly ducked into one of the stalls, listening as a pair of heels clicked across the marble floor. A faucet turned on and then off, then a few minutes of primping, no doubt, and finally the sound of a door opening and closing. I peeked out, listened, and then exited, tiptoeing down the short row of stalls, looking for any telltale shoes, Milo's or not. I was alone. So, I did my business, wiping myself with toilet paper so soft, I could have draped it over my shoulders as a shawl.

Nothing to see here, so I left and, keeping an eye on the staircase, started to explore, pausing at each door and listening. Do I dare peek inside, and risk finding a couple in flagrante delicto? Why was I using fancy words? This place was getting to me. Anyway, I didn't have to make that decision, because at the other end of the hall, not far from *Messieurs*, a door was open, revealing a sitting room. Who else but the rich need a special room for sitting? I took another look down the hall and, coast clear, went inside. Fortunately, I didn't need to turn on the light as there were sconces on the walls, bathing the room in a cozy glow.

How compromising could an unlocked room be? What did I think I'd find? A noose, a wrench, a candlestick? Colonel Mustard and Miss Peacock lounging around? Maybe an elephant tusk displayed on the mantel? I stood in the center of the room and turned around in a circle, taking everything in: the finely crafted furniture, the Oriental rugs, and the framed art and photography displayed on the fleur-de-lis-papered walls. Hello!

Standing out among the artsy fare was something that did not seem to fit: a plainly framed, boldly colored caricature, a couple dressed in safari clothes, complete with pith helmets, astride a huge elephant, its tusks curled, the eyes the sort that would follow you around the room. The riders, I knew, were Mitzi and Milty Morrison.

"Are you fond of street art?"

Now I knew what it was like to jump out of my skin. I whirled around to find the gracious hostess standing in the doorway looking bemused. I realized that my mouth was open, but no words were coming out. Then I collected myself and went into my default mode. Babbling.

"Oh, Mrs. Morrison, I'm so sorry, I was looking for a restroom, the one in the mudroom was occupied and I really needed to . . . anyway, I turned the wrong way and found the men's room, *messieurs*, and then I noticed this room and it looked so inviting, with those cool lights and everything, so I—"

I didn't know this woman, but it didn't take me long to size her up as a snob and a bully who was enjoying my discomfort.

"Oh, no need to apologize, Miss—?"

Oh, crap. The gang of three had gone over everything but my alias if something went south, like it was going now. But I was quick on my feet, as sore as they were.

"Cochrane, Elizabeth. Lizzy."

This was the real name of Nellie Bly, so, technically, I wasn't lying, right?

"Well, Lizzy, no harm done."

Mitzy strolled into the room, tall and willowy, probably late middle age but could have been older. With these folks, you never knew. She wore an emerald green ankle-length gown and matching shoes. Silk or satin, I couldn't tell. Her jewels sparkled in the dim light, and her auburn hair was swept back in a chignon. Classy.

Standing next to me, she pointed at the caricature and began to regale me about its provenance, as though she were a doyenne at one of the museums in town.

"My husband, Milton, and I are Friends of the Zoo. We had this drawn during one of its fundraisers."

"I take it you weren't really posing on an elephant? He sure looks real."

When I'm in uncomfortable situations, making stupid remarks is right up there with my tendency to babble. But Mitzi just smiled.

"No, Lizzy. Kubwa is very real and will be the new star draw at the zoo, no doubt. And, no, we weren't actually astride him."

Her thought balloon read, "You moron."

"Interesting name. Does he live at the zoo?"

"Oh, yes, he's a new resident. Milton and I were among those who helped facilitate his transfer from Africa. They're endangered you know, so it was a privilege to have played a role in providing him with a safe environment where he can thrive."

"He's sure a big one, at least from the picture."

"Kubwa is seven and a half tons, hence his name. *Kubwa* is Swahili for *giant*."

Then just as quickly as she had arrived, Mitzi turned on her stilettos and sashayed to the door.

"Don't be long, Lizzie. We have a full house tonight, so it's all hands on deck."

Then she glided out, leaving me to ponder my next move.

When I returned to the party, a makeshift dais had been installed next to a set of purple velvet curtains.

I had restocked my tray and was painfully plodding around the partygoers, who plucked pâté and petit fours from me without so much as a "Thanks! How're those feet doing?" Then Mitzi strode through the crowd, which parted like the Red Sea, stepped onto the dais and raised her arms. Silence descended and she announced, "People! It's time for the auction. Please deposit your written bids on the items that you desire."

With that, Mitzi and one of her minions tugged on gold tassels on the sides of the curtains, which opened to reveal a long table draped in matching purple velvet. A dazzling array of goods—designer clothing, bags and shoes, jewelry that sparkled under the track lighting, and I spotted a few pieces that looked like ivory. There were intricately carved urns and vases, framed oil paintings and so much more—all awaiting new ownership. This was not your granny's garage sale. Wow. I was dazzled.

The partygoers were transformed into a pack of hyenas let loose on prey, and I had to dodge and weave through the crowd while holding my tray of canapes over my head. Cilla came to my rescue and guided me into an alcove out of the fray.

"What the hell is this, Cill? Where did all this stuff come from?"

"Well, while you were snooping around upstairs, an armored car arrived and trucked all these goodies in. They're being auctioned, with the proceeds going to SOS. Mitzi's been trolling for donations all year. She's really good at it."

I stared at the scene before me—all the lords and ladies pawing over the booty and slapping their bids down hither and thither. My mom would have compared it to a sale in Filene's basement, where feverish shoppers would enter into mortal combat for an off-the-rack rayon blouse.

"All this stuff was donated by this crowd? Are they regifting?"

Cilla gave me one of her looks.

"No, Nellie, that's not how this works, at least not for Mitzy and Milty. Once a year, they hold one of these soirees and the silent auction is the big draw. Everyone wants an invite, so they spend a lot of time sucking up to them to snag one." Cilla pointed to the luxury-laden table and lowered her voice. "Those items are exclusive, and money contributed by the wealthy grovelers is what pays for them. They can't get these things themselves. You're not going to find them at the mall. I tell you, Nellie, those two are well connected. I'd love to know more about their supply chain."

My feet were throbbing.

"How long is this shindig going on? If the auction is the highlight, can we split when it's over?"

Cilla cast a look toward the back of the house.

"Well, that would depend on Finn. He's still in there, but I didn't want to poke my head in too many times. I got to tell you, Nellie, these poker games can go on into the wee hours."

Wonderful.

"Finn has been sitting on his butt all night, guzzling expensive booze and probably has won enough of the pot to retire. Me? I'm hungry, tired, and can no longer feel my feet. What do we have to show for it?"

Cilla tugged me closer and again lowered her voice. "I have a few nuggets, and I'll bet you collected a few upstairs, even if you don't know it. Finn's a great reporter, so I'm sure he's got some good stuff too. I think we should get together tomorrow and compare notes. I'll ask Finn to invite Wendy. Maybe she's off on Sunday. We can meet for breakfast."

"No! I am planning to sleep late and then take a long soak in the tub."

"Okay, fine, how about brunch then? Meanwhile, you hold down the fort here and I'll go check on Finn and the boys."

As she teetered off, I sank farther into the shadows of the alcove and stuffed a *petit four* into my mouth. *Milo, what have you gotten us into?*

That's when the lights went out, followed at first by surprised murmurs and then an overpowering stench that sent the revelers gasping and running for the exits. It sounded like a herd of elephants, which seemed to be the theme of the evening.

In the crunch, a few cell-phone lights came on, and I could hear Mitzi moaning across the room. Well, I was the help, right, so I might as well help, although the air was so foul I was feeling dizzy. I felt for a napkin from the buffet table and covered my nose and mouth, which only made breathing harder. What to do? My choices were to get trampled trying to get out the door or having to face whatever had happened to Mitzi.

"Nellie!" Suddenly, Cilla had appeared by my side and was tugging at my arm. "I think Mitzi's been hurt. Let's try to help."

Yeah, my thoughts exactly.

Cilla dragged me along in the dark, dodging panicky partiers and maneuvering around the auction table, where we found Mitzi curled in a fetal position, moaning and gasping.

"Milton!" she shrieked. "Where are you? Get your ass over here!"

Cilla sunk down on her knees and flashed her cell-phone light in Mitzi's face.

"What are you doing?" Mitzi shrieked, knocking the phone out of Cilla's hand. "Help me get up, dammit!"

The fresh night air was mercifully drifting through the now open door and the stink was starting to dissipate. Then the lights came back on. Mitzi was sitting up, her legs spread in a most unladylike fashion, one of her beautifully pedicured feet bare, her face a canvas of smudged makeup and drool. Then she resumed her shrieking, her eyes bulging, hyperventilating while pointing at the table where only moments ago had laid an array of dazzling treasures.

"They're gone! Somebody call nine-one-one this instant!"

Then she passed out.

CHAPTER SEVEN

Creatures of habit and, for most of us, possessed of a limited budget, we skipped the posh brunch bistros in the village for Starbucks. The sausage egg muffin and other breakfast fare were still warm and edible at eleven o'clock, and we washed everything down with our favorite beverages.

Topic, of course, was the Morrisons' misbegotten party of the previous evening. While the ritzy revelers had stampeded out the door not long after the lights went out and the bedlam started, Finn, Cilla and I had hung around to get as much intel as we could, despite the stench that was still heavy in the air.

Somebody had called 911, and once the cops arrived, Mitzi was awake but not very lucid. While Milt ministered to her, the two officers, who looked like rookies who got stuck with the night shift, turned their attention to us. When they realized that none of us had anything relevant to contribute, we were sprung.

Wendy had agreed to join us for brunch and had come armed with a few tidbits that had not been reported by the media, at least those who actually cared about a NIMBY fund gala hosted by the venal and vacuous luminaries of the village.

"The security they hired for the party wasn't exactly from Blackwater," Wendy told us, inhaling the aroma of her chai tea. "They were rent-a-cops who were found tied up and stuffed in an upstairs closet."

"Wow, I didn't hear about that," Cilla said.

"That's because Madame Morrison didn't let anyone know," Wendy said. "She told the cops who showed up that her hired guns must have run out the back door."

"Why?" I asked.

"Apparently, the Morrisons didn't want any of their circle to know they were stupid enough to hire a couple of beach bums on the cheap to guard a table filled with valuables worth a gazillion bucks."

"They were insured, right?" Finn asked, his notebook out and pen in hand.

Wendy shrugged. "Not my turf, but I'd say yes. The folks who donated that stuff will want a full accounting, I'm pretty sure. Anyway, the loot is probably long gone by now."

Cilla sighed. "Poor Mitzi. She must have been terrified. Can you imagine being knocked down and pinned against the floor while thieves get away with a fortune?"

That part had made the news. Among the scant details, it was reported that the stench had been caused by a stink bomb, but not much else was known about the "brazen home invasion" at the Morrison manse.

"Am I wrong, or is this posh little village suffering from a crime wave?" I asked. "I know I'm not in Kansas anymore, but is this normal?"

"No, it isn't," Wendy said.

Finn pointed his pen in her direction. "So, do you think there's a connection with Milo?"

That question tickled my memory banks. "You know, I was looking at the jewelry, and a few of the pieces sure looked like ivory to me, not that I'm an aficionado."

Again, Wendy shrugged. "Could be. Too early to tell."

Then it was time for more show and tell.

Cilla retrieved a pink leather journal from her shoulder bag. "I jotted down a few notes after I got back," she said, wiping away crumbs from a mini vanilla scone with a napkin. "The chitchat last night was just gossip about Milo, but nobody I talked to or overheard seemed to have a clue about what happened to him."

"What about his business ties?" Wendy asked.

"Well, the funny thing about Milo is, even though he loved to hobnob and party, no one was actually close to him. At least, that's the impression I got. Lots of acquaintances and hangers-on and hotties, but no real friends."

"What about those girlfriends?" Finn wanted to know. "With all that dough, you figure he'd have a bunch of trophies tucked away."

"That's the point, Finn. He had lots of supermodels and starlets and society babes competing for his attention, but they never lasted long. But getting back to the party, what I found interesting was the auction. It's the first one I've been to since I hit town, but there was something shady about the armored car that delivered all the swag."

I held up my palm. "Wait a minute, Cilla, you saw the stuff being delivered?"

"Isn't that what I just said, Nellie? I just happened to have slipped out the front door to have a smoke—"

"A smoke? You don't smoke."

Cilla rolled her eyes. "Well, they don't know that, do they, Nellie? I always keep a pack of ciggies in my purse. You never know when a prop will come in handy, like last night. Anyway, I stood in the shadows, holding my fake Virginia Slim, and I watched the delivery guys hauling the stuff out the back of the truck. They were all dressed in black uniforms and caps. Nobody spoke, but they moved like they were on some kind of military mission. Black ops maybe?"

Finn stopped scribbling. "What do you know about black ops, Cilla? You cover high society."

Cilla gave him a sly smile. "Wouldn't you like to know."

Wendy pointed at Cilla. "I've been meaning to ask you, why weren't you covering Milo's yacht party? Didn't you get an invite?"

Cilla nodded. "Of course I did. But there are a lot of parties going on right now, and I had a prior commitment—one where nobody died." She looked a bit disappointed. "If only, right? Anyway, about last night, I don't think anybody noticed me, so I took a few shots of the crew—and the armored car."

With that, Cilla picked up her phone and called up the pictures she'd taken. We passed the phone around, and I had to admit, the crew looked a bit sinister. But what did I know?

"Okay, Cill, these guys do look a little shady, compared to, say, Brinks or Dunbar, but is that all you got?"

She gave me that look again. "Did any of you notice what's missing on the truck?"

Wendy held out her hand and I deposited the phone in her palm. She stared at the image for a few seconds and then nodded.

"No license plates, for one thing. Did you notice if there were any logos?"

Cilla shook her head. "It was dark, but the lights at the entrance gave me a clear view. When I slipped out after they arrived, I checked out the front and the other side of the truck, while they were busy unloading, and there wasn't any logo or ID anywhere. No front license plate either."

Cilla took a breath. "But I did get some shots of the auction table, under the radar, of course," she said with a wink.

Unfortunately, my uniform had no pockets, so I'd had no place to stow a cell phone and take photos. Good for Cilla.

"Any idea where the Morrisons got all the merch?" Wendy asked.

Cilla filled her in about Mitzi's genius at raking in donations, and her refusal to ever divulge her donor list.

"I used to think Mitzi kept her donors shrouded in a cloud of secrecy because she didn't want any competition, but now I'm not so sure," Cilla said.

Wendy continued scrolling through the photos.

"Last time we all met, I gave you an overview of the illegal poaching of endangered animals and how tough it is to nail these cartels that are smuggling animal parts for goods and medicine. It goes beyond elephants, Nellie. We're not only talking about pachyderms and rhinos and big cats, but there's a huge trade in sea turtles, crocodiles, even snakes, especially pythons."

"Pythons?" I asked, feeling my chest tighten.

"I can tell you that about a half million python skins are exported every year from Southeast Asia, bringing in one billion, a big incentive. At that rate, how long do you figure this species will survive?"

Nobody responded but the answer was clear.

"But it's not only pythons and it's not only about snakeskins. There is a market for rattlesnake venom, and there are plenty of gullible or desperate folks out there who consider this a wonder drug. In fact, it can kill them."

"You're saying that it's illegal to mess with rattlesnakes?" Finn asked.

"I'll give you an example," Wendy said. "In Arizona, rattlesnakes are considered the property of the state, so trying to sell them or milk them is illegal. Now, let's talk about those sea turtles. Their shells are prized for jewelry and high-priced knickknacks. The problem is, the average consumer often has no idea that she's buying a necklace or earrings that are made from endangered creatures. Not all the boutiques who sell this stuff know, either, but you can be sure that some of them do, and look the other way. They are complicit."

We all let that sink in.

"I guess you can't tell anything about the items from just looking at my pics, right?"

"No, but I'll need you to send those shots to me—all of them, Cilla, and I'll see what I can dig up. This may be the break we need to connect the dots to the smugglers."

Then it was my turn, and I told everyone about my chat with Mitzi and her joyride on Kubwa the elephant, but what did that prove?

Sure, she and Milt had connections and the money and clout to relocate a valuable animal from Africa, but did they break any laws?

I mean, he still had his tusks.

Finn was up next. He looked beat and was nursing a venti cup of what looked like strong black coffee, no frills, and no food. He kept his sunglasses on, no doubt covering a set of bloodshot eyes, and rubbed his hand over the dark stubble on his jaw.

"Well, Finn, how much did you rake in before the lights went out? "I asked.

He peered at me over the rims of his glasses and took another sip of the bitter brew.

"I was beating the fancy pants off of them, but if I didn't slow down, I'd still be there," he said. "Those pricks hate to lose. It's not only about the money for that bunch."

"How much did you lose, Finn?" Cilla looked worried.

He shrugged. "I broke even, and that seemed to satisfy them."

"So, no dirt about Milo?" Wendy asked. "What a waste of time, but you get points for trying."

Finn removed his sunglasses and rubbed his eyes and I could tell that he had a hell of a hangover.

"Oh, it wasn't a waste, Wendy. I was just saving the best for last.

"These guys, they're all alpha pricks, and that means they not only have to win, but they can drink anybody under the table," he said, taking a gulp from his cup. "They get suspicious if a player doesn't match them shot for shot, you know?"

He shrugged, again rubbed his eyes, and replaced his sunglasses. "Anyway, John Jeffers was sitting in—"

"John Jeffers?" I asked. "I quoted him in our first story. He said that Milo seemed fine at the yacht party." Dame C had also called Jeffers a fool.

Finn waved his hand. "Yeah, well, after a few belts J. J.—"

"J. J.?"

"Jeffers, Nell. He tells us that old Milo was acting strange—moody and not the usual life of the party. He spent most of the time down below. Get this, he even left his date for the night—a Victoria's Secret model, I think—he left her high and dry on deck. Jeffers said she got so mad that she went below and he could hear her pounding on the door to the cabin, so, he goes to the top of the steps and watches her hammering the door with one of her stilettos—a Milo original, no less, he says—and she's yelling, 'Milo! Milo!' and a bunch of X-rated words. She was swigging from a bottle of Cristal so I guess he left her high, but not dry."

"You think she was planning on christening him?" I asked.

We all exchanged a glance. Was I joking about that? Good question. So, we all turned to Wendy, who maintained her poker face.

"Okay, Wendy," I ventured. "We've been sharing, but you've only been educating us about the scourge of smuggling endangered animal parts. That's good to know, but we're trying to stay ahead of this story, and we need something quick. Tomorrow's our deadline, remember? Can you help us connect the dots—at least a little? Who exactly are we dealing with?

The theft at the Morrisons, right under Mitzy's nose, would be a good place to start."

Wendy just sipped her chai tea.

"Come on, Wendy," Cilla said, smiling that smile. "We know that Milo had a piece of ivory shoved down his throat and had cement in his boots, even if you won't confirm it. Could he have been struck with the proverbial blunt object—like a champagne bottle?"

Wendy took a deep breath. "I know nothing about champagne bottles."

"Well, you do now!" Finn's voice had an edge to it.

"Look, I'm in a tough spot here. The chief is planning a press conference next week, and I have no idea who will be there. The feds or some other agency? The DA? No arrests have been made; that I do know."

"But you can confirm or deny what we already know, Wendy," Finn said. "That would be a start, give us something to run with tomorrow."

Wendy had been doodling a swirly thing on her notebook, but looking at it upside down, it didn't seem to be a code, just something to do with her hands.

"You don't think anyone will know it's me leaking this intel?" she asked. "Just because I work downtown doesn't mean that nobody's seen me meeting with you guys. I'm not the only surfer in the department, you know. I've been careful, but still."

"You want to make chief of detectives someday, Wendy?" Finn asked, peering at her from behind his shades. "Then play ball with us. That was the deal. We've given you some good leads. It's time to share."

Wendy gave him a fierce look.

"I want more, Finn, if you expect me to stick my neck out."

"You want more, Wendy. Good, because I haven't finished. Jeffers told us that Milo's date made such a scene that everyone started milling around Jeffers, including—get this—Mitzi and Milt Morrison. So, Mitzi brushes past Jeffers and goes below, grabs the model by the arm and twists the bottle out of her hand, and then not so gently shoves her up the steps. Well, Vicki—the Victoria's Secret babe—wasn't too happy about this, but Mitzi, being an alpha female, takes charge. She went to the cabin door, but it was locked, and all the windows to the cabin were shuttered. Not a peep from inside either, Jeffers says."

Finn took a breath and another slug of coffee.

"Of course, what happens on the *Muse*—that's Milo's boat—stays on the *Muse*. Except last night, when Jeffers decided to run his mouth. And, I gotta tell you, Milt didn't seem too happy about Jeffers's loose lips. He kept glancing my way as though he was the only one who remembered I was a reporter. So, I tried to look shit-faced, which, as time went on, is precisely what I was. Anyway, Milt finally managed to shut Jeffers up. You know, 'Hey, are we gambling or gabbing? Play your bleeping hand.' Like that."

Finn fixed his gaze on Wendy. "So, detective, what do you say? How about you throw us a bone—or, in this case—a tusk?"

We all turned to Wendy, who seemed ready to surrender.

"Okay, I'll confirm what you know so far," she said. "But that will have to hold you for a while, until I know what the blowback will be after you print this. I'm just happy you're not online."

Cilla held her phone up. "No, but I do keep my readers posted through Twitter and such, Wendy. The *Crier* might be old school, but it does have one foot in the twenty-first century."

"Actually, Cill, you use that stuff for your society sh— stories," Finn said. "We're still working on Cap'n Jack to acknowledge we're even in a new century."

Wendy sighed. "Okay, fine. But that's the deal. You can keep snooping, but I've got to keep a low profile until after the press conference. Then we'll regroup and go from there. Agreed?"

We all nodded.

"Works for us, Wendy," I said. "But you know what would be really terrific? How about you get us a copy of the autopsy report?"

She looked at me with wide eyes and open mouth.

"You want me to leak an autopsy report? Are you crazy? I'm guessing that's what the press conference is going to be about. You'll just have to wait."

Finn held up a hand. "That's fine, Wendy, we won't get greedy. Well, not for another day or two. By then, we'll be hungry again, so—"

"Maybe we'll find some more loose lips!" Cilla chirped.

"Yeah, well, don't expect me to be filling them with pâté and petit fours," I said. "I'm still recovering from last night."

That's when my cell phone buzzed. A blocked number. I answered.

"Nellie? It's Cate. Come to the house immediately and tell no one."

Then she was gone.

Everyone was staring at me now.

"Wrong number?" Cilla asked.

I stood and stuffed my phone in my purse and took a last swig of my latte.

"Sorry, folks, but I've got to run."

I guess the game was afoot, a very apt turn of phrase, considering.

CHAPTER EIGHT

It was early afternoon when I arrived back at my place, or I should say, Dame C's place. I parked my Mustang in the ten-car garage, and when I emerged, there she stood, one hand on her hip, the other clutching a lethal-looking gardening tool, decked out in full pruning attire.

"It's about time! Follow me."

Cate led me up the cobblestone pathway, past my granny flat and up to a decorative wishing well that sported a quaint little bucket dangling from a rope. My nose wrinkled and it wasn't from the salty air wafting off the coast.

Not good.

"Do you smell that, Nellie?" Cate had stopped abruptly. "There is something dead down there. I know that smell."

I scooted over to her and felt a chill run down my spine.

"That's a working well, Cate? I thought it was just for show."

She glared at me.

"Of course it's a working well. Style should always have substance, and that's where I draw my water for the plants. I cranked the bucket into the well, and that's when I noticed that horrid odor. I yanked the bucket back up and you can see for yourself what's in it."

Did I want to do that? I was never a crime reporter and I didn't much want to start now. But curiosity got the better of me.

I walked over to the well, holding my breath, and peeked down into the bucket. The afternoon sunshine played off the surface of the water, which had a definite pinkish tinge. I walked back to Cate.

"Okay, I see what you mean, but maybe an animal fell into the well?"

I had a terrible thought and started over to my cottage, but Cate grabbed me by the arm.

"Your cats are fine, Nellie, I checked. Those worthless felines are napping, as usual. And why would some feral creature wander into my yard, bleeding, and fall into my well? It makes no sense."

I thought about that.

"Cate, we don't even know if that's blood. Maybe it's rust?"

Another glare. "For one thing, the bucket is made of wood and does not rust. For another thing, the water is pristine. I make sure of that. No, Nellie, I tell you, that is blood, and something—or someone—is down there."

I circled the well and returned to Cate. "Someone? You are suggesting that a stranger could just wander onto your property and dump a body down there?"

"No, I have excellent security—cameras and alarm systems—and as you can see, a natural barrier out back. Beyond the wall is a very steep and rocky hill leading down to the beach. No one would be foolish enough to try it. Besides, I have security installed over there as well. I've asked Quigley to review the feeds. He knows all about that sort of thing."

Hmmm, Quigley had many talents, it seemed.

"Okay, what now? Do you want me to call the cops?"

Cate's green eyes blazed, and her pale face turned a bright red.

"Are you mad, Nellie? Of course not. It's bad enough that you have to deal with the authorities at all."

How did she know that?

As if reading my mind, Cate said, "Of course I know about your furtive meetings with that detective—Miss Nebuchadnezzar—"

"Nakamura—"

"Whatever. We should have kept this to ourselves, Nellie. Not that I owe that bastard anything."

"That bastard?"

"Milo, of course."

"You think whatever—or whoever—is in the well is connected to Milo's death?"

Cate heaved a deep sigh. "Well, of course I do. Maybe it's some sort of warning?"

"Warning? What does Milo's murder have to do with you?"

Cate smiled enigmatically, as she no doubt had done as femme fatale in those B movies to great effect.

But I was getting tired of all the drama.

"Look, Cate, if you know anything about what happened to Milo, you'd better spill it. You could be next on the list, you know."

And then it occurred to me that I could get caught up in the net too. Maybe sleeping in my car wasn't such a bad idea.

"Nonsense, Nellie. But we'll have time to chat later on, for our next session. Now, we will find out what Quigley has discovered on the feed and how soon his friend can come by."

With that, Cate turned and started walking along the path back to her house.

"Friend? What friend?"

Cate stopped and turned to face me, again sighing. "Really, Nellie, do try to keep up. Quigley's friend, Freddy. He'll retrieve whatever is down in that well and we'll take it from there."

"Are you serious? If there is a body down there, that's a crime scene. You can't—"

But Cate was moving again, waving me off. "No need to fret, Nellie. Freddy is a very resourceful fellow. You'll see."

Quigley found zip on the security feeds, so that left Freddy, whoever he was. He arrived just as the sun was setting, parked his truck on the circular driveway, and then retrieved a toolbox from the back. Cate and Quigley were there to greet him, while I held back, using my journalistic chops to size him up.

Speaking of which, Freddy was short but sinewy, with the look of a jockey. It occurred to me that maybe he rode horses at the Del Mar racetrack. At this distance, it was hard to tell his age, so maybe he was retired? They walked up the driveway, where I had been tucked away behind a palm tree, observing the scene. Cate bellowed, "Nellie! Where are you? Get out here!"

I stepped out, feeling a little foolish. Why was I being so furtive? But there was something about Freddy that was a little off-kilter, even from a distance. Vibes. But Cate didn't seem to notice and led the way up the cobblestone path.

"There you are." Cate halted the troops and introduced me to our guest without giving up his last name.

The fading rays of sunlight lit up Freddy's red hair like a wildfire and his pale blue eyes shone hard and bright. An unsettling combination. I shifted into full babble mode.

"Pleased to meet you, Freddy. Cate, uh, Dame Cavendish tells me that you are well-informed about wells. I mean, I've heard of chimney sweeps, but not well sweeps, if there is such a thing. What is it that you do?"

Cate, Quigley, and Freddy stared at me and then exchanged a look. In unison they said, "Plumbing."

"Ah, of course, plumbing. Septic tanks and subterranean stuff?"

Freddy stared some more, then said, "Sure."

Cate clapped her hands. "Enough chitchat. It will be dark soon, so let's get on with this."

But Freddy was staring at me. Then he tossed his head, sending Cate and Quigley a silent message.

"Nellie, why don't you tend to your cats?" Cate said. "No need for you to waste your time out here. It's the cocktail hour. Off you go."

Well, for Pru and Pat it's more like the catnip hour, but clearly Freddy didn't want me around. It occurred to me that he was as suspicious of me as I was of him. Interesting. Our antennae were up. I excused myself and strolled over to my place just as my cell phone chirped in my pocket.

Inside, I perched on the settee and looked at the screen. Cilla had texted. "What's going on? We need to have a plan before deadline tomorrow."

The kitties were mewing and circling their food bowls, so I doled out the Friskies and filled their water bowls. The litter box would have to wait.

I called Cilla and she answered on the first ring.

"Well, it's about time, Nell. I didn't dare call you, because I didn't know what you were up to, and I didn't want to interrupt. But then I started to worry and—"

Cilla babbles too.

"I'm sworn to secrecy, but we could be getting a big break on the story, depending," I said.

"Depending on what?"

"I can't tell you yet, Cill, but if it's what I think it is, I'll need to convince Cate—"

"Cate? Dame Cavendish? Did she dish?"

I took a deep breath, wondering what was happening back at the well.

"Look, Cill, I'll call you as soon as I have something to report, okay? You know, I'm in a tough spot, what with my day job, and my side gig as Boswell. Then, there's that nondisclosure form she made me sign. It's complicated."

A few seconds of silence and then: "Fine. At least we've got the tusk and the cement snowshoes angle, but all we can say is we've got a reliable source. We can't name Wendy. And there's that press conference coming up next week. If we can add another juicy tidbit, we'll be ahead of the pack. Can we do that, Nellie?"

"Maybe."

If Freddy did find a body down there, that was a crime scene and police business, nondisclosure form or not. Damn the memoir and hello Mustang, my new home. Would it come to that?

CHAPTER NINE

After a quick dinner of sliced apples and gruyere cheese, and a glass or two of Chablis, I had retired to the loft, trailed by the kitties, who curled up in their beds over in a corner. It wasn't that late, a little past nine, but no one had come to report what Freddy might have dredged out of the well. I shivered at the thought. I was feeling restless so I started roaming around the room, admiring the vintage forties-style furniture that, true to Cate's tastes, embodied both form and function, including a rolltop desk set by the window. Okay, I'm a snoop, by profession, but I'd been too busy with work and my Boswell duties to poke around up here. My clothes were either hung in a small wardrobe against the wall or stuffed into a dresser. But now I was intrigued.

The desk had three drawers on either side, and a wider one set in the middle, below the roll top, which had a skeleton key poking out of the keyhole. I moved the matching chair, made of walnut, I think, and gently rolled up the top. It wasn't locked. Feeling a tad guilty, I walked over to the stairs and listened, but all was quiet. I knew that Cate had a spare key to the granny flat, but would she be snooping around when I was here? Unlikely. I returned to the desk, sat down, and started rifling through the items stored inside. There was a stack of yellowed letters tied with a red satin ribbon, and below it, a scrapbook. Now I did feel like a voyeur. On the other hand, if Cate was concerned about her privacy, why let a stranger take up residence without locking the desk? Had she just forgotten?

Well, curiosity might kill my cats, but I was a biped, so I put the letters aside—I had some sense of decorum—and lifted out the scrapbook, which had a pastel floral cover and smelled of dried rose petals and stale air. I slowly turned the pages, where old photos were held in place by yellowed tape, as was a collection of faded newspaper clips.

The older photos were black-and-white and showed a young Cate in a variety of settings. In one she was standing in a chorus line, one long leg kicking out, her arms entwined with her fellow chorines. In another, she was seated in a canvas chair looking coquettishly over her shoulder, glossy platinum hair cascading. A movie set. There were several shots of her at now long-shuttered nightclubs, sitting with a variety of men in tuxes, smoke circling over their heads, half-drunk cocktails on the table. Some of the faces in the faded pictures were familiar—Clark Gable? Tyrone Power? My mom was a film buff, so she'd know.

I ran across several clips from *Variety*, as well as some from the gossip columnists, proclaiming this new starlet or ingenue as the next big thing, promoting their soon-to-be released films. My mom might have recognized the names, but I was drawing a blank, except for Cate, of course. Except she wasn't Dame Cavendish back then. She was billed as Catherine Carlisle soon to costar with the dashing Rex Reynolds in the thriller *Murder at Midnight*. I kept turning pages and, as the years progressed, the nightclubs and soundstages were replaced with glitzy society shots. Cilla would love this stuff. And so would my mom, come to think of it.

Cate was posed with a variety of men, young and old, over the years. Her husbands? Lovers? Gangsters? Who knew? She was a confection, in satin gowns, dazzling jewels, and furry wraps. There was, and still is, something ageless about Dame C, almost as though she isn't of this world. Of course, I knew better. Right now, she, Quigley, and Freddy were probably tucked away in the aviary, examining whatever he had excavated.

The scrapbook seemed to end abruptly circa the 1950s. Maybe there were more? I closed up the desk, figuring I'd finish my snooping later. I had a lot to do the next day. But maybe one last peek? I opened the long drawer and there lay a short stack of movie posters, featuring, who else? Miss Catherine Carlisle. There she was, in a steamy embrace with Rex Reynolds, half hidden in the shadows, a revolver clutched in his hand. *Murder at Midnight*. Their names writ large. Coming soon!

I went over to a corner of the room where I kept my laptop and brought it over to the bed. I got comfy, leaning against the feather pillow and sitting in the lotus position, the computer in my lap. I tapped in "Catherine Carlisle" on the search engine but only Wikipedia seemed to have any info on Cate's alter ego, and that was brief: a studio glam shot of her and short copy noting that she had appeared in a few B pics, naming a few of them, all quite forgettable. She had decorated the arms of various actors, directors, and wealthy gentlemen, including a few reputed to be mob-linked, but no apparent scandals, at least none worth any salacious headlines. No hints as to what caused her sudden departure from Tinseltown, although I had to wonder how much she'd been missed. There were so many starlets back then who were here today, gone tomorrow. It made me wonder if Cate and I had at least one thing in common—big dreams but scant rewards. But I still had some time, didn't I?

Maybe it was time to check in with Mom and see what she knew about Miss Carlisle, aka Dame Cavendish. But first, it was time to get my butt over to the main house and hope Freddy had discovered something down in that well that would get me off the dead beat once and for all.

CHAPTER TEN

Before leaving my cottage I grabbed a small flashlight I kept on a table by the door and then locked up, leaving the guard cats in charge. Good luck with that. I flicked on the light, keeping it aimed at the cobblestone path, as there were no exterior lights on at Cate's place. Odd, considering her top-of-the-line security gizmos. Wouldn't she at least have a motion detector out here? I considered taking a detour out back to the wishing well, but that familiar shiver kept me moving in a straight line. Halfway to the door I paused and listened. A few gulls squawking and the distant sound of the surf, but otherwise it was a quiet late-summer evening.

Standing at the back door, I hesitated and listened some more. Peering inside the glass panes, I couldn't see any light and I assumed Cate's fleet of seed sacks were all snoozing in their various lairs. What to do? If my benefactor/landlady had wanted me to know what they had discovered, wouldn't she have dropped by? Maybe it was a false alarm and she felt foolish. Or—

It occurred to me to check on Freddy's truck out front, so I aimed the flash down at the ground and followed the path to the driveway, also oddly unlit. But Freddy's truck was gone. Now what? I looked over at the garage, where I kept my Mustang. I turned off the flash and crept over to the garage door, which was open a few inches. So much for security. Inside was a cavernous space where, in addition to my Mustang, sat an array of vintage vehicles—vintage with a capital *V*, unlike my heap, which was aging with a small *a*. There was the Bentley Quigley used to motor Cate here and there, along with others that clearly were meant for show—a Mercedes-Benz, a Jaguar, a Porsche, a Ferrari, and—I moved closer and flicked the flash to illuminate the other model names—an Alpha Romeo, an Aston Martin and, wow, a Ford Model T. My poor little pony must have felt so inferior out here among such splendor.

I knelt and peeked inside, but it was too dark to see anything, and I didn't hear any voices. What was that smell? What I did determine was that a reasonably lithe person could scoot herself through the opening between the garage door and the ground.

Well, as they say, in for a penny, in for a pound, so I crawled through the space and immediately recognized the smell as the same one that had wafted up from the wishing well. Yuck. I stood and waited for my eyes to adjust to the darkness, and then noticed a faint light that seemed to be seeping from behind a closed door, tucked away in a corner of the garage that hadn't been immediately visible to me. I moved carefully in my sneakers, not wanting to turn on the flashlight, and managed to make it to the door without breaking my neck.

That foul odor was even stronger now and I shivered trying to imagine what lay on the other side. I was about to try the knob, when—swish!—it was opened from inside, and Quigley loomed over me, glowering. I just shrieked, which brought Cate into the mix.

"What are you doing in here, Nellie?" she hissed from behind Quigley, who continued to glower. "Did I beckon you?" Her eyes shifted to my hand. "What is that you're carrying? A weapon?"

I looked down at the flashlight and handed it to Quigley.

"Just a flashlight, Cate. It's loaded with batteries." Then I added, "Why? Do I need a weapon?"

That seemed to give Cate and Quigley pause and they exchanged a glance. Finally, she maneuvered past her aide-de-camp, grabbed my arm and tugged me inside, slamming the door shut and locking it.

"What the hell, Cate?" Would Johnson treat Boswell like this? "I was curious about what Freddy found and was coming around to ask you. But everything's so dark, and then I noticed that the garage was open a few inches, so I was worried. What's going on? And what's that stink? Is that why you opened the garage a crack, to air it out?"

Again, the two exchanged a look.

"The security system doesn't seem to be working," Cate said. "We'll have it checked out in the morning. No need to worry. Now, why don't you—"

I glanced over her shoulder and, in the dim light, noticed something set in the middle of a table, but it was covered up. The stink was coming from over there, but when I tried to get a better look, Quigley stepped in front of me.

"You heard what Dame Cavendish said, Ms. Bly. You need to go back to your place. Now."

That old-timey radio voice gave me the chills.

"I don't think I will, Quigs, so let me by. Now."

Quigs? Oh my, I was getting as plucky as Cilla. This seemed to amuse Cate for some reason, but old Quigs did not look happy.

Before he could respond, Cate took charge.

"Very well, Nellie, I suppose you have the right to some answers," Cate said as she pointed a well-manicured finger in my face, "with the caveat that everything you see and hear tonight is kept in strictest confidence. Agreed?"

Here we go again. Reporter vs. ghostwriter. That creeped me out, too.

"Fine," I said as I pointed a not-so-well-manicured finger in her face, "unless I can get the same intel from another source. We're talking about murder, and I get the feeling that this is all about Milo. Am I right?"

Cate and I spent a few more minutes negotiating my intel access, but she didn't answer my question about Milo, at least not directly. Instead, she led me over to the wooden table. A bare, low-watt bulb was hanging over it.

"Madam, I must object—"

Before Quigley could continue, Cate strolled over and yanked the cover—a cleaning rag—from the blob that rested on the table.

What was that thing?

"Is that a—?

"Yes, Nellie, but as you can see, it's not beating—at least not anymore."

I took a few steps closer. "Milo?"

That seemed to amuse Cate. "No, Nellie, I can promise you that Milo was never a bleeding heart. And this one isn't human. Am I correct, Quigley?"

"It comes from a mammal, Ms. Bly, perhaps from the big cat family."

Cate grimaced. "Big cat, small cat, they all should be exterminated, if you ask me."

I was trying to process this and asked Quigley, "How do you know this?"

His expression could only be described as imperious as he informed me: "I just know, Ms. Bly."

I did the math, such as it was.

"Okay, so we have a piece of ivory from an elephant tusk, and now we have what seems to be a heart from a big cat? The ivory ended up down Milo's throat, and this," I gestured to the blob, "this ended up in your wishing well. Do you think it's time to call the cops, Cate?"

That's when the sound of an engine, more than one, came to life outside the door, the garage door slammed down and the light went out. Not good.

I clicked on my flashlight and ran to the door, unlocked the deadbolt and turned the knob. Nothing. The engines continued to purr and roar, an odd mix, but I didn't hear any sputtering, which is mainly what my car did, when it wasn't knocking.

Cate and Quigley were right behind me.

"Well, open the door, Nellie! What are you waiting for?"

"It won't budge." I kept yanking on the knob, but the damn door held fast. "Does this room have another exit?"

"No," Cate said. "This is my craft room and I do not like to be interrupted when I'm in here. I sealed the door to the house years ago."

Cate shoved me aside and started yanking, and then Quigley stepped up and she let him take over.

Meanwhile, those powerful engines were cranking out all those fumes. How long did we have until carbon monoxide overcame us?

"Did you bring your cell?" Cate was starting to hyperventilate.

"No." I flashed the light around the room and spotted the canvas cover that was lying next to the heart. I ran over, grabbed it and then stuffed it into the crack beneath the door, frantically looking around for other scraps.

Cate and Quigley got the message and followed my beam as we stumbled over each other trying to find anything we could stuff in the crack.

"There's a workbench against the back wall," Cate panted. "There are rags and paper towels I keep there for my crafts. Hurry!"

Cate got to the bench first and started hurling cloths in our general direction. I caught a few and ran back to the door, stuffing them into the crack, instinctively holding my breath. The job done, we stepped back and caught our breaths and I wondered how many other cracks were letting the odorless poison inside the room. Then I returned to the door for another round of yanking when I noticed another smell. I leaned down near the stuffed crack and sniffed. Nail polish remover? How could that be?

Then I heard the garage door being opened and I didn't know whether to be relieved or scared shitless.

"What should we do?" Cate whispered. "Maybe they're coming back to finish us off!"

"I doubt that, madam," Quigley said. "We haven't been in here that long."

Okay. It was time to make an executive decision. If they were the bad guys, we were done for anyway.

"Who's out there?" I shouted.

I heard footsteps coming in our direction and then the knob rattling from the other side.

"Who's in there?" It was a raspy voice that sounded familiar.

"Freddy!" Cate was beside me now. "Get us out of here at once!"

"Catie? That you in there?"

Catie?

"Yes, of course it is, and Quigley and Nellie are with me. We've been locked in. Please shut the engines off immediately. We could have been killed!"

The footsteps receded and then came back.

"Yeah, I hear engines too, but the sound ain't coming from the cars in here. None of them is running."

What?

"Freddy, it's me, Nellie. We can't open the door. Is there something obstructing it? Do you have a flashlight?"

"Nah, that's why I came back. I must've left it here, maybe near the well. But it's so damn dark. What happened to your power?"

"Whoever did this to us knocked out the power and shut the garage door. Then we heard the engines and figured we were done for."

I was still smelling that nail polish odor mixed in with the stench of a decaying organ.

"Freddy, feel around the door. Is that glue I'm smelling?"

We waited.

"Feels like some gunk crammed in along the doorjamb. That must be one hell of an industrial grade."

Fast-drying too, it seemed, although we were inside awhile, examining the heart.

"You're a handyman, right, Freddy? Can you get the door off?"

Before he could answer, Cate shouted, "Of course he can! Now let's stop the nattering. Freddy, get moving!"

Freddy got moving. It took him a couple of minutes to rifle through his truck out front for the right tools and another five to pry open our door.

The stink was making me nauseous.

What was the stuff? I doubted that it was super glue, not that I'm an expert.

While the glue kept stinking, those irritating engines kept up the ruckus, so once we were out of the room, I flicked on my flashlight and started to search for what must have been a recorder.

"What are you doing, Nellie?" Cate asked, standing in the center of the garage, hands on hips.

"I'm trying to find the recorder that's playing that damn engine noise. It's got to be tucked away somewhere here."

But Cate wasn't having it.

"That can wait until daylight. The batteries will run down anyway. Quigley and I have work to do, so why don't you and Freddy run along?"

In the dark it was hard to read Freddy's expression, but he obviously knew what he had dug up. Or did he? Maybe it had been in some kind of container? Why were they keeping him in the dark? Or were they?

"Are you kidding, Cate? I saw what Freddy dug out of that well. Human heart or not, we need to call the cops and report this. At the very least, it's vandalism, at the worst, it's—"

"It's revenge of those delinquents I ran off my property last winter."

"Delinquents?" I asked.

"A bunch of hooligans," she hissed. "The water from the hose I soaked them with was very cold." She shook her head. "Kids these days."

I let that sink in.

"Are you telling me that a bunch of kids planted an animal heart in your well? Are you serious? And why would they wait all these months to get back at you?"

I could sense that Cate was rolling her eyes at my idiocy. "Why, Nellie? I'll tell you why. Revenge, as everyone knows, is best served cold. Now, enough of this nonsense. We have work—"

"So a pack of delinquents cut your electricity, snuck into the garage, planted the recorder, and sealed up the door while we were inside? Is that what you're telling me?"

I could see Cate and Quigley mulling this over, but before they could respond, Freddy gathered up his tools.

"I'll check out the fuse box, Catie, then I'm outta here."

I needed to find that recorder, but there was no way I could do that with Cate and Quigley around. So, I'd play it cool and check out the garage tomorrow before I drove to work, assuming, of course, that a bomb hadn't been planted under the hood of my car.

"Have it your way, Cate, but this was no prank. Someone is trying to send you a message," I said.

Cate flicked her hand dismissively and strutted back into her craft room, Quigley bringing up the rear. In the darkness, she called out, "Night, night, don't let the bedbugs bite!"

"Are you crazy?" I said. "You're going back in there?"

But Cate had already closed the door, well, as much as she could manage, considering the damage.

Freddy was already outside.

"Wait up!" I sprinted to catch up to Freddy, who was very nimble. He half turned and said, "Yeah?"

By the time I caught up, he was unlocking a compartment in his truck and shoving his tools inside. He slammed the compartment closed and turned around.

"You know what you dug up in that well, right?"

The moon was out and cast a glow on his face, those eerie eyes giving me goose bumps.

He shrugged. "I hauled a canvas bag out of the well. So what?"

"So what? Didn't you hear what I said in there? It was a heart—not human—but Quigley thinks it came from a big cat. Doesn't that pique your curiosity?"

He shrugged again.

"Nah, my curiosity ain't piqued. I don't get piqued. Catie gives me a job and I do it, no questions asked. The pay's good.

End of story. Now I gotta check out the fuse box, if ya don't mind."

"Fine, but one question, okay?"

"What?"

"That didn't smell like ordinary glue. You're a handyman, right? What was that stuff?"

Freddy gave me a cold, blue stare and I shivered.

"Horse glue. See ya."

Horse glue? Maybe he *was* a jockey.

"Are you kidding me? They still use horses to make glue?"

Freddy was already moving, but said over his shoulder, "Yeah, for special uses. It's strong stuff."

Then he disappeared into the shadows. Horse glue? Elephant tusks? A heart from a big cat? What was going on? Did I want to find out? I could still pack up and get the hell out of Dodge, couldn't I? But if I quit now, where did that leave me? Back to zero. Not an option. I had to honor my namesake.

CHAPTER ELEVEN

The next day I hauled myself out of bed an hour early to give myself time to poke around the garage for that damn recorder. But as I was getting dressed, I reconsidered. Did I expect to discover one of those big honking reel-to-reel jobs sitting on top of my hood? And that garage was big, with all sorts of nooks and crannies.

I wasn't even sure what I was looking for. A microrecorder? Some teensy-weensy number crafted by James Bond's master inventor Q? Maybe it was designed to self-destruct and vaporize. Why was I wasting my time? Whoever had terrorized us the night before was no avenging kid, no matter what Cate thought—if she did indeed think that. Meanwhile, I had to get to the paper.

Maybe the gang could help me figure this out.

I got in the Mustang, cranked the ignition and was relieved that there was no BOOM! My nerves were shot, and I promised myself that I'd brew a nice pot of decaf tea as soon as I landed.

When I arrived, I found Finn pecking away on his laptop, Cilla spooning heaps of sugar into her coffee and, behind the counter, Cap'n Jack stuffing his face with a fast-food breakfast sandwich. As soon as I entered, announced by the little tinkle bell on the front door, all eyes turned my way, in breathless anticipation, no doubt.

Bounding out of his seat, Finn raised his hands.

"You got our lede, Nell?"

"I got something," I said. "But I have no idea how it fits in."

We gathered around a vacant banquette by a window, where the usual crowd of worker bees bustled along to their shops and offices. I took a deep breath.

"For starters, a strange little man named Freddy fished the heart from a big cat out of Dame C's wishing well, then we were attacked by an unknown intruder, who sealed us inside C's craft room, and started a bunch of car engines—well, we thought they were car engines—and then the strange little man came to our rescue by battering down the door, which, he said, had been sealed with horse glue."

I took another deep breath and surveyed the faces before me.

"A cat's heart?" said Cilla.

"Horse glue?" asked Finn.

"What have you been smoking, Bly?" roared Cap'n Jack. "I don't pay you to smoke reefers!"

Okay, I deserved that.

Maybe I should have used more finesse in telling my tale. I tried again, filling in the gaps, and explaining that Dame C seemed to dismiss the whole incident.

"So what does all this have to do with Milo?" Cilla asked hopefully. "Did you connect the dots?"

"Well—"

"We've got till three to pull this story together, damn it, so there better be some goddamned dots!" said Cap'n Jack, who still had the remnants of his breakfast sandwich stuck in his beard. He glared with his beady, red-rimmed eyes, and I could smell the Bloody Mary he must have transported from O'Toole's to wash down his sandwich.

"I don't know about dots, but there may be a common thread—wildlife. First, Milo was found with a piece of ivory stuck in his craw, then all that fancy loot, including some ivory pieces, were stolen at the Morrisons' party right from under their noses. Then Freddy hauls out a bag with the heart of a big cat. At least according to Quigley." I felt myself deflating. "Okay, maybe I'm clutching at straws."

"Dots, threads, goddamned straws now!"

Cilla raised her well-manicured hand and stopped Cap'n Jack in mid-rant. "Cappy, maybe Nellie's right. There were a lot of exotic items at that silent auction, and didn't Mitzi tell you about that elephant, Kwonzi—"

"Kubwa," I corrected.

"Right, Kubwa, who's at the zoo now?"

"That's what Mitzi said," I said.

Cap'n Jack was swiveling his egg-shaped head to and fro, trying to keep up.

"So, Nellie could be right about the common thread. Wildlife."

Finn, who'd been idly doodling on his pad, asked the obvious question. "But so what? Big cats, elephants, ivory—how does any of this connect to Milo? If he was in with a cartel, we need more proof than that. And what about the Morrisons? How are they connected? If they are connected, that is. I'm thinking Dame Crazydish knows more than she's saying. Can't you crack her, Nell?"

I shrugged. "I don't know what game she's playing, Finn. I mean, I get a panicky call from her to meet at the house about some odd smells coming out of the wishing well and now she's back to being coy about what they found. She even shooed me away when Freddy first showed up."

Cap'n Jack stood up and announced, "We got enough for now—the ivory and the cement overshoes." He turned to Finn. "How about that stuff you heard at the poker game, about Milo locked inside his cabin and that underwear model?"

Finn considered this and shook his head. "If I went with any of that, the La Joya swells would shut us down and we'd be left out in the cold. Plus, if I write anything about Milo's date hoisting a champagne bottle while trying to break down his door, I hope you got a lot of insurance, Cap. We'd get sued for libel."

"And we'd end up looking like a cheesy tabloid," I added. "Besides, the ivory and cement angles alone will put us on the map, assuming we break this before the chief holds his news conference. Wendy didn't know when he plans to do that, but he could be ready to put the skids on our scoop."

We were quiet for a while, and then Cilla proposed a solution to our quandary.

"We can't take a chance, guys. Why don't I post a teaser on my Twitter and Instagram accounts—about the ivory and the cement? At least we'd get it on the record, right?"

Finn twirled his pencil. "How many followers you got, Cill? What's to keep our competitors from taking your teaser and running with it, like it was their scoop? They're the big guns, we're not."

That's when Finn's cell chirped. He looked at the screen and raised his eyebrows.

"Well, what do you know," he said. "Incoming call from Detective Wendy Nakamura."

Phillippe Perreau was dead. Very dead. Dangling from the crystal chandelier in the main room of the La Joya Gallery des Art, the distinguished curator was twirling around above his vast collection of rare artifacts like an aerial act from the Cirque du Soleil. At least, that's what Detective Wendy told us as we assembled at our usual spot at Starbucks by the Sea. A night watchman had discovered him in the wee hours, alerted by a howling dog—Phillippe's pooch, Rodin.

Like Milo, Phillippe had been accessorized.

"Oh my God!" Cilla's saucer eyes were working overtime. "He had a piece of ivory stuck down his throat, too?"

"Would you keep it down!" Wendy hissed, looking around the patio for eavesdroppers. "No one knows about this yet."

"Why the hell not, Wendy?" Finn pointed his pen directly in her direction. "Perreau's a big wheel around here, he's found hanging on a chandelier, with a bone in his craw, and this is all hush-hush? Are you kidding me?"

Wendy was staring at the steam rising from her cup of chai tea.

"You were the one who called us, Wendy." Finn was leaning in, keeping his voice low. "I hate to sound like a broken record, but we're staring down a deadline today. You can't just dangle a shiny object in front of us, then clam up. What's going on?"

We waited. Finally, Wendy looked up at us and took a deep breath.

"I called to head you off before you went to print, Finn. This is way bigger than we thought. There are other players."

"Yeah, like who?"

"Like the Department of Fish and Wildlife, that's who. This is what they do, go after poachers. They've been sniffing around, but usually they're investigating all those rug stores that keep popping up and disappearing when the heat's on. But this is different. This is a gallery, a very respected one, and Phillippe Perreau is a town father, not a playboy like Milo."

I took a swig of my black tea lemonade.

"Are we talking about smuggling animal parts again?" I asked. "Cartels?"

"We are still off the record," Wendy said, zeroing in on Finn, who shrugged and put his pen down.

"Okay, for now."

"I'm part of a task force that's been formed. State, feds, they're covering all the bases."

At this, Finn slammed his hand down hard on the table, jiggling everyone's beverage.

"You're on a task force? You didn't think that was worth telling us?"

Wendy held up her hand. "Calm down, Finn. I just found out myself. But this is big and they're keeping things under wraps for now."

"How big? What exactly has the force been tasked with?" I asked.

"Poaching has always been a problem, especially in coastal areas," Wendy said. "But our area has become a hot spot for smuggling animal parts, and the task force wants to track down who is behind it."

"And with bodies popping up," I said, "I guess our hot spot is getting a lot hotter."

Wendy nodded. "We need to identify the pipeline before anyone else gets hurt."

"You think Milo and Perreau—this is about payback?" Finn asked. "Sending a message? Don't mess with the cartel?"

"Wait, who says it's the cartel that is sending a message?" I asked. "Maybe its conservationists trying to punish poachers and profiteers."

"Well, that's precisely what we need to find out, isn't it?" Wendy said.

Cilla stopped nibbling her cake pop. "Are you saying that Phillippe's death—murder—won't be reported?"

"I didn't say that, Cilla. Chief Leonard—"

"Chief Lamont 'Lamo' Leonard. Terrific." Finn snorted. Wendy glared.

"As I was saying, the chief is planning a press conference tomorrow to announce Perreau's death, which is being spun as suspicious, but with no details. No hanging from the chandelier, no ivory down his throat. The same with Milo. All the chief will say is that the case is still being investigated.

No mention of the ivory or the cement boots. They're trying to connect the dots. And the chief will not be drawing any connections between Milo and Perreau. They're being treated as separate incidents." Wendy looked at each of us.

"So, we go back to the *Crier* and tell Cap'n Jack to fill page one with society crap?" Cilla shook her cake-pop stick in Finn's face.

"Hey!"

My head was spinning, what with the crazy night in Cate's craft room, horse glue fumes, Mitzi's silent auction, sinister delivery guys, and theft, and now this. Was I in over my head? Of course I was, but I couldn't admit that, least of all to myself.

"So, Wendy, we're left high and dry?" Finn was as angry as I'd ever seen him.

"Look, I didn't think I'd be on the spot before," she said. "I thought Milo got caught up in some nasty business with some sickos. A good case for me and a good story for you. Maybe we could help each other, under the radar. But now? I'm on the task force and everybody will be watching me. In this crowd I'm the rookie. I can't risk it."

Finn smacked the table again and we all jumped. "Here's what we're going to do, Wendy. We'll go with our original plan—the ivory and the stuffed shoes, which we truly did hear from another source, by the way. We'll keep the Perreau stuff—the ivory stuck in his craw—off the record, unless we get that from another source too." Finn glanced at me, but Wendy didn't seem to notice. Some cop she was.

"We're going to do our jobs, Wendy," Finn said before turning to Cilla and me. "You agree?"

We did.

CHAPTER TWELVE

By 6:00 a.m. the next day, the *Crier* was plopped onto La Joyan doorsteps, or general vicinity, and stuffed into sidewalk boxes throughout the village.

At 11:00 a.m. Chief Lamont "Lamo" Leonard was scheduled to brief the media on the dual—but supposedly separate—demises of Milo, the playboy shoe magnate, and Phillippe Perreau, patron of the arts.

Not long after the circulation folks had finished their rounds, the cell phones of the *Crier* crew had started chirping, chiming, or otherwise waking us up.

My call came in around 6:25, my ears greeted with the dulcet tones of one Sylvia Sheldon, ex-Bronx detective sergeant and current aide-de-camp to Chief Lamo, er, Leonard.

"What the !#$%* do you think you're doing, Bly, you and your pals at that rag you call a newspaper?"

My ear started throbbing.

"Deputy Chief Sheldon? I am honored that you would reach out to a humble obit writer such as myself."

Actually, I wasn't surprised in the least. We might be low on the media totem pole, but an obit was an obit, as in dead people, and Sylvia was a cop. She didn't miss much and kept track of the dear departed no matter where the obit ran, especially in this tony enclave.

"I go out to get my papers—including that throwaway of yours—and I see this?"

Our headline read: "Museum Curator Perreau Found Dead." The subhead: "Second La Joya Luminary to Die This Week. Foul Play?"

"Where did you get that stuff about Milo? The ivory and the cement shoes? And what about Perreau? You didn't get any of that from us, Bly, so spill, goddammit! Who leaked it?"

The decibels kept rising.

"As for the headline, it was a simple question," I said calmly. "Was foul play involved in both deaths? What's the big deal? I'm sure your boss will be filling in all the gaps at the news conference. Secondly, the details about Milo? We have our sources—and we don't have to tell you who they are, as you well know. Did we get anything wrong?"

"That's not the !#$%* point and you know it, you and your pack of dummies. We get to break the news in these cases, not you. By eleven, it's going to be a !#$%& three-ring circus, thanks to you. We're already getting calls!"

I felt giddy.

So we did get the scoop on Milo's murder and Perreau's death—in his case, minus the ivory down his throat. Score one for our team. More to come, soon.

"Look, Depu—"

"This isn't over!"

There was no slam, so she must have been on her cell phone, but it still registered as a slam. Then my phone meowed—yes, that's what it does—and the caller ID read "Finn."

"Hey, Nell, you won't believe—"

"She called you too?"

Finn was chortling, or maybe it was a guffaw. "Yeah, Syl called Jack and Cilla too. We have arrived, Nellie. We'll be the stars at Lamo's briefing."

"He'll eat us for brunch, Finnian, and spit out our bones. Not that I'm complaining. We did get the big scoop. But didn't you tell me that Leonard is a vindictive prick?"

Oh my, would you listen to me? Such language for a sweet, small-town girl.

As for my warning, I imagined Finn shrugging as though he gave a damn.

"Bad optics, Nell. He won't do that, because he hates my guts and doesn't want to give me the spotlight."

"Yeah, Finn, you are telegenic."

"Damn right. Anyway, my guess, he'll just ignore us and find another way to screw us."

Something to look forward to.

"Okay, Mr. Optics, what's your plan?"

I could sense another shrug.

"We show up and take it from there. Bask in the glory. Get some respect for a change."

That's when I heard my door slam shut downstairs and the muffled sounds of feet on my staircase, followed by, "Nellie! Get out of bed this minute!"

"Who the hell is that?" Finn said. "Where are you? Oh, never mind. Tell Dame C I said hi."

Then he was gone, and she was there, standing in my doorway, in all her glory, from the feathered turban on her head to the matching slippers on her feet.

"I told you not to print that story! Now they will come after us, don't you see?"

My brain was still wrapped in cobwebs from interrupted zzzz's, but I managed to get out of bed, tug on my bathrobe and slippers, and take a deep breath. Coffee. I needed coffee. What I got was a hysterical Cate, now pacing my room.

"What are you talking about?" I walked into my mini-bathroom, turned on the faucet, and splashed some water on my face. I grabbed my brush and started raking out the snarls on my disheveled head, but when I looked up into the mirror, there she was—hovering behind me like Freddy Krueger. I twirled around, holding my brush like a pistol, and suddenly felt very foolish.

"Are you listening to me? You and your friends will be targets now, as well as Quigley and myself, thanks to you. They know you are on to them and they must know you live on my property."

Her high-pitched screech was now downgraded to a hoarse whisper, as she spun around and started peering out the windows. My kitties managed to sleep through it all, but they had weathered their share of tornados back in Kansas, so this was no big deal. As for me, the dynamics of our relationship seemed to be an ever-fluctuating yin and yang, with Cate and I trading off being cool or crazed. She had that effect on me.

"Cate, who will be after us? Should I be taking notes?"

"No notes!" Cate started pacing. "Your story implied that the two deaths—Milo and Philly—were connected. And you wrote that Milo had a piece of ivory in his throat and cement in his shoes. How dare you!"

Philly?

"How dare I? We didn't name you as the source."

"That's not the point. Those details were meant for my memoir and your ears alone. You betrayed me!"

"No I did not." Now I started pacing in the opposite direction. "You can't just drop these tidbits and expect me to ignore them. I have a job. Besides, who's going to guess this came from you?" I stopped pacing. "If you knew about Milo, I'm assuming you also know about Perreau's murder? Cate, do you know who is behind this?"

Now Cate stopped pacing and her expression was a combination of surprise, anger, and confusion. She did have quite a range.

"Murder?" she asked. "What are you talking about?"

I just stood there, wagging my finger at her.

"Are you angry that I found this out without your help? We do have other sources, Cate."

She took in a deep breath and slowly let it out. "Very well, yes I do know about it. Are you going to print that, too? That Philly didn't hang himself?"

"Yes, if you'd like to confirm it. We promised our source that we wouldn't write about that unless we got it from someone else. I'm guessing it isn't likely to be you."

Cate moved a few steps closer and lowered her voice. "I will say nothing for publication. Unlike you, I know when to keep my mouth shut."

At that moment my cats yawned and stretched and scampered down the stairs, expecting breakfast. And I had to get to the paper and huddle with the gang before the news conference.

"I need to get ready, Cate. Chief Leonard—"

"Another fool!"

"Yes, so I'm told, but he's holding a news conference this morning and I need to be there. I'll keep you posted—"

"You'll keep *me* posted? That's rich."

"But I'm not, Cate, so if you'll excuse me?"

With that, she spun around and headed to the stairway, telling me, as she descended, "This is not over, Nellie Bly. We will discuss this later."

Then the door slammed shut, Patience and Prudence meowed, and I headed downstairs to tend to coffee and cat food, making a mental note to buy chains for the doors. But knowing Cate, she'd probably just tunnel in from a secret portal under the house. On the other hand, Cate was telling me that we were in danger from—well, who knows? Cate seemed to have an inkling she wasn't willing to share. Maybe I needed door chains for multiple reasons.

For this, I left Kansas?

If Chief Leonard had indeed intended to snub Finn and the rest of us, he got upstaged by assorted other outlets, including from overseas. Milo and Perreau had both been well-connected globally, and this story was rapidly expanding beyond our little village. As soon as we entered the conference room, we were set upon by our fellow reporters, with calls of "Hey, Finn!" and "Cilla!" Well, them, not me. No one seemed eager to chat with the proprietor of the dead beat, although, oddly enough, the story du jour did involve dead people. On the other hand, maybe it wasn't so bad staying under the radar.

While Finn and Cilla were basking, I roamed around the room, bobbing and weaving through the tangle of camera equipment, on up to the podium, which was still empty. I wondered who'd be flanking the chief. The DA? The Department of Fish and Wildlife? I didn't have long to wait. Striding into the room was Deputy Chief Sylvia Sheldon, in full command mode, until she spotted me and, even more alarming, the scene beyond: Finn and Cilla holding forth and stealing what was supposed to be Chief Lamo's thunder. She was not happy.

"Morning, Deputy Chief," I said, giving her my most sincere smile. She glared at me and I felt my brain burn. She headed to the podium, adjusted the mic, and clapped her hands together, causing everyone to go silent.

"Members of the media, please take your seats."

Sylvia cast her dark eyes on each of those in attendance until they were settled in, flipping open their notebooks, turning on recorders and other gizmos, while the camera folks got ready to roll. I joined my crew, which had managed to secure three spots in the front row. We had arrived.

"This is a busy day for Chief Leonard, as you must know, so this will be brief. There will be two minutes allotted for questions, so keep them short, understand?"

As much as Sylvia tried to polish her elocution, at least in public, her New Yorkese always bubbled up to the surface and went full tilt when she was pissed. The early-morning phone call was a prime example. Chief Leonard, on the other hand, never even tried, clearly proud of his days on the mean streets of the Bronx, where the two of them had scrambled up the ladder, no doubt, elbowing everyone else to the pavement. We had our mayor to thank for having poached them from the Big Apple to the Jewel of the Sea.

At the sight of the chief bounding onto the stage like a pit bull, Sylvia retreated to the back. How to describe Chief Lamo? A fire hydrant, but with a lot of spit and polish, especially on his bald pate, which beamed under the reflected glow of the lights. As short as he was, the chief spoke in a bass that rolled like thunder throughout the room. My brain was twice assaulted.

I turned to look at Finn, but he seemed as cool as ever, while Cilla had a frozen smile that I knew masked her anxiety. But the chief didn't even give us a glance, just slapped down a sheet of notes, gripped both sides of the podium with his meaty paws and started playing to the cameras.

"We got two dead. Milo Malovich, the shoe guy, and Phillippe Perreau, from the La Joya Gallery—" the chief glanced down at his cheat sheet "—dess Art."

Dess?

He went on to fill in the dates of the dual demises, but quickly added, "Let me be clear, folks. We are investigating these as separate cases, so don't start spinning this as a serial psycho running amok. We got—"

"What about that piece of ivory stuck down Milo's throat and the cement—"

"And what about Perreau? How'd he die?"

The chief's face made like a steamed lobster. "Am I finished? Did I ask you for questions? So shut the !@#$&* up!"

"Yeah, but the *Crier*—"

Boom!

"I don't give a @#$%& about that rag, buddy." With that, the chief cast his eyes on Finn, and I almost expected my pal to combust. But Finn just sat there, doodling in his notebook and grinning. That really pissed off Lamo, who said, through clenched teeth, "Okay, O'Connor, you wanna come on up and take over? You wanna do my job?"

Finn looked up and seemed to be considering this: "Well, it does pay more than my job, so maybe—"

The chief smacked the podium so hard I ducked, expecting splinters to start flying my way.

"Shuddup, you two-bit hack! And don't think I won't find out who leaked this to you."

I looked around the room, but there was no sign of Wendy, thank goodness.

Then Finn stood up.

"Are you telling us that I got it wrong, Chief? If I did, I'll write a correction. But, if I got it right, then, you owe us the facts—on both of these homicides."

The chief's froggy eyes bulged. "Homicides? Did I say anything about homicides? Where you get that? More leaks?"

Finn grinned. "So they are homicides—both of them?"

Then the dam burst and the chief was getting pelted with questions, all of them shouted and sounding like the Tower of Babel. I distinctly heard, amid the cacophony, a question about the Morrison auction heist, which had been reported in the local newspaper's society page, along with mentions in various social-media posts.

Meanwhile, Sylvia looked genuinely alarmed that her old pal was about to have a stroke. She quickly took her place by his side and gently reclaimed the mic.

"If we do not have order, you will all leave now." She then patted the chief on the shoulder and whispered something in his ear. He took a deep breath and nodded.

"The shoe guy, Milo, was fished out of the harbor and the museum guy, Perreau, was found inside, hanging from the chandelier. Could be a suicide. We're still investigating—"

"Milo had a hunk of ivory shoved down his throat, Chief," Finn said. "What about Perreau? Any common thread?"

Before the chief could leap over the podium and go for Finn's throat, Sylvia grabbed his arm and again whispered in his ear. He took another deep breath.

"Like I said, we're investigating. That's all I got for you now."

He grabbed his cheat sheets and stomped off, disappearing into the wings. Sylvia then took command.

"We will inform you when we get more information, but, I'll remind you, this is an open investigation and we will do nothing—" she turned her gaze to Finn "—to jeopardize our work. We also will be vigilant in identifying anyone in our department who might be compromising this investigation. They will be dealt with to the fullest extent of the law, believe me."

With that, Sylvia left the podium and also disappeared into the wings. When we turned to leave, I spotted Detective Wendy Nakamura, standing in the back of the room, her face as white as a beached whale. Would the brass be able to find out that Wendy had been the one to tip us off about Perreau's death—before Cate even had the chance? I guess we'd find out soon enough.

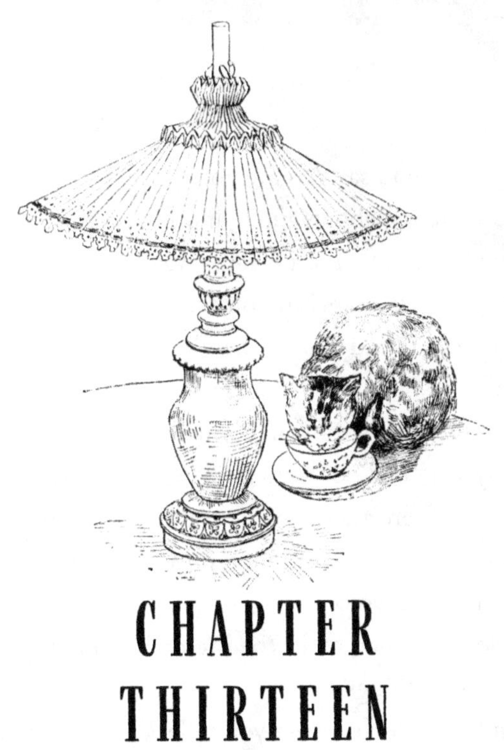

CHAPTER THIRTEEN

"Shit! What was I thinking?"

Wendy and our gang were again seated around the patio table at Starbucks by the Sea, enjoying the sunset. Well, enjoying might be an overstatement, as Wendy hardly looked joyful. Though I hadn't known her long I had sized her up as cool and unflappable, but at this moment she was neither.

Finn sat there sipping a Frappuccino and doodling in his notebook.

"Hey, Wendy, no need for buyer's remorse. You weren't our only source, you know, and we did some of our own digging. Plus, we kept our word about not using the Perreau stuff." Finn took another swig, adding, "For now, anyway."

Wendy gave him a look that could be called withering.

"Easy for you to say. You've got nothing to lose. This is my career we're talking about, Finn, and I'm on that damned task force." She leaned in. "For now, anyway."

Cilla, who was munching on a chocolate biscotti, reached over and patted Wendy on the hand.

"Don't be silly. You'll do great on that task force. And think of all the juicy stuff you'll bring back to us."

Wendy snatched her hand away. "Are you crazy? I can't do this anymore. There are too many players now and too much at stake. Did you notice the foreign press there today? This isn't small-town stuff anymore."

Cilla looked stung and I tried to defuse the tension but no doubt just made things worse.

"Wendy, we don't expect you to leak us information. That wouldn't be ethical, right? But if we were to turn up some nuggets on our own, maybe you could confirm or deny? Would that be okay?"

"No! It would not be okay, Nellie. I've got a lot of people breathing down my neck now, with Sylvia Sheldon leading the pack. She suggested me for the task force, did you know that? 'It will be good for your career, Wendy,' she told me. Sure it will. Are you familiar with the phrase, 'Keep your friends close . . ."

". . . and your enemies closer," Finn said. "I thought she was your mentor."

Wendy gripped her iced tea and took a swallow.

"I don't know what to think anymore, Finn. But I need to lay low for now. I don't know who to trust."

Cilla looked hurt.

"You can trust us, Wendy. We've got your back."

"Sure," Finn said, "but we've also got a job to do, and we need to move on that Perreau angle. Hell, now Lamo is spinning this as a possible suicide. Are you kidding me? Does he think he can keep a chunk of ivory shoved down Perreau's throat a secret? Why the cover-up?"

Wendy didn't answer right away, just took another big sip of iced tea, and I could almost see the wheels spinning in her head.

"I have no idea what that jerk is up to, Finn," she said. "You may be giving him way too much credit. He's not very bright, but he did manage to convince the mayor and city council that he was this big crime buster from the Bronx with a ton of street cred. I'd say Lamo is making it up as he goes along, because he's no detective. Now, give him a set of brass knuckles or a taser, that's more his style, I'm guessing."

We were all mulling this over when Finn broke the silence.

"Where does that leave us? We got two stiffs and we know the cases are related, and maybe there will be more. If a cartel is involved, who knows where it's heading?"

I was reminded of Cate's paranoia this morning, but was it paranoia? I decided to brief the gang on her latest theatrics.

"Cate thinks someone is after her?" Cilla's saucer eyes were luminous in the fading light.

"She seems to be convinced that she and Quigley might be targets, but she won't give me any details. She's saving everything for her memoir, if she lives long enough to finish it. At least, that's what I think she's worried about, that someone might try to shut her up, if they know how much she knows. Cate even hinted that I could be on the list, because I live on her property. Who knows? Maybe it leaked that, as her ghostwriter, I'm privy to her secrets." I felt that chill again. "I'll have to admit, that gives me the creeps. Especially after what happened in Cate's craft room the other night."

Wendy almost choked on her tea. "What happened in Cate's craft room, Nellie? Who's holding out now?"

I raised my palms. "No, Wendy, I wasn't holding out on you. It's just that so much has been happening, we had the story to write, and then you called about Perreau—I would have told you."

She tilted her sleek head. "Well, Nellie, no time like the present."

And so I began my tale of stinky smells, a severed heart, a mysterious little man and horse glue.

That night, tucked away in the loft with the kitties snoozing nearby, I was feeling restless. Wendy had listened to my wacky tale with a poker face and then stood and excused herself, with the vague assurance that she'd stay in touch. Finn, Cilla, and I were left with another deadline bearing down on us and even more pressure to keep our momentum going.

On my way home I had stopped at the hardware store and purchased two chains that I secured to the front and back doors. I was relieved that the main house was dark, and I assumed that Cate and Quigley had gone out for the evening.

Cate wouldn't be happy about the chains, but I'd deal with that later. Meanwhile, curled up on the bed with a mug of chamomile, better to soothe my nerves, I again turned my attention to the antique desk filled with Cate's memorabilia, which probably would end up in her memoir. Catherine

Cavendish, society dame, aka Catherine Carlisle, showgirl, and B-movie actress.

My movie-buff mother might be a good source of intel, but what time was it now in Paris? Or had she moved on to other parts unknown? With Nora Nottingham Bly, it was hard to keep up. She'd leave me cryptic texts about her travel plans and occasionally I'd get a postcard. Africa, India, Asia? By the time the postcard arrived, she'd be on the go again. Nora would have fit right in with the expats of the twenties, who spent their days roaming from one salon to another, writing, drinking, and reveling in their bohemian lifestyles. Alas, she had to settle for backpacking through Europe with her fellow Bennington College trust-fund pals, sending dispatches of her adventures to travelogues that had agreed to publish them for a pittance.

The trust fund had been set up by her wealthy parents, who met their end while skiing in the Alps when an avalanche came tumbling down. As it turned out, her folks were deeply in debt, and the trust fund didn't last long. The bank took the country house, the cars, the jewelry and art, leaving Mom broke. Ever resourceful, she was able to leverage her contacts in the travel world to finance what turned out to be a successful career as a photojournalist. Until I happened, that is. Oops! My mother was a free spirit who considered monogamy an unnatural state. I should also point out that she hadn't a clue who had fathered me, a mystery to this day. Where would I even look?

Anyway, I was born back in the States, where Mom established a circle of artists, writers, and musicians who took us in on a revolving basis, while she tended to my education and found work freelancing for several New England publications. Once she landed a full-time gig at the *Manchester Union-*

Leader as a general assignment reporter, we finally settled down in a cozy little cottage on a hill. By that time I was twelve and Mom thought it was time for me to enroll at a public school, an experience that made me feel like an alien invader. I adjusted, although I never was able to come up with a good answer when asked, "Who's your daddy?"

Once I headed off to college, Mom decided that she had socked away enough for her to resume her days as a globetrotter, freelancing tales of her adventures. Flash forward, and that's where we are today. I now use Facetime to chat with her face-to-face, but as I didn't know what time zone she was in at the moment, I just texted her: *Hidy ho. What do you know about a vintage starlet named Catherine Carlisle? Love, Nellie.* Maybe she had some intel that I wasn't able to find on the internet.

My phone meowed at around 3:00 a.m., an occurrence that appeared to be the new normal for me. I clicked on my bedside lamp and tapped the message icon: *Hidy ho yourself. Why do you want to know?*

Cryptic and inquisitive, that's my mom. Rather than spending the rest of the night tediously exchanging texts, I responded: *Facetime?*

As it happened, she was back in the US, settled back into the little cottage up on the hill, and now preparing her tea and hummus on whole-grain toast, with a side of fresh fruit, chia, and flaxseed. I know that because we now were Facetiming.

"Why are you asking about Catherine Carlisle, sweetie? Isn't she dead?"

Mom filled her teacup and sat down at her little kitchen table, lifting her face to the screen. She wasn't young anymore, but well-tended, her sleekly cropped silver hair accenting a classically sculptured face sporting high cheekbones and luminous blue eyes. Even at this hour, she looked well-rested and energized. Me, not so much.

"You remember I told you about my landlady, Dame Catherine Cavendish? I'm staying in her guest cottage and helping her write her memoirs. Anyway, I was nosing around in a desk up here in the loft, and found a bunch of clips and photos, a movie poster—and what was apparently her stage name—Catherine Carlisle. I'm thinking that eventually she'll haul these out for her memoir. You are an encyclopedia when it comes to old movies. I couldn't find much about her on the internet."

Mom spread a schmear of hummus on her toast and thought about that.

"If I recall, she usually played the bad girl in those B-movies—conniving, predatory, you know the type, and then, kapow! She has a few dying words and then the screen fades to black." Mom sipped her tea. "Of course, that could describe a lot of these actresses back then, and some of them were better known. I don't think she stayed around long enough to make her mark. Maybe her option wasn't picked up. You know, Nellie, there's a busload of farm girls arriving in Tinseltown every day."

Well, I knew the rumor that she was the daughter of a Queens butcher, but I doubt the press agents back then would have included that in her bio.

"So, no scandals? I mean, she was photographed with a lot of slick-looking guys. A few of them looked downright sleazy, but probably loaded."

Mom nibbled on a strawberry and shrugged.

"You mean gangsters? Well, sure, they were always around, from what I hear, laundering their loot in Hollywood, pressuring some producer to get roles for their girlfriends. But I can't really recall anything about your landlady. Maybe she kept it all under the radar."

Hmm, that sounded like Cate, all right. But then something else occurred to me.

"I'm working on a story that might involve the smuggling of endangered animals—"

"I thought you were writing obits?"

I filled Mom in on the murders and the ivory connection. "It's turning into a big story. You didn't read anything about this, maybe online? We just broke the story."

At that, Mom gestured to what appeared to be a stack of newspapers on the floor by her feet.

"I've been a bit off the grid, Nellie, in the rain forest, actually. I've got to catch up on the news. But this sounds exciting. I can tell you, from my travels to Africa, that this type of smuggling is a huge problem and very hard to contain. It's like Whac-A-Mole." Then Mom gave me a hard stare. "But wait. Are you in any danger? It's bad enough I had to worry about all of those tornados when you were in Kansas."

Well, that was a good question, but I did not have a good answer.

"No, I'm fine, Mom." I mustered confidence. "But I need to get some sleep. Got a big day tomorrow. Let me know if you hear anything, okay? I'll send you our story. Maybe you can tap into your network."

She sipped her tea. "I'll see what I can do, sweetie, but please be careful. These smugglers are cutthroats."

We signed off and I tried to get back to sleep, but that was not to be. Just as I was drifting off, I heard a fierce rattling coming from downstairs, the kind of noise that sounded like a door being pushed against a chain, followed by, "Nellie Bly! Let me in this instant!"

I thought about tugging the covers over my head and hoping she'd go away. But from what I know about my looney landlady, she'd just drag a ladder over to my window and pound on the glass.

"Nellieeeeeeeeeeeeeeeee!"

I was beginning to feel nostalgic about tornados.

As soon as I disengaged the chain, Cate pushed through, nearly knocking me to the floor. Wrapped in a kaftan and turban, her feet tucked into multicolored feather mules, she glared at me, wagging a bejeweled finger in my face.

"Cate, it's the middle of the night. What are you—"

"Why did you tell that origami woman about the event in my craft room, Nellie? What were you thinking?"

What?

"Origami woman? What are you talking about?"

She rolled her eyes and sighed. "Don't play dumb with me. That Oriental detective, Origami."

Now it was my turn to sigh.

"Her name is Detective Nakamura, and the proper term is Asian, not Oriental. She's a citizen of the USA, born right here in San Diego."

"Let me tell you something, Nellie, loose lips sink ships! Don't you understand that?"

How old was this dame?

Before I could respond, Cate was stomping her feathered feet into my sitting room and depositing herself in the comfy chair.

I sat down on the settee and tried to collect my thoughts.

"We've been exchanging information regarding the case, Cate, to the degree that Detective Nakamura can share. I filled her in on what you call 'the event' in your craft room—"

"Prank! I should have said prank, because that's what it was, not a high crime. We do not need the police sniffing around."

"I'm confused, Cate. First you say that we all may be in danger, then you say you don't want the cops coming around? When did Wendy—Detective Nakamura contact you, anyway?"

"She had the temerity to show up here this afternoon without so much as a phone call—"

"You have an unlisted phone number, Cate, so what else was she supposed to do? I'm sure she was concerned about your safety."

She waved her hand. "Well, I did not admit her into my house. Fortunately, there are no neighbors to have witnessed me, Dame Catherine Cavendish, being interrogated by the gendarmes. That woman just stood there, trying to intimidate me, asking a lot of foolish questions. I sent her away. I have my rights, you know."

"Cate, you do understand that there have been two grisly murders, and you clearly know more than you're telling. This is more important than your memoir, so you don't get to hoard critical details—"

"Hoard? What are you talking about?"

I let out a deep breath. "I think that you and Quigley know something about these murders—or suspect something. If that's true, then you could very well be in danger." I added: "That's assuming that you didn't kill anyone. Did you, Cate?" I was half kidding but suddenly felt better about the door chains. What did I actually know about this woman?

"Are you mad? Do you actually believe that I am capable of murder? If you do, then I want you to pack up and leave immediately!"

Uh-oh. Might have gone too far. I held up my palms in surrender. "No, of course I don't think that, Cate. But you need to work with me here. We've got two bodies and there could be more coming. If you do know something, tell me."

Cate folded her arms tightly around her body, maybe in a protective gesture. I almost felt sorry for her. Almost. But her coy act was getting old.

Then she surprised me, leveling me with a fierce stare. Rage, fear, guilt? Cate leaned forward and spoke in a hushed tone. "Very well, Nellie. Let me tell you a story."

CHAPTER FOURTEEN

I raised a hand, signaling Cate to wait and scampered over to the front door, making sure I had engaged both locks. I then went to the kitchen sink and splashed cold water over my face. When I got back to the settee, she had laid out two martini glasses, a sterling silver tumbler, a small container of olives, and a set of silver toothpicks. Huh?

"Where did you—?"

"In the lowboy dresser, of course." Cate waved to a corner of the room. "I like to be prepared for every contingency."

Cate started shaking the tumbler and was in the process of unscrewing the lid to the olive jar when she frowned at me. "Well, Nellie, where is your tape recorder? Your notebook? I have no intention of repeating myself."

When I returned from the loft with my tools, Cate was munching on an olive, looking thoughtful.

"Where to start?" she mused, more to herself than to me. "I've had such a colorful, exciting life, you know, but most of it has been lived under the radar. Very hush-hush."

"How about we start with your career as a B—I mean, femme fatale in Hollywood?"

Her glass halfway to her lips, she asked, "You know about that, do you? And, by the way, my dear, there is no shame in B-movies. Many of them are unsung gems—although I must admit, mine tended to remain unsung. But that was not my fault. I was brilliant. The camera loved me. But I had dreadful directors and leading men." She waved her hand in the air. "Anyway, are you telling me that you've seen my films? They're not easy to find, you know."

I took a swig of the booze and felt a warm sensation in my tummy, but I needed to pace myself if I was going to navigate Cate's usual meandering memories. "My mother is a fan of old movies, noir especially, and she was quite impressed that I was staying here and writing your memoirs."

Okay, that was a bit of an exaggeration, but Cate loved to be flattered, so Mom wouldn't mind.

"I see," she said. "Well, I had my share of fans, but my career was short-lived, and I'll tell you why."

I had no idea how any of this was connected to the murder and mayhem we were experiencing in La Joya, but I hoped that she'd get to the point before the sun came up.

"Even as a starlet I was never cast as the ingenue," Cate said, rolling another olive between her thumb and forefinger. "I was always the femme fatale, as you so astutely noted. The bad girl. The dangerous dame. The siren who lured sailors to smash themselves on jagged rocks."

With that Cate savagely speared an olive with one of the toothpicks. I pitied her leading men.

"But as I said, my films were not creating much of a buzz, so the studio's press agent, a rather tawdry fellow named Stan, suggested that I could burnish my bad girl image by keeping company with—well, I guess you could call them gangsters."

Oh my.

"Now, I'm not saying that I mingled with the A list of bad boys, you understand, Nellie. They were more like lieutenants—not thugs. They were all dressed in tailored suits and expensive shoes and flashed a lot of cash at the clubs and the racetrack. They liked to have a certain type of woman on their arm and, well, to be honest, I fit the bill. Straight out of central casting. Of course, I was just playing a part, but a girl had to do what she had to do back then to get ahead."

At that, Cate knocked down the rest of her drink and poured some more. She was in no way impaired.

"In any event, I played my part well enough and I managed to accumulate quite a treasure trove of expensive jewelry." She held her elegant hand out and inspected the large green stone that sparkled in the muted lamplight. "Unfortunately, my brilliant performance as a gun moll did absolutely nothing to help my career. Quite the contrary. The studio did not renew my contract, and I was out on the street."

Cate took a big sip of her drink and seemed lost in the memory.

"What did you do then?" I checked my microrecorder and it seemed to be humming along, while I held my pen aloft to jot notes—a backup in case the recorder suddenly crapped out.

Her sad eyes regained their focus, their dreaminess replaced by a barely contained rage. "What did I do then, Nellie? The answer came soon enough, when Alphonso—"

"Alphonso? You mean Al Capone?"

Cate gave me a sour look. "Of course not. How old do you think I am? Besides, I already told you, I did not mingle with the crime bosses, just their minions. Anyway, Alphonso Anaconda, one of my 'boyfriends,' told me what a shame it was that the studio had dumped me and maybe he could help me out. I reminded him that I still had my jewelry and I could pawn it when my money ran out. But Alphonso had a different idea."

At that, Cate started to chomp viciously on an olive.

"He offered you money to tide you over?"

She almost choked on her olive. "He certainly did no such thing. In fact, he laughed in my face and informed me that the jewelry didn't belong to me, never had, and that I was being cast in a new role."

Another dramatic pause. I prompted, "He got you a part in a movie?"

Cate let out a shriek, and I heard the sound of little cat paws clicking on the hardwood upstairs.

"No, Nellie, pay attention! Alphonso was not my hero; he was a villain. Do you know what the role was?" She was hissing now.

"Ingenue?" I regretted that as soon as the word left my lips.

"Mule!"

Okay, I was pretty sure Cate wasn't referring to that old movie about a mule named Francis.

"Smuggling?"

She nodded, her turban slipping down her brow. "I was to smuggle cocaine. Can you imagine? I had been playing the part of the femme fatale and now I was expected to become a bona fide member of the underworld."

She drew in a deep breath.

"You know, I wasn't born with a silver spoon in my mouth, Nellie. I grew up in Queens, New York. My mother took in laundry and my father was a butcher. Believe me, I know what it was like for him, having to pay protection money to those thugs. What was I thinking? Throwing in with those mobsters just to become a star? I was a fool, and I was ashamed."

Cate fiddled with her turban.

I waited.

"They had set me up from the start, Nellie. They were grooming me to smuggle cocaine and who knows what else, and I'm sure I wasn't the only down-and-out player they exploited this way. When they thought I was ready for the job, they made sure that the studio dumped me and left me high and dry, ripe for the plucking."

Wow. Was any of this true?

"What did you do?"

Cate stabbed another olive with her silver toothpick, and I was picturing Alphonso on the other end.

"What could I do? No one said no to Alphonso. He'd been so charming, so dashing, in a flashy way, but now, before my very eyes, he had become this beast. I was terrified. So I agreed to do his dirty work—but of course I was just stringing him along. I needed to escape that town and disappear. And that's what I did."

I waited.

"We made arrangements to meet the next day, but that night I made other plans. You know, Nellie, I hadn't only kept company with gangsters. I had a few other swains on the line as well, and one of them was a well-connected shipping magnate who just happened to be in town. Long story short, I called him, and he sent his limo to fetch me. I was absolutely terrified that Alphonso and his goons were watching my bungalow, but apparently I had played my part well. The cowed chorus girl who was eager to please. My shipping magnate and I set out on the yacht before dawn for the Greek isles, and that's where I hid out for several years. I was no longer Catherine Carlisle. I was Catrina Katsis. I married him. Well, he was a lot older than me, rather short and stocky and certainly not a matinee idol. But he did save me, so I felt that I owed him. He was a dear fellow, Nellie, and I did feel sad when he died. He was buried at sea."

I gave her a look.

"Oh, for heaven's sake, Nellie, I didn't kill him. He had a heart attack. I was young and he was well into his eighties by then."

"So Mr. Katsis left you a rich widow?"

She sipped her martini and shook her head.

"No, dear. You see, his children absolutely loathed me and blamed me for his heart attack. Well, that was somewhat true. He did die in the saddle, so to speak, but it's how he would have wanted to go, don't you see? Anyway, they made sure that I never saw a penny. If poor Katsy had ever written a will, I never was able to turn it up, and I'm sure his vile progeny and their lawyer made sure I never would."

I considered this. "So you were broke again, Cate?"

She looked at me and shook her finger in my face.

"Have you been paying attention, Nellie? I had my jewelry, of course."

"You smuggled the jewelry onto the yacht? The rocks that Alphonso said never really belonged to you?"

"Well, of course I did, Nellie, and they did belong to me. They were gifts from my gentlemen friends. And I should tell you, I had them appraised and they were indeed worth a fortune. I'm sure that Alphonso was quite put out with me when I disappeared and he never got those glorious gems back. A pity. But that was small potatoes compared to the cocaine I stole from him. Serves him right for trying to exploit a naïve young woman."

I took a minute to digest all that. "You snatched the cocaine? You actually became a drug runner?"

Cate's eyes popped and her mouth opened as though I had just punched her in the gut. "Of course not, Nellie. What do you take me for? I do have principles. No, I dumped that poison over the rail once we were out to sea. Think how many lives I saved, me, an unsung heroine."

"Unsung? It didn't occur to you that Alphonso knew you took off with the drugs? You didn't think he'd come after you?"

"Well, I do admit to having been young and foolish back then," Cate said, taking another swallow of her drink. "But I didn't think he'd find me."

I took another sip and checked the recorder again. Still rolling.

"On the bright side, Cate, Alphonso has probably long since claimed his horns and pitchfork," I said. "What's a gangster's life span anyway?"

"Remarkably long, as it turned out, but he is dead, albeit fairly recently. I've kept tabs, discreetly of course. In any event, in the passing years since Katsy died, I have had a few more husbands and a few more surnames, and moved around in rather rarified circles, staying under the radar, as I said. You know, I am quite a talented actress and very good at reinventing myself and disappearing into my character."

Okay, so where did this leave us?

"Cate, if you've managed to stay under the radar, how were you able to nail down a contract with a publishing house for your memoirs?"

She chuckled. "Well, Nellie, you'd be surprised how much one can discover under the radar. You see, I know where all the bodies are buried, and I've crossed paths with a lot of colorful characters. My memoir will be quite a tell-all from that B-movie femme fatale who mysteriously disappeared one night. Where did she go?"

I opened my mouth to ask the logical next question, but she held her hand up. "Don't worry, Nellie. The truth will set me free at last and earn me a tidy sum. My publisher adores salacious stories and was willing to pay me a pretty penny for mine."

"Cate, this is a fascinating story, but what does any of this have to do with Milo and Perreau?"

Cate was silent for a time, sipping the last of her martini.

"Well, Nellie, that's a very good question. You see, Alphonso might be dead, but I'm told by reliable sources that before he departed this world, he left a letter locked in a safe-deposit box, addressed to his son, Alphonso Junior, a psychopath, from what I'm told, who has tentacles in many areas of the underworld."

Cate shivered and wrapped my afghan around her shoulders.

"So what was in the letter? Did you find out?"

Cate nodded and tugged the afghan tighter.

"Oh yes, Nellie, I found out. It was a blood oath with very clear instructions. Find Catherine Carlisle and kill her."

I felt a cold tingle crawling up my back.

"Wait a minute, Alphonso sent his brood after you?"

Dame C nodded.

"Oh sh—I'm ghostwriting your memoir, Cate. That means I'll know where all the bodies are buried too."

She nodded again.

"True, but don't worry, Nellie. I won't tell my readers where I can be found and your name won't be mentioned. You are the ghostwriter, after all. Junior and his minions will never find us."

"What are you talking about, Cate? If they're connected to the murders here in town and sending you a message indeed, playing with you Godfather style—horse glue?—Well then they've already found you. Has it occurred to you that someone who works for your publisher might have leaked your address? No offense, but your publisher isn't exactly in the big leagues, am I right? We're talking tabloid tales of Tinseltown, I'm assuming. Don't you think they can be bought?"

Cate seemed a little spooked at that, but then shrugged it off.

"I'm only working with one editor, Nellie, and she seems quite professional and discreet. I wouldn't worry. Besides, maybe this has nothing to do with me after all. Maybe Alphonso's blood oath and his crazy son are not connected to any of these murders and the mischief at my house. But I am serious about writing this memoir and I expect it to be completed." She looked into her empty glass. "Even if it is published posthumously." She raised her eyes to mine. "Are you still in, Nellie?"

After Cate finally left, shortly before dawn, I staggered up the stairs and collapsed into bed, hoping to steal a few hours before I had to get up and start another merry day of crime fighting. Thank goodness I didn't have any new subjects to celebrate on the dead beat, as we were weaving the latest demise—Phillippe Perreau—into our continuing story about Milo.

I was midway through a bizarre Alice-in-Wonderland-like dream involving Cate as the red queen, a talking horse, and marauding elephants minus their tusks when my phone purred.

I blinked at the screen, which read 9:15, and realized that I was a tad tardy to work.

"Nellie, where are you?" Cilla sounded anxious. "I've been worried. Are you okay?"

Hell, no.

"Had a late night, courtesy of Crazy Cate, so I am sending you on a mission: Ask Finn to set up a meeting with Wendy. It's trading time."

There was an interval of silence on the other end of my phone and I suspected that Cilla had covered the mouthpiece on hers and was passing on my message. Then Finn came on the line with, as usual, no preamble.

"What's up, Nell? Jack's been waiting for our next bombshell. You got one?"

"Maybe. Cate told me quite a tale in the wee hours and I do believe that Wendy would find it of interest—maybe enough to trade what's been happening on her end. Can you set something up for today?"

Finn, I could tell, was ruminating.

"I'll need a headline, Nell, something to motivate her, without giving the story away. Feed me."

Morsels.

"Okay, how's this? Maniac mobster might be the murderer. Does Wendy appreciate alliteration?"

"The hell with alliteration. Are you serious? What mobster?"

"It's a long story, Finn, and I'm too brain-dead to share right now. Just set up the meet and I'll enlighten the gang. Now I'm going to rejoin the living with a gallon of caffeine and a hot shower. See you soon."

Before Finn could argue, I signed off and headed downstairs, my kitties now awake and hungry, following at my heels. My front door was still secure, and I hoped that Cate was still sleeping. But with her you could never be too sure about anything.

With Prudence and Patience busy munching their breakfast, I headed back upstairs to shower and dress, then locked up and walked quickly to the garage, hoping that the door's motor wouldn't wake Cate up. A light mist hovered, the marine layer casting a dreary cloak that made me uneasy. I felt the same way about the garage. Once inside, I did a quick 360-degree look-see before heading to my Mustang, then checked under the car and looked into the interior. No boogeymen seemed to be lurking, but I wasn't proficient at searching for bombs, and would have to take my chances.

I turned on the ignition, holding my breath, and then drove out, lowering the garage door and hoping that there would be no further breaches.

Making my way down the twisty turny hill, I continued to marvel at the magnificent coastal view, even when muted by the mist. In Kansas, I had to learn how to maneuver through a lot of crappy weather, so this was no big deal. Still, I took it low and slow on the turns, and then was greeted by large raindrops that splashed onto my windshield, forcing me to slow down even more. I had become accustomed to flat plains, and Southern California's steep hills still gave me the willies.

As my car limped along the wet pavement, soothing me with the rhythmic movement of its windshield wipers, I listened to the familiar patter of NPR. A few seconds later I was startled by the appearance in my rearview of headlights advancing toward me. Rush hour was past, but this scenic road was popular with the tourists emerging from their B and Bs to head to the village. Nothing sinister about that, right? But there was something off about this particular traveler, whoever it was. Visibility was limited, and the headlights, filmy in the mist, had an odd pattern of slowing and then revving up. When the high beams flashed, I figured it was time to pull over. Or was it?

Maybe the driver was just impatient behind a car doing considerably less than the speed limit. But I was in the slow lane, so why didn't they just pass me? Not good. The rain was heavy now and the sky darker, and then it happened. Just as we came out of a curve, my follower careened into the left lane, staying even with me. A glance told me that the windows were deeply tinted, so I couldn't see inside. My brain went into overdrive when I imagined the passenger, if there was one, aiming a gun at me and blasting me off the road. *Take a deep breath, Nellie, keep calm.* Then the car—a dark-colored sleek-looking machine with a powerful engine—cut in front of me, causing me to brake hard and send my heap spinning. As I tried to take control, my Mustang smashed into a guardrail that overlooked a steep ravine. I had no airbag, and my seat belt didn't stop me from banging my head on the steering wheel. Then it all went black.

When I came to, I was lying on a stretcher inside an ambulance, being attended to by an EMT, who started asking me questions, I suppose to determine how serious my head injury was. Concussion? Fractured skull? As it turned out at the ER a bit later, I just had a bump on the forehead, but before they released me, I was cautioned about the signs of concussion and advised to take it easy. They also said that I shouldn't drive, but that wasn't an option, anyway. The front end of my Mustang, they told me, was bashed in and tangled up with the guardrail. Just what I needed. I signed my discharge papers and was about to call Cilla for a ride. As it turned out, that wasn't necessary, because I was told that a Mr. O'Connor was waiting for me out in the lobby. Finn? What the hell?

"What are you doing here?" I said as a nurse's aide rolled me in a wheelchair into the lobby.

Finn was leaning against the wall, fiddling with his cell phone, and grinned at the sight of me. "Wow, Nell, I figured you'd learn how to drive in bad weather, what with dodging all those twisters in Kansas."

I extricated myself from the wheelchair and sent the aide on her way, feeling a bit wobbly. But Finn came to the rescue, taking my arm and leading me through the lobby out to the exit.

"Finn, how did you find out I was here?" I tried again.

"I went out for doughnuts and the traffic report came up on the radio, something about an accident involving a blue Mustang on the route you usually take to work and—"

"How do you know what route I take to work?"

Finn gave me a look. "I know where Cate lives, so that's the route you'd be taking, right? Anyway, you hadn't shown up at work yet, so I figured I'd head to the scene to check it out. But there were jams everywhere, a lot of fender benders—nobody knows how to drive in the rain in SoCal—so by the time I got there, you'd already been loaded in the ambulance, and it was heading to the hospital, sirens on."

"How did you know it was me in the ambulance?"

"What's with the twenty questions, Nell? I saw your car smashed into the guardrail. And before you ask, I know your car. You've got that dumb bumper sticker—'Kool Kitty from Kansas.'" He rolled his eyes. "So, yeah, I knew it was you. Who else would have a sticker like that?"

He had an answer for everything.

"And you followed me to the hospital?"

Fortunately, the rain had stopped, and Finn walked me over to his car, a shiny red BMW. How rich was this guy?

"Your car was pretty banged up, so I wanted to make sure you were okay."

He helped me into the passenger seat, took his place at the wheel, and off we went.

I lay back against the seat, grateful that the painkiller was finally kicking in to ease my throbbing headache.

"What happened back there?"

"Not sure." I groaned. "It all happened so fast, but now I'm remembering it in slow motion."

I gave him the lowdown, trying to remember as many details as I could.

"You made a police report, right?" Finn asked. "Suspected hit and run?"

"I haven't had the chance to do anything. I still have to get my car towed."

"Any witnesses?"

"The EMTs told me that a good Samaritan pulled over, probably right after I crashed into the guardrail. He said it was raining hard and there was a lot of fog, but he did see the taillights of a car zooming down the hill." I felt that familiar chill.

Finn gave me a sidelong look.

"What?" I said.

"I'm just thinking, with all the crazy stuff going on, especially at Cate's place, maybe—"

"Maybe what? The driver was trying to run me off the road and down the ravine?"

Holy shit.

"Could be this good Samaritan scared him off," Finn said.

"Finn, do you think they were trying to kidnap me or kill me or both? If it hadn't been for that rail, I'd have gone into the ravine and my heap could have burst into flames."

Even I could hear the hysteria slowly rising in my voice.

"Calm down, Nell. I shouldn't be scaring you. Maybe it was just a couple of frat boys out for a joyride. They hit and they ran. But without any actual witnesses to the crash, I doubt the cops will come up with anything. I mean, the way you tell it, they swerved into your lane but didn't actually smash into you. Your car was damaged when you tried to get control, but they got out of it without a scratch, so no evidence. If that's the way it happened."

Calm down. Easy for Finn to say.

"Are we still on with Wendy? I mean, were you able to set something up?"

"You still want to do this, Nell? Yeah, we're on, and I haven't told her yet about your accident—if it was an accident—but still—"

A large and colorful bump had bloomed in the middle of my forehead, only partially concealed by my bangs. I was sitting at a corner table inside Starbucks by the Sea, holding a cup of Wendy's ice against my owie.

It was early evening and we had huddled here, having taken refuge from another rain shower. I felt soothed by the splatter of raindrops against the window.

The hot tea helped too.

Wendy joined us after her shift and we filled her in on my crash.

"Should I be worried? I have to drive that road to work every day. Should I rent a Hummer until I get the Mustang back?"

Maybe one outfitted with bulletproof glass. It seemed like a good idea.

Wendy considered this as she breathed in the steam from her chai tea and then glanced through the notes she had taken.

"The windows were tinted, right? And you didn't get any ID, only that the car was dark colored, maybe black, and looked expensive? A powerful engine?"

"That's about it. The good Samaritan had nothing to add either, and I wasn't rammed, just cut off. I guess the crash itself was my fault. So, they won't have any scratches or dents on their car. Where does that leave me?"

Wendy shrugged. "At a higher insurance rate?"

"Very funny."

"Could just be an isolated incident of some idiots giving you a hard time for driving too slow in the rain," said Wendy. "Or . . ."

Finn, Cilla, and I waited. Dramatic pauses seem to be a thing now.

"Or what?" I finally prodded.

"Well, I don't want to spook you, Nellie, but you recently had another scare at your landlady's place, right? An animal heart in the well, horse glue, fake carbon dioxide? No way to tell if they're related, but you might want to stay on high alert for a while, just in case."

Agreed.

It's always good to be on high alert when impending death is heading your way. How is this helpful?

But Wendy had already moved on, turning over a page in her notebook.

"Okay, folks, you got my attention with that headline, Finn. Something about a maniacal mobster murderer? Fill me in."

Finn put down his Frappuccino and smiled like a hungry wolf.

"The word is *trade in*, Wendy, not *fill in*. Even stephen. Quid pro quo. Like that."

"So, tell me what you've got. If it's that good, I'll trade."

Cilla's violet eyes were wide with bewilderment. "Am I the only one left in the dark here? What maniacal mobster murderer?"

Finn gestured to me.

"Don't ask me, Cill. That's all I got from Nellie." He smiled that smile again. "Well, Ms. Bly, we're waiting."

Now the spotlight was on me. Taking a deep breath, I began recounting my tale of Dame C's caper, right out of a B- movie, replete with smugglers, mobsters, shady characters, and, finally, Alphonso Anaconda Jr. and the blood oath bequeathed him by Snake Sr., sadistically toying with us until he tires of his game and sends us to sleep with the fishes or whatever he might have in mind. After I had finished, I looked from Finn to Cilla and then to Wendy, all of whom were staring at me as though I had gone quite mad. Hey, don't blame the messenger, folks.

Finally, Wendy took a deep breath. "Alphonso 'the Snake' Anaconda? Are you shitting me?"

True, when she said the name out loud it did sound pretty silly.

"I shit you not, Wendy. That was the name of Anaconda Senior, Dame C's gangster boyfriend back in the day. Before I came here, I took another look at her memorabilia and, sure enough, that's how he was identified in one of the glitzy nightclub photos I came across. She was at a table with him and a lot of seedy but snappy dressers and their girlfriends. Or molls. Who knows? I also Googled him and found a couple of references to him as being a high roller in Vegas and a patron of the cinema in Hollywood. As in blackmailing or bribing his way into the studios, landing parts for his flavor of the month, or some more nefarious deal with a mogul. Of course, this was all vintage tabloid fodder, so basically rumors."

"So what about Anaconda Junior? The one you say is stalking Dame C?" Wendy asked, still taking notes.

"Zip. If he exists at all, I couldn't find anything. Unlike his daddy, he seems to be lurking in the shadows."

Wendy smacked her pencil down on the table.

"So how does that help me, Nellie? What do we have to trade? A dead low-level gangster and his potentially sociopathic son who might be but a figment of Dame C's imagination?"

Finn snagged one of the cake pops from Cilla, who squealed, "Hey!"

Popping the cake into his mouth, Finn pointed the empty stick at Wendy.

"That's not the point, Wendy. Here's the thing, Nellie just gave you a lead and, correct me if I'm wrong, you guys don't have any leads. Now you do. Just because Junior has been lying low doesn't mean he doesn't exist. He's a snake, right? He'll keep lying low until he's ready to strike." Finn made a fangy face and hissed.

"Besides, Cate might be cuckoo, or she might be cagey, or both. Maybe she's spinning this as publicity for the release of her memoir. But my gut tells me that if she says Junior is out there, I'm taking it to the bank. Obviously, we can't do anything with this stuff, at least not yet. But you can. You've got the resources to sniff around." Finn turned to Cilla. "And you, Ms. Society Scribbler, I'll bet you can run down a few sources who might know something about him. Who knows what you'd turn up?"

Cilla was thinking this over, I could tell. She did love a challenge.

"Maybe, Finn." Then she smacked him on the shoulder. "Now buy me another cake pop. A girl can't live on lattes alone, you know."

Finn tossed the cake-pop stick into the air and caught it with his fist.

"I'm good for it, Cill, but let's seal the deal with the good detective. What do you say, Wendy? Was this worth a nugget or two? We need something for the next edition, and we don't want to lose our momentum. Hey, we're the Woodward and Bernstein of this caper. We gotta deliver."

Wendy was staring into the steam from her cup, which probably wouldn't still be steamy if I hadn't appropriated her cup of ice for my boo-boo.

She looked up at us. "Okay, take notes. But you did not get this from me, understood?"

We all nodded, opened our pads and held our pens aloft in breathless anticipation. Who knew when this opportunity would come again?

"A sculpture. Female dancer. Ivory inlay. A thirty-two-piece ivory chess set. Carved ivory ornaments from Japan."

Scribble, scribble. Then we waited.

"That's a partial list of goods that the state investigators confiscated from the Museum des Art. Phillippe Perreau's place. The Fish and Wildlife department's been staking out the place for months and even planted an officer inside as a doyenne—a real grandmotherly type. You'd never suspect that she was a veteran with a long list of busts. Anyway, they were all ready to drop the hammer when Mr. P gets himself hoisted on that chandelier and fed a piece of ivory."

Wow.

"How big was the haul? Must have been more than a few trinkets, right?" Finn asked.

Wendy nodded.

"They turned up more than three hundred pieces from the gallery, and our fake doyenne was able to track down a warehouse out in El Centro. Booty worth about one point three million. And get this, she also found a ledger detailing about one hundred pages of ivory sales invoices."

"Talk about the elephant in the room," Cilla said, chuckling.

"Not only elephants," Wendy said. "The state ban covers mammoths, mastodon, walrus, warthog, whale and rhinoceros horns. Perreau's stash also included hippopotamus teeth, another no-no."

Warthogs?

Finn flipped another page of his notebook over.

"So what was he facing? A long stretch in the pen?"

Wendy shook her head.

"No, that's the thing. There tends to be a high bar for felony convictions, so he was likely facing misdemeanor counts, along with stiff fines and community service. For a first offense, anyway. Perreau probably would have pleaded out, because it was his first offense, at least, that we know of, at this particular gallery. He could have been involved in other hauls, who knows? He won't be able to tell us. But one thing is for sure, Perreau must have pissed off people in high places. We've got forensic accountants going over his books, but it's likely that with the fines, he would have gone under, and his reputation, of course, would be trashed. That could have been enough to get him to flip and rat out his pipeline."

"Also reasons for Perreau to kill himself—except there's that chunk of ivory in his throat," Finn said. "They were sending a message."

"Who?" I asked. "You're saying that his suppliers, a cartel maybe, killed him to shut him up? How did they know you guys were onto him?"

"Good question," Wendy said. "Our plant has never been compromised, and she doesn't have a clue. But it's interesting that they went for Perreau, in a very splashy way, and not her. Too much heat, I guess. But I agree, the bad guys were trying to send a message to all the other Perreaus—or Milos—out there."

Wendy gave us each a stern look.

"You use this information, you'd better come up with another source, because I'm not letting you tank my career, understand? And that Anaconda lead better pay off. If I can crack this, I'll be golden."

We were silent for a few minutes. Then Finn piped up.

"We'll have to run this by Cap'n Jack, Wendy, but maybe we could say something like, our source insisted on anonymity, because he or she is fearful for their life. I mean, that sounds like a civilian, right? Are you fearful, Wendy?"

She snapped her notebook shut.

"No."

CHAPTER FIFTEEN

Once Wendy had left, we all got refills and Finn made good on his promise to replenish Cilla's cake-pop stash, while the storm pounded hard against the windows. Southern California usually is bone dry, but Mother Nature seemed to be making up for lost time. None of us seemed eager to venture out into the storm.

"So, what's the plan?" I asked as I dunked my tea bag. "Wendy gave us some good stuff, but how much of it can we use, with just one anonymous source? I know Cap'n Jack's all about his bottom line, but still. Do we tell him that Wendy's our source?"

Finn and Cilla both spoke at the same time and their answer was a loud "No!" Some of the patrons gave us the eye.

"Will you guys keep it down. What's the problem with telling Jack?"

Finn, who had traded his Frappuccino for a more sensible black coffee, was his usual blunt self.

"He's a drunk, that's why."

Cilla nodded, rather sadly.

"Finn's right, Nellie. We've known him a lot longer than you, and I love the guy like a father, but when he ties one on, he's a terrible gossip. True, that's one of the reasons why I love him. But telling tales at the tavern is one thing. Can you imagine what would happen if he starts babbling about Wendy?"

Loose lips sink an up-and-coming detective's career.

"Point taken, but what about my point? Jack loves getting scoops and reeling in the ads, but not at the expense of making a fool out of himself and the paper. The *Washington Post* demanded at least two sources on Watergate, right?"

That's when my phone purred, and I jumped.

I checked the screen and it was an incoming text from my mom.

Anaconda Junior is bad news, Nellie! He's a crazy killer. Let's Facetime.

"Holy shit," I said, handing Finn the phone, where he and Cilla took turns reading the text.

They both looked confused.

"Nora? Who's Nora?" Finn asked, handing me back my phone.

"Oh, that's Nellie's mom, back in New Hampshire." Cilla looked at me. "She is back, right?"

I nodded.

"Yes. My mom's a big fan of old-time movies, especially B-movies. She told me she'd sniff around about Dame C. Then I texted her today about old man Alphonso and his son." I raised my phone. "Well, now we know that Junior does exist and he's as nutty as Cate says he is."

I felt that familiar chill down my spine.

"How the hell does your mother know about Junior?" Finn shook his head as though his brain was filled with cobwebs.

"Nora is a globe-trotting travel writer and photographer," I answered. "She'll go anywhere for a story. I've seen the pictures. She just got back from the rain forest, and Lord knows what she was doing there. She knows all sorts of characters, some likely deeply rooted in the underworld of smugglers."

"Are you saying that she might have crossed paths with Snake Junior?" Finn asked. "What are the odds of that, Nell?"

I shrugged.

"Nellie, we've got to Facetime her right now!" Cilla said, her violet eyes popping.

"What, here?"

"No, of course not, silly. Let's get in Finn's car. It's more comfy and mine leaks." She turned to Finn. "Okay with you?"

We gathered the remnants of our drinks and snacks, ventured out into the storm, and scrambled into Finn's ritzy ride.

Cilla ducked in back, and I climbed into the passenger seat, rain pounding on the windshield. I got on my phone and was soon face-to-face with Mom, who seemed a tad surprised that I had company.

After I introduced Finn, my no-nonsense mother got right down to business.

"As I said, Nellie, under no circumstances are you to get in spitting distance of this maniac, do you hear me?"

My mother has always had a laissez-faire approach to parenting, and I was a free-range kid growing up.

This surprised me.

It was Finn who responded, gently taking the phone away from me.

"Look, Ms. Bly—Nora. May I call you Nora? We're the Three Musketeers here and we'll always have Nellie's back, I promise. If you've got intel on this guy, maybe we can help the cops get him off the board. What do you say?"

"I appreciate that you and Cilla are there for Nellie, but it's she who is living with Catherine Carlisle and therefore could be a target as well. My daughter told me about this so-called blood oath against her landlady and I can tell you, Mr. O'Connor—"

"Finn."

"Finn. I can tell you that Alphonso Anaconda Junior does not take prisoners, nor does he leave witnesses."

Before Finn could respond, Cilla grabbed the phone out of his hand, and chirped, "Hi, Nora. It's me, Cilla. Long time, no see. How was the rain forest?"

Finn and I groaned in unison and waited for the small talk to segue back to the main topic.

"So, Nora, how do you know this creep?"

"I've never had the pleasure, Cilla, but I have my sources. Naturally I cannot reveal them. Alphonso Anaconda Junior is one of the premier traffickers of endangered wildlife contraband—ivory, potions, skins—and he's ruthless. He's a psychopath. Why, if he even suspected that—" My mother seemed to remember that her daughter was sitting a few feet away and changed the subject. "Anyway, no story is worth crossing paths with this monster."

I thought about this and reached back for my phone, which Cilla reluctantly handed me.

"Do you think he's in town? Stalking Cate—or me?"

"Could be."

"And what about you? Is there a chance that Junior knows you've been asking about him?" I asked.

At that point, Finn grabbed the phone out of my hand.

"Whoa, whoa, whoa!" he said. "Did I miss a reel? Nora, I thought you were a globe-trotting photographer and travel writer. What gives?"

"I am, but I am also an environmentalist. Anaconda is a predator and a smuggler; I would never think of confronting him directly—even if I knew where he was hiding out. But any nugget of information I have collected, I will—and have—passed on to the authorities."

"So you're an informant?" Finn was incredulous.

It was my turn to take the phone away from Finn.

"Are they on his trail?"

"According to my sources, the authorities have been pursuing him for years. But they are not about to share the status of their investigation with me. After all, I'm a journalist."

I could hear the pride in her voice.

"How is it possible that we're all in Junior's crosshairs?" I asked.

"I don't know, Nellie, but I'd guess it is because of your affiliation with Cate. Please, take my warning to heart. Junior is a sadist—the sort who loves to torment the mouse before he devours it. Now I have things to attend to and must go. Be safe, my dear. Good night."

Then she was gone and there were only the sounds of raindrops beating against the windshield.

It was Finn's turn to chauffeur me home, and he dropped me off around nine, the rain having downscaled into a steady drizzle, occasional flashes of lightning, and rumbles of thunder off in the distance. I was relieved to find that Cate's house was dark.

I unlocked the door and flicked on the light to find my kitties poised over their empty food bowls. If they wore wristwatches, they'd be tapping them.

I peeled my raincoat off and hung it on the hat rack by the door, fed and watered the felines, and then put the kettle on. My over-the-counter painkillers were starting to fade, so I took out the bottle from my shoulder bag and popped a couple more with tap water. I felt weary to the bone and just wanted to change into warm, dry comfies and slip into bed. But the best laid plans of Nellie Bly—

The sharp knock on the door scared the dickens out of me, and even my usually mellow cats hissed in unison. I peered out the half-moon window carved into the door. There stood Quigley, tall and regal, holding a very large black umbrella. He was carrying something in a tote bag, and I could only hope that it did not contain an animal part.

I opened the door and was immediately hit by a wet chill as the rain gained traction and the thunderstorm seemed to be getting closer.

"Good evening, Ms. Bly," he said in those clipped, stentorian tones. "I was waiting for you to return so I could give you this."

He then handed me the tote bag, which was rather heavy and very warm.

"Ah, thanks, Quigley."

I looked beyond him, back at the house, but it was still dark.

"Madame has retired for the night, but heard about your unfortunate mishap this morning," he said.

How did Cate know about my unfortunate mishap? It wasn't on the news. It was just another hapless motorist driving too fast in the rain and crashing into a guardrail. But at this point, I knew better than to ask questions.

Cate had her sources.

"She wanted you to have this potion—homemade you know—to help you as you heal."

He then bent down to get a better look at my forehead, which my rain-slicked parted bangs now revealed. "I trust that you didn't have any serious injuries?"

"No, I don't think so." I looked down at the tote bag, which emitted a soothing warmth against my skin. "Did you say 'potion'?"

Quigley straightened up and nodded. "Yes, Madame brews this from the plants and herbs in her garden. All organic, of course."

"What's in it?"

"I have no idea. It's her secret recipe. Just drink the potion; you'll feel better in no time and you'll sleep soundly."

I took another look at the tote bag.

"She brews this in her craft room?" That sort of gave me the creeps, given that I still had unpleasant memories of an animal heart on the workbench.

Quigley looked offended. "Of course not, Ms. Bly. Dame Cavendish doesn't believe in cross-contamination. She does her brewing in a separate room."

"My, she certainly has a lot of interesting hobbies."

"She likes to keep busy." Then Quigley bowed. "Have a good evening and do enjoy the potion."

Before I could respond, Quigley had pivoted and was striding back toward the house, his umbrella held ramrod straight, despite the wind and rain whirling around him. I looked up at the night sky and saw a bolt of lightning, followed by Thor's hammer. My heart jumped and I hurriedly closed and locked the door. The cats were in their gargoyle stance, motionless and staring at me with luminous eyes. Kitties of the corn. I always had a feeling that they were a jump or two ahead of me in the foreboding department.

Then the kettle started squealing, causing me to jump again, and I considered sampling Cate's potion. Maybe it would soothe my jangled nerves. I would have preferred one of my landlady's shakers of martinis, having developed a taste for that potion, courtesy of Cate. What if the potion was spiked? I took a silver thermos out of the tote bag, unscrewed the cap and took a sniff.

Steam scented by floral notes caressed my nose. Seemed harmless enough, and I'm sure that Samuel Johnson wouldn't have tried to kill Boswell, right? It's not as though I knew too much. Well, not yet, anyway. And didn't Cate hire me to record her stories for posterity?

Trailed by Pru and Pat, I made my way up the stairs and into my room, placing the thermos on the bedside table next to my china mug. I looked around and everything looked in order. I checked the locks on the windows, which were secure, and pulled the blinds shut. After changing and slipping under the quilt, it was time for a nightcap. Unscrewing the top of the thermos, I poured half of the magic elixir into the cup and took a tentative sip. It went down as smooth as silk, warming my tummy. I took another sip and sank back onto my feather pillow.

Then I started thinking about Wendy, the fearless detective, who, at our first meeting, had admonished me to face my fears. Get back in the water. That really pissed me off. She didn't even know me. I had to admit, the very thought of getting back in a car and driving solo down that winding hill filled me with dread. But how long could I expect Finn and Cilla to be my personal Ubers? Then I thought about Cilla, who was scheduled to pick me up tomorrow in her prized pink Caddy convertible, which she had inherited when her aunt, a Mary Kay star, passed on. Cilla tended to that car as though it were her baby, but the baby was getting long in the tooth, its rooftop torn and leaky, in the unusual event that we get rain. Still, she kept a tarp tucked away in her trunk. I sure hoped she remembered to use it, so I wouldn't have to sit in a puddle. I also hoped she remembered to take her allergy pill, lest she spend our drive having a sneezing fit, courtesy of my kitties.

I had drained my cup a couple of times and was starting to feel mellow, ready to drift off into dreamland, lulled by the rain pelting against the window. I don't know how long I slept, but I do know when I left dreamland. That was when my kitties started hissing, mewling, and making strange feline sounds that told me to get my ass out of bed. But my brain wasn't getting the message, and my feet felt like I was wearing lead shoes. I opened my eyes, and everything was a blur, with thunder crashing and lightning flashing. But why were the cats going crazy? They were Kansas kitties. Fearless. I looked over at them in the dark and they were skittering around the hardwood floors in a frenzy. What the hell?

I tossed off the quilt, swung my legs over the bed and got a grip on the mattress, easing myself up. My head was spinning, although the pain was gone. I pitter-pattered barefoot over to the front window and listened. All I heard was the rain. But the cats were clearly hearing something else. I took a deep breath and opened the blinds. Winds whipping the trees. A stormy night sky.

"What's up with you guys?" I gave the kitties the stink eye. "Did you break into the catnip?"

Then I walked over to the rear window, which overlooked the backyard and the fabled wishing well. The very thought of that well gave me goose bumps. I listened. Rain and thunder rumbling. I opened the blinds and, illuminated by a flash of lightning, there it was, staring in at me from the other side of the window. Horns, flashing yellow eyes, white luminous fangs. I opened my mouth to scream, but nothing came out, and for the second time in twenty-four hours, everything went black.

The next sensations I had seemed to cover all of my senses simultaneously: harsh light trying to breach my closed eyes, licks on my face, purring sounds—my phone?—and loud knocks pounding somewhere below me. Where was I? I opened my eyes and quickly closed them again, as the morning sunshine blinded me. I pushed away Pru and Pat, who seemed to be trying out some version of kitty CPR. My phone stopped purring, but the knocks continued, and I could hear a faint hollering outside my front door.

A familiar voice. Cilla!

Then my phone started purring again and I dragged myself over to the night table and grabbed it before it went to voice mail.

"Nellie! What's going on? I've been banging on this door forever. Are you okay?"

No, I was not, but where to start?

"Sorry, Cill, I've had a really weird night. I'll let you in."

I grabbed the side of the bed and hoisted myself up, had a dizzy spell, and collapsed on top of my quilt. Not a great start to the day.

I gingerly walked down the stairs and opened the front door. Cilla was wild-eyed.

"Oh my God, Nellie. What happened to you?"

I hadn't looked in the mirror yet, but I surmised that I didn't look too good. What was in that potion anyway?

"I'm fine, Cilla. Well, no, I'm not. I need some fresh air and caffeine."

She looked closely at me and sniffed.

"Are you hung over?"

That was a good question. Was I hung over? Maybe it was all a drunken dream. But just to be safe, I wanted to get the hell out of Dodge as quickly as possible.

"Give me a second to clean up and get dressed and we'll make a quick stop at Starbucks. Call Finn and ask him to join us."

We convened at the coffee shop and were greeted by our favorite barista, Gracie, who took our orders. It was too wet to sit outside, so we crowded around a table by the window. Finn and Cilla stared at me and, once again, it was story time. Once upon a time—

When I finished, Finn had a question.

"What the hell did that loony dame put in your drink?"

"Why would Cate drug me, Finn? I'm writing her memoir and she's been feeding me information."

"She's been feeding you something, all right!" Finn smirked.

"You did pass out, Nellie," Cilla agreed. "If it wasn't that potion, then maybe you do have a concussion."

I shook my head and instantly regretted it.

"My noggin's a little sore, Cill, but I haven't had any symptoms of a concussion. I think I just got spooked. You should have seen this thing."

Finn and Cilla exchanged a look.

"You're sure this wasn't a dream, Nell?" Finn said. "I've gotten wasted a few times and had some wild visions."

Gracie called out our order and we went to claim our breakfast and beverages, which I hoped would clear my head.

"I'm not imagining things, Finn," I said, back at the table. "I mean, at first I thought it might have been a nightmare. But it was real enough. Something was out there."

Finn had opted for strong black coffee and an egg-and-cheese biscuit, and he was busy dabbing at an errant yolk dribble.

"Okay, do I have this right?" he asked. "Quigley gave you the potion, you then drank said potion, fell asleep, and then were woken up by your cats, who were having a fit in your room. You got out of bed, there was a lot of thunder and lightning, and then you saw—or thought you saw—some googly-eyed monster peering in at you. Like that episode of *Twilight Zone*, where William Shatner opens the airplane blinds and comes face to face with a gremlin. Like that?"

"Well, when you put it like that . . . But how do you explain my cats' behavior? They're not skittish. They slept through their share of tornados in the storm cellar without so much as a meow."

Finn shrugged.

"How about this, Nell? We drive on up to your place and check out the turf. My guess is, if you did see someone out there, he or she was wearing a costume and using a ladder to peek into your window. Now that would fit the crazy stuff that's been happening at Casa Cavendish. Maybe we find ladder marks and footprints."

Sounded like a plan, but I did wonder—what would be worse? Finding evidence of an intruder, or not finding evidence of an intruder?

That was the question.

I opted to ride with Finn rather than risk sitting on a damp seat in Cilla's Caddy.

I was relieved not to find Cate puttering in her garden. Maybe she was puttering in her craft room, making bird feeders, or concocting potions in a caldron in another room. Maybe she was still snoozing.

With Dame C you never could tell.

We parked down the road from her driveway and made our stealthy way up the path leading to my place, ducking around to the back. So far, so good.

"Lucky that it rained last night," Finn said. "If there are dents in the ground under your window, maybe you weren't hallucinating." He gestured. "Lead the way."

Sure enough, there were gouges in the mud, directly under my back window—but more disturbing were the footprints. That is to say, the three-toed cloven hoof prints.

"What the hell are those?" Finn said, crouching down and pointing. "Did Satan drop by?"

Cilla had arrived and joined me in scooching down beside him, equally perplexed. She whipped out her cell phone and started snapping pictures.

Finn stood and chuckled.

"What's so funny?" I asked.

"Are you kidding me, Nell? Three toes and a cloven foot? Your creeper must have a Party City in his hood."

Cilla frowned. "But Halloween isn't for months, Finn."

"Fine, so he shopped at a costume store or ordered it from Amazon. The point is, this schmuck is no criminal mastermind. He's hokey."

"That doesn't mean he's not dangerous, Finn," I pointed out. "Not if he's involved in those murders. And, don't forget about that blood oath against Cate."

Finn just shrugged. "I wonder where the ladder went?"

Good question.

The three of us circled the backyard and peered over the ledge and agreed that the wishing well was too small a place to stuff a ladder. Maybe whoever it was had just thrown it in his car or truck. I had passed out at that point and didn't recall hearing any engine being cranked up.

With the wind and the thunder, nobody would have heard it.

"One thing we know," Finn said. "Whoever this was left those prints there to scare the shit out of you, Nell."

"Well, it worked."

"He's sending you a message."

"What message? I'm just a boarder here, Finn. I don't have anything to do with any blood oath or a grudge against Cate."

"You're more than her boarder, Nell," he said. "You're writing her memoir and maybe someone—Snake Junior, for instance—thinks that she knows where all the bodies are buried. Maybe literally."

How did I get myself into this mess?

"When I agreed to write her memoir, I thought it would be some Hollywood Confidential-style pablum about the rich and sleazy, not murder and mayhem. And besides, nobody even knows I am writing her memoir."

"Maybe whoever this is hopes to scare Nellie off," Cilla said. "Make her move out and eliminate a witness. Cate is pretty isolated out here."

"Yeah, well, from what you told me, Nell, this Quigley is probably more than her butler. He sounds like he might be a bodyguard too."

"I wonder what Cate will have to say about my night visitor? I'm sure she'll have a few ideas."

A familiar voice came from on high.

"Oh yes, people, I do indeed."

We all looked up at my bedroom window to find Cate staring down at us, her turban-wrapped head poking out.

We convened in my cozy little parlor, with Cate claiming the comfy chair, Cilla and I side by side on the settee, and Finn straddling a chair he had dragged in from the kitchen, his arms crossed over the back.

Pru and Pat were lounging on the staircase, their heads poking through the banister railing, glaring at us, or maybe just at Cate, the cat hater.

Dressed in a kaftan emblazoned with birds of paradise and matching feathered mules, Cate was not in hostess mode, so no martinis were offered. As it was still morning, that was just as well.

"Well, Mr. O'Connor, we finally meet," said Cate, eyeing Finn hungrily. "I must say, you are as dashing as your picture in that column of yours—'Sunset and Vine?' So many memories of that fabled corner."

"Nothing so glamorous. It's 'Sunset and Pearl.' That's where our office is located. And thanks for the kind words, Dame Cavendish. Call me Finn." He gave her his devilish smile, but fortunately did not wiggle his eyebrows.

"You are most welcome, and you may call me Cate."

Cilla rolled her purple peepers.

"Now, let's get down to business, shall we?" Cate said, turning again to Finn. "As to your belief that I know where all the bodies are buried, well, that's for me to know and you to find out. Once my memoir is published, do drop by and I'll gift you with a signed copy."

Then she turned to me. "You are interested in what I observed last night—regarding your nocturnal visit—I'm assuming that's what you were all prattling about out there?"

"You saw something last night?"

"Well, Nellie, I didn't witness the incident, but I did see the culprit speed away, driving right around my circular drive. The nerve. Anyway, I was up in my bedroom, which overlooks the driveway, and I couldn't sleep, with all that thunder and lightning and Phillippe flapping about."

I held up my hand. "Phillippe?"

"Yes, my other parrot, a magnificent specimen, but very high-strung. He was—"

"You have a parrot named Phillippe? Phillippe Parrot—sort of like Phillippe Perreau? Is that a coincidence, Cate?"

She gave me that "Please do keep up, Nellie" look. "No, of course not. Philly gifted me with this glorious creature to thank me for my support of the gallery. You know, I am one of their biggest donors and I have attended many of his fundraising galas over the years."

Philly?

"As I was saying, Phillippe—the parrot—was flapping and squawking and my head was splitting. So I went to the bar to make a martini and was passing the window when I heard this engine—at first I thought it was thunder—and I looked out and there it was—a dark-colored car speeding away. Of course, it was a stormy night, so I can't be sure of the color, but it did look dark from my vantage point. And that engine made a fierce roar."

"Did you get any ID?" Finn asked, his notebook out and his pen at the ready.

"No, but I heard what happened to poor Nellie—the crash? Could this be related?"

"It could be," Cilla said. "That's how Nellie described the car that drove her off the road."

Not for the first time, I wondered how Cate always seemed to be so close to the action.

"Cate, what were you doing in here?" I asked, rubbing the bump under my bangs. "I know that you own this cottage, but I am your boarder and I do have a right to some privacy."

Cate looked stricken. "Well, that's gratitude for you. I came to check on you, Nellie, and to find out if my potion had helped. Imagine my surprise to find the three of you out there poking around in the mud."

How to respond? I felt a combination of anger, violation, and guilt, but before I could say anything, Finn came to the rescue.

"Fair enough, Cate," he said, giving her that smile. "But we've got a story to file in the next couple of days, so do you have any idea who this character could be?"

"You mean do I associate with lunatics who run around on three-toed cloven hooves wearing monster masks?" She sighed. "I may be a woman of a certain age, but my hearing is excellent, so yes, I heard you down there. Anyway, during my B-movie years, I appeared in my share of dreadful monster melodramas, although I don't recall anyone wearing this particular ensemble. But if I had to guess, I'd say it was most likely Junior or one of his minions." She turned to me and held up a finger, whose clawlike nail was coated bright red. "I told you about that blood oath, Nellie. This is the type of stunt this maniac would delight in—tormenting his victim before he strikes."

I was surprised that Cate was talking about this with two other reporters present.

"I thought you wanted to keep all this hush-hush?"

Cate waved her hand dismissively. "Oh please, Nellie, don't pretend that you haven't already spilled my beans to your friends here," she said, then glared at me. "But what I say in this room stays in this room, do you all understand?"

"Unless we get the information from another source, Cate," Finn said. "That's how this works."

Cate's cheeks reddened and I had the feeling that she was having second thoughts about the dashing reporter with the devilish grin.

"You will do so at your own peril," she said, lowering her voice. "You have been warned."

Cate was good at creating an atmosphere of dread, and my bowels were churning.

"How the hell did I get in Junior's crosshairs?" I said, standing up. "All I wanted was a place to stay. You're the one who was hooked up with his father, not me."

Cate made soothing sounds that no doubt helped calm her feathered flock. "No, no, Nellie, I'm the victim here—or the intended victim. He's just using you to get to me."

I sat back down and thought about that.

"How many enemies do you have, Cate? Has this happened to you before?"

She wrapped her arms around herself and sighed deeply. "Well, I have my detractors. As you know, I've led a very colorful life and encountered people who had connections to the underworld. That will all be told in my memoir. In any event, this is why I've been keeping a low profile and live way up here. I can't risk anyone suspecting that I'm writing the story of my life."

"Yeah, well, I'd say somebody leaked," Finn said. "And you, Cate, have us at a disadvantage."

Cate's eyes narrowed the way my cats do when they feel threatened. "Why, Finn, whatever do you mean?"

"What I mean is, you know something that you're not telling us and that's putting my friend Nellie in danger. I don't like that."

Cilla nodded, her red curls shimmying. "Maybe you should move out, Nellie, and bunk in with me." Then she looked over her shoulder at my cats and frowned. "I'll get stronger allergy pills."

My pals really did have my back, which made me feel all warm and fuzzy. But only for the nanosecond it took me to see that Cate did not like the way this was going.

"Don't be ridiculous. Nellie will be fine. Isn't this what all of you do? Skulk around and dig up dirt? That's your life's blood."

Again, with the blood. Then she turned her gaze to me.

"And I'm sure that you do not want to spend the rest of your career churning out obituaries of the rich and tedious. I'm offering you a way out, Nellie. I'll even give you a ghostwriting credit—in smaller type, of course."

Obits. Ghosts. Why do all of my jobs lately involve death?

But I had to admit that Cate was right—I wouldn't move out and abandon the memoir. As Bette Davis used to say, "No guts, no glory." As long as my guts remained intact, I was all in.

CHAPTER SIXTEEN

It was late afternoon and Wendy's day off. She had agreed to meet Finn and me at the paper to hash over what we had so far. Cilla was out on a mission, trying to sniff out the mysterious drivers who had delivered the goods for Mitzi's auction. Finn and I had decided to keep Cilla's sleuthing under the radar for now. The stakes were high for Wendy and, with her participation on the task force, her allegiances might have shifted. We'd have to tread more carefully until we were sure we could trust her.

We assembled on the deck, not far from where Cap'n Jack was snoozing in his hammock. Wendy seemed unusually subdued. I asked if she'd had the chance to question Mitzi about the auction heist and those shady drivers.

"I went to her McMansion and hit a stone wall," Wendy said, glancing over at our slumbering editor in chief. "What's with him?"

"Cap'n Jack?" Finn said. "Sleeping off his liquid lunch as usual. Don't mind him. Anyway, what about Mitzi?"

"If she knows anything, she's not talking. In fact, she said that she doesn't deal with the 'hired help' directly." Wendy made air quotes. "One of her assistants makes the arrangements for her soirees, but all of her vendors, from the drivers to the caterers and waitstaff, are vetted, she said. As for the 'unfortunate incident—'" more air quotes "—Mrs. M. assured me that the goods were all insured, and didn't I have more important work to attend to?"

"Wow, that's a strange response," I said. "Aren't people usually complaining that the cops aren't doing enough to get their property back?"

Wendy nodded. "Yeah, but it did give me an opening to ask her about Perreau," she said. "I suspect that he donated some of his stash to her auction, but when I started that line of inquiry, she shut me down. 'The identity of our donors is confidential, unless they say otherwise,' she said, and what did the theft have to do with Perreau's tragic death, anyway?"

Wendy shook her head as though it was filled with seawater. "I wasn't authorized to discuss the details of the case with her, so I let it go. I figured I'd talk it over with Deputy Chief Sheldon."

"And?" Finn prompted.

"And nothing," Wendy said. "When I met with Sheldon last night, she told me to let robbery handle it. When I brought up a possible connection to Milo and Perreau's murders, she said if robbery turned up anything suspicious, she'd handle it herself."

Wendy breathed in deeply.

"There's more, isn't there?" Finn asked.

She nodded, her dark eyes staring down at the table—angry eyes. "I'm off the task force."

"What?" I sputtered. "Why?"

Wendy didn't answer right away and there was nothing but Cap'n Jack's snores to disturb the silence. Finally, she looked up at us, but there were no tears in her eyes, only fire.

"Why do you *think* it happened?" Wendy directed the question to us both.

"Are you telling us that Sheldon found out that you were leaking information to us?" I asked.

"No way can Sheldon prove that, Wendy. No way," Finn said.

Wendy clenched and unclenched her fists and I could tell that she was struggling to maintain that cool control she liked to project.

"She didn't say that in so many words, Finn. What she did say was that I wasn't a good fit, that I needed more seasoning, and that from now on, I'd be working with the cold-case unit. What do you make of that?"

Did I feel guilty? Sure, but Wendy was a grown woman, and no one had forced her to do anything, right? But that's not what I said.

"If Sheldon found out that you were leaking intel, wouldn't she have fired you outright?"

Wendy shook her head. "No, she wouldn't do that, Nellie. 'Cause you're right, she has no proof. If she accused me, I'd file a complaint with the union. She knows that and it could get messy. This way, she just tells me I'm too green to take on this big responsibility and sends me to the graveyard. Passive aggressive. Brilliant."

"I'm so sorry about this, Wendy," Finn said. "But it doesn't mean you have to stop working on the case, does it?"

Wendy squinted her eyes. "Go on," she encouraged.

"With your new assignment, nobody will suspect you're still looking into the active murder case, so it'll be easier for you to sniff around. And we can still join forces. If you break this, with a little help from us, you'll be back on track for the stellar career you deserve." Finn knew how to grease somebody's wheels. "This could be a blessing in disguise."

Too much.

Wendy pounded the table and then used her thumb and forefinger to make a handgun gesture. "If you say anything about turning a lemon into lemonade, I swear to God I will take out my gun and shoot you."

Finn raised his hands in surrender. "Fair enough."

That night, after locking up my wee cottage and drawing the blinds upstairs, I slipped under the covers, but my mind was racing. Wendy had left telling us that she'd think over our offer of continuing our collaboration. Finn and I had stayed out in the courtyard, listening to Cap'n Jack saw wood while we kicked around our next moves. It was quitting time when I realized that we hadn't heard anything from Cilla yet. She'd been gone all day, poking around, but didn't actually tell us where she intended to poke.

"I'll follow the bread crumbs," was all she'd said. That was Cilla's work process and it usually paid off.

I tried texting her. No response. Then I tried calling her. Zip.

I tried to calm my nerves, telling myself that maybe she hadn't turned up anything, and, given it was quitting time, decided to go home or out on a date. Cilla was always in motion, so why worry?

Well, worry is what I do. I kept calling her every hour or so, trying to silence the dread I was starting to feel. Eventually, I nodded off, my phone tucked under the sheets, still in my hand. I was somewhere between wakeful and dreamland when I felt a sensation in my palm and heard a purring sound. The kitties? Then my eyes popped opened and reality hit me in the gut. The ID on the screen read Cilla.

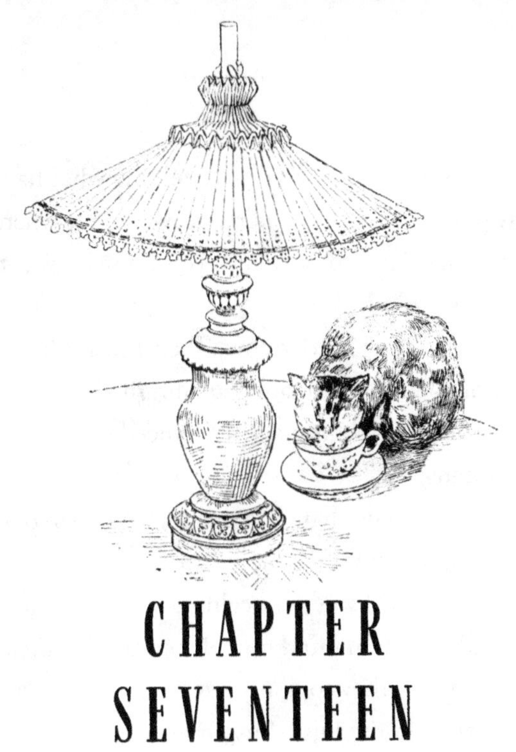

CHAPTER SEVENTEEN

I could barely hear her. She was whispering and there was a lot of background noise, but I could tell that she was scared. No, terrified.

"Where are you?" I found myself whispering too. "I can't hear you, Cilla."

My panic was rising and I had to tamp it down so I could be of use to her.

Cilla raised her voice just enough for me to understand what she was saying.

"I'm in a trunk, Nellie. A car trunk." She was crying and hyperventilating. "I don't know where they're taking me. I didn't even get to see them. I can't let them hear me." Her voice was raw. "Oh, Nellie, you've got to get me out of here!"

My mind was racing. "I will, but tell me what happened."

"I was poking around the party crowd about where to find reliable drivers, asking for a friend, you know? I was trying to get a line on Mitzi's drivers."

She was breathing harder now. Then I heard her scream.

"What happened, Cilla, are you all right?"

"They went over a bump and I bounced and hit my head," she said, sobbing.

Okay, enough chitchat. I needed to get her out of that trunk, and fast, but how?

"Listen to me, Cilla. Try to calm down. Are you tied up?"

"No. And they didn't find my cell because I stuffed it in my pocket. But I think they took my bag and that had my burner in it, for when I do my hush-hush stuff, you know? See, they don't know I have another phone, so—"

She was getting hysterical and starting to babble. I had to calm her down and get her focused.

"Okay, Cilla, do you hear anything or smell anything that can give me a clue where you are right now?"

A train whistle would be good, but what were the odds of that?

Another pause, and then she said, "I smell salt water. We're near the ocean."

"Look around the trunk with the light from your phone," I said, "Is there a latch you could pull?"

I could hear her labored breathing. How much oxygen did she have left in there?

"Okay. Looks like there's something I can tug on, maybe to get out. But it's a curvy road, I can tell by getting tossed around, and they're not driving super-fast, but they're driving fast enough. How will this help if I end up breaking all my bones or killing myself?"

I thought about that.

"Do you hear any traffic?"

It was after midnight.

"I don't think so."

"Okay, then we can probably stop worrying about you getting run over. How about this? Is there anything in there that you could wrap around yourself to cushion the fall?"

Cilla was quiet for a minute, probably feeling around for something that could do the trick.

"Well, I'm lying on something padded," she said. "It's not attached to the floor. I think it's a tarp."

I didn't like the sound of that, but let it pass.

"Okay, Cilla, how about you wrap yourself in the tarp, wait for the car to slow during a curve, then pull the latch and roll out. Keep your head covered."

Silence.

"Cilla?"

I heard a deep breath.

"You need to move now."

Another deep breath.

"Here goes nothing, Nellie!"

I heard a faint pop, wind, and what I imagined was a thud, then nothing. I had lost our connection.

I waited. Then I called Finn.

We sat in his car on a side street near the cove and waited, trying to make some sense out of what had happened to Cilla.

"So, she was sniffing around, following up on some leads she dug up at the party," Finn said. "But where was she heading?"

"I have no idea."

"Well, wherever it was, someone must have been watching her. But who?"

So many questions. Before I could answer, my cell meowed and I jumped.

It was Cilla.

Long story short. Cilla told us that she had hurled herself out and hit what turned out to be a dirt road, had the wind knocked out of her, rolled a few yards, managed to get up with no bones broken, but sore as hell, unwrapped herself and then ran across the road to what was a low sea wall leading to the beach. She hopped over it, and pounded the sand in the opposite direction of where her kidnappers were driving. She managed to reach a beach house with lights still on and a friendly older couple eager to help.

Cilla gave us directions to the beach house and we fetched her. She was disheveled, shaken, and hyper when we loaded her in the car. We drove along the coast, pulling into a twenty-four-hour diner, a beacon in the darkness. As we entered, I breathed in the aroma of comfort food and immediately felt a warmth infuse my stressed-out body.

Seated in a booth, with a steaming cup of strong coffee—likewise for Finn, and Earl Grey for me—Cilla began her tale.

"I was driving around and looking for this warehouse, out in Otay Mesa. I was asking around about where to find reliable drivers to make deliveries, you know, asking for a friend, and they all mentioned a place called Overdrive. But I got lost. No GPS in my car and no one to ask. It was getting dark and there was all this fog coming in. All of a sudden I saw these flashers coming up behind me. I thought it was the cops, so I pulled over. Then I heard a door open and close and footsteps. When I rolled my window down and looked out, someone with a ski mask grabbed my hair and pushed a rag in my face. It smelled awful. And that's all I remember."

We kicked around the pros and cons of calling in the cops. Normally, when someone gets drugged and stuffed into a car trunk, the logical thing to do is to report it, right? But, as Finn and Cilla pointed out, these were not normal times, at least for us.

"Look, like I said before, someone got the word that Cilla was nosing around about delivery services," Finn said. "Had to be what happened."

"But who?" I asked, wishing I could read the tea leaves in my cup but finding only a single sad little teabag.

"I don't know, Nellie, but Finn is right," Cilla said, warming her hands on her mug. "Why else would they snatch me?"

"Okay, so those people you asked about delivery services?" I said. "Anyone seem suspicious?"

Cilla shrugged.

"These society folks. They're hard to read, you know? Usually, I just cover their parties, talk about the food and the fashions, and once in a while include a blind item in my column that might raise some eyebrows. But nothing criminal, and I don't name names. I'd never get invited to another party if I did. Still, with all the money these people have, I'd bet there are a few crooks in the mix. No clue who, though."

Finn gulped down the last of his coffee, plunked down his mug, then tapped his knuckles on the table.

"Here's what I think we should do," he said. "If we go to the cops, what are we going to tell them? Lamo will probably accuse us of concocting a publicity stunt to rev up readers for our 'rag.' Or, maybe we scare off the bad guys. Let's stay cool and keep digging."

I almost choked on my tea.

"Easy for you to say, Finn. Cilla's the one they stuffed in that trunk. She could be dead by now. What's to keep them from trying again?"

As terrified as Cilla had been during her wild ride, now she just seemed pissed off at the memory.

"Let them try, Nellie," she said, her violet eyes shooting laser beams my way. "If I'm onto something, I'm going to go after it, like a goddamned bloodhound. Or bulldog. Or whatever." She slammed the palm of her hand down on the table, causing our waitress to gawk at us from behind the counter.

"Besides, I think they were only trying to scare me, whoever they were," she said. "Why would they bother with masks if they were going to whack me?"

Mentally and physically exhausted, we agreed to consult with our favorite detective the next day and maybe convince her to help us retrieve Cilla's car, assuming it was still where she had left it.

CHAPTER EIGHTEEN

The good news was that Cilla had secured her driver's license and house key in a secret pocket that her abductors had not found. She told me that she always did this when she was nosing around outside her usual haunts. Still, she couldn't be sure that whoever had snatched her would not find another way to track her down, outside of the office, so Cilla had arranged to crash—I mean, stay—with a friend until she felt safe enough to return to her place. But she remained dogged in her quest to follow the trail. Bulldog? Bloodhound? Whatever.

But speaking of crash, the next day, I spent part of the morning arranging for a loaner car and ended up with a nondescript Toyota sedan. Driving to work, on the lookout for maniacs, I decided to treat myself to a blueberry scone and a nice mocha latte to prepare myself for the demanding day to come. I parked the car in the little Starbucks lot and headed inside, placed my order, tipped Gracie, and turned around to find myself staring into the face of the one and only Deputy Chief Sylvia Sheldon.

"Well, good morning, Syl," I chirped, using her nickname mainly to piss her off. "What brings you to our little village?"

She actually snorted.

"I got your jewels right here, Ms. Blight." Fortunately, the breakfast crowd had thinned, so just the two of us were in line.

"Ms. *Blight?* Really, Syl?"

I sidled over to fetch a couple of sweeteners, thinking that maybe I could also snag a plastic stirrer for self-defense if need be. When I turned around, there she was, eyes like burning coals searing my brain. Maybe an exaggeration, but she gave me the willies.

As petite as she was, Sylvia had long ago embraced her inner minotaur. She poked her index finger into my solar plexus and it felt like a drill bit. I flinched and instantly regretted it.

"Assaulting an innocent citizen?" I looked around the bistro, but my only potential witnesses had their heads stuck in laptops and smartphones.

"Innocent?" Her index finger was now retracted and curled into a fist that she held by her side. "You almost gave the chief a heart attack, you and the rest of you hacks."

I raised an eyebrow. "I had no idea that Chief Lamo—Leonard—was so fragile. But, come to think of it, he did seem a little off his feed at the news conference."

Our banter was cut short by the sound of my name being called and I made my way to the pickup place, where my latte and scone were waiting. I scooped up the order, but the minotaur stood between me and the door.

"So, what do you and your pals plan to run for Fake News Friday this week?" she hissed.

Do minotaurs hiss?

I glanced over at Gracie, who was observing this heated exchange and looking alarmed.

"Hey, I'm talking to you!" Sylvia snapped.

Fearing that Gracie was about to call in the troops, I spoke in what I hoped was a calm voice of reason.

"You are making our barista very nervous, Syl. If you want to chat, then let's do it out on the deck. May I pass now?"

Sylvia gave Gracie a look, smiled, and walked over to her, taking out her wallet and making sure that our barista had a good view of her badge. I don't know if this reassured Gracie or convinced her that a SWAT team was about to descend, but she forced a smile and proceeded to take Sylvia's order.

Then Sylvia turned back to me and purred, "I'll be right out."

As much as I wanted to call for backup, there was no time to beckon Finn or Cilla. But maybe there was a remote chance that Sylvia had something of use to offer. Should I tell her about Cilla's abduction? But the look on Sylvia's face when she slammed out the door and headed my way quickly made up my mind.

Hell, no.

She settled in on the deck and I toasted her with my latte.

"First of all, Syl, we don't write fake news. Let's be clear about that, and, might I add, Chief Leonard didn't correct our story when Finn asked him if there were any mistakes in it."

Sylvia slammed her palm down on the table, something I'd grown used to with Finn, so I was already anchoring my beverage from spillage.

"That's not the !#%&* point!" she said, waving a chocolate croissant in my face. "You jumped the gun, with no credible sources and no confirmation from us. You are impeding our work and attracting those paparazzi, who are turning this investigation into a circus!"

"We're just doing our jobs," I said, taking a bite of my scone. "You and I both know that the Milo and Perreau murders—"

"Who said anything about murder?"

"Oh please," I said. "How long do you think you can keep this covered up? We already reported that Milo had a chunk of ivory stuck in his throat, and nobody's buying that Perreau, the pillar of the arts community, hanged himself from a chandelier. We know he had a chunk of ivory stuck down his craw too."

Another palm slam. "Who told you this? There's a leak in our department, isn't there? Well, I'll tell you something, and you can spread the word—we will find the leaker and prosecute to the fullest extent of the law!"

I thought about Wendy toiling away in the cold-case unit. Did Sylvia suspect her? After all, Wendy had alerted us about Perreau's murder.

"We have our sources, Sylvia, outside of the cop shop."

"You need to keep your nose out of police business," she said, standing up and gathering her trash.

"All I'm asking is, you throw us a bone now and then and you'll have some control over the narrative." Well, not really. "You could be quoted as an official source and we can solve these murders together. Maybe head off more mayhem."

She leaned down close to my face. "You'll get a dose of mayhem if you don't stop messing with me."

That was more of a growl than a hiss.

With that, she gathered up her food and drink and stomped over to her ride. And what a ride it was. A cherry-red Ferrari. I'm no car buff, but I'd seen a few of these babies around the village. Wow. How much were deputy chiefs making these days?

I got up and gathered my trash and noticed for the first time some handwriting below my name that had been scrawled on my cup. It read: "See me. G."

G? I looked back at the bistro and figured that must have been written by Gracie, because she had taken my order, and the handwriting for my name and the message was the same. Had I left her a hundred-dollar bill instead of a dollar? Not likely, as I couldn't remember the last time I had even seen a hundred-dollar bill. I went back inside and got in line behind an earnest young woman who seemed to be holding forth about the evils of gluten.

Finally, I stepped up, raised my empty cup and cocked an eyebrow. "What's up?"

The barista looked around, determined that no one was paying attention to us, and called out, "Trevor, could you take over for me? I'm taking my break."

A lanky teen with bushy red hair who was puttering around in the beverage prep area sidled over, and Gracie exited from behind the food counter and grabbed a bottle of water, beckoning me to follow. We sat down at a table out on the deck.

"I read what you wrote about Milo, the designer shoe guy." For some reason, Gracie was whispering, her dark eyes darting around the empty deck.

I waited, not wanting to spook her. She bit her lower lip and took a big swig of water.

"This might not be anything, Nellie, but it's been on my mind."

I nodded and smiled, letting her know that I was eager to hear what she had to say, but not being too pushy.

"Well, the other night, the Morrisons had a birthday party on their boat for one of their friends, and I was part of the waitstaff."

Hmmm, not much of a mourning period for fellow socialites Milo and Philly, but eat, drink, and be merry, right?

"You moonlight?" I asked.

I didn't know Gracie all that well. Mostly, we just chatted about new beverage concoctions and the latest seasonal pastries. Now I learned that she was enrolled in the culinary arts program at the local community college, worked parttime at Starbucks and, when she could fit it in, signed on with caterers, mostly serving the society folks in La Joya.

"It was getting crazy," Gracie told me about the night in question. "Everybody was getting drunk, and Gretchen—she's the caterer—was scared to death we'd run out of liquor. Some of the guests were hurling over the railing, because it was really windy that night and the boat was rocking. I'm a fisherman's daughter, so I had my sea legs, but I couldn't wait to get off that boat."

Gracie said that she had to use the restroom, but there was a long line, so she decided to go below in hopes of finding another restroom. The Morrisons had strung up a rope across the steps leading down to the cabin. She guessed it was their private quarters but figured that no one would notice if she snuck down there.

"That live steel drum band was so loud, my head was aching, and I just wanted a few minutes to myself. It was dark down there, but I always carry a little flashlight in my pocket for emergencies. I roamed around until I found the master bedroom. The door was closed, but when I tried the knob, it wasn't locked. I wasn't sure what to do. Should I knock? What if there were people inside—you know."

Gracie looked embarrassed at the very thought and raked her sculpted sea-green fingernails through her unicorn-hued spiked hair.

"Well, I had to pee really bad, so I took a chance and knocked, and when I didn't hear anything, I opened the door and stuck my head inside. It was dark but seemed empty, so I slipped in and closed the door and used the flash to find the bathroom. I was scared to death that someone might walk in and think I was trying to steal something. In this kind of business, you have to be careful."

Gracie did her business and returned to the bedroom, using the flash to retrace her steps. Despite sea legs, she had to struggle to keep her footing as the boat was heaving a lot now. That's when she stumbled and fell against something hard that had slid out of the closet and pinned her to the foot of the bed. It turned out to be a trunk.

"It was really heavy," she said. "I tried to push it back into the closet, but the stupid boat kept rocking and I was afraid that it would crash into me again and hurt me if I couldn't get out of the way fast enough."

She kicked it hard, with just enough time to roll away before it came crashing back, this time into the bed frame. Gracie's flashlight was rolling around on the floor, still lit, so she grabbed it. But curiosity got the better of her and she started wondering about that footlocker.

"I was raised to be honest and I've never stolen anything in my life, Nellie, but all I wanted to do was take a peek. I mean, it's fun to gossip about the hosts, you know. Harmless stuff. We all do it. Anyway, I crawled over and felt for the clasp, figuring it was locked. Well, when it smashed into the bed frame, the lock must have broken off . . ."

She grabbed her water bottle and was hydrating like crazy.

"And?" I prodded.

"You wouldn't believe what was inside, Nellie. I mean, it was packed tight with those peanuts so nothing would break, but when I went to feel what was in there, I almost cut myself on something sharp. It was just poking up, so I tugged at it and I pulled out this tusk—well, a part of one anyway. It was shiny and white and glistened in the light. I poked around some more and there were a lot more of those bones and other stuff wrapped up tight. It was spooky somehow, and I wanted to get out of there and fast. I shut the trunk and tried shoving it back into the closet, but that wasn't working, so I just got up and left. I figured that the Morrisons would think that the trunk had been knocked loose by all that rocking." She held her hands up. "It's not as if anything was going to be missing."

Gracie said that she left the bedroom, hoping that nobody was watching, and ducked back under the rope leading upstairs. Her story made me wonder.

"Gracie, have you heard any gossip about ivory being smuggled around here?"

She gulped down more water and looked scared.

"Well, not me, personally, but my dad hears all sorts of things," she said. "He's a fisherman and sometimes gets hired to go out on charters as a guide to show tourists around the harbor."

"Who hires him?"

Her frantic look told me she wasn't going to answer that one.

"My dad's an honest man, Nellie, but that doesn't mean he won't be at the wrong place at the wrong time, you know? I'm worried about him—that maybe he's seen stuff that he shouldn't have. I mean, after reading about that shoe guy, Milo . . ."

Before I could respond, Gracie glanced at her watch, a Disney model featuring the Little Mermaid. A gift from Dad? Appropriate for a fisherman's daughter.

"I've got to go," she said, starting to rise. "I don't like leaving Trevor alone too long. He's still in training."

I gently grabbed her arm before she could walk away.

"Gracie, let's give Trev a chance to hone his skills for a few more minutes," I said. "This is important. You remember Wendy, who hangs out with us now and then? Pretty, black hair? Chai tea?"

Gracie shot a worried glanced back inside, but sat back and wrinkled her brow. "The surfer chick?"

"That's the one. Anyway, she's a police detective—"

Gracie's eyes widened. "A cop? Like that horrible woman who was harassing you in there? Sylvia? That's the name she gave me for her order."

I waved my hand. "A cop, yes, but no, nothing like Sylvia, believe me. Wendy's been investigating Milo's murder."

Well, Wendy was technically off the case now, but she had been investigating, so it wasn't a lie.

"I'm thinking that you might want to have a chat with her, not here, but somewhere private. Just tell her what you told me. What you found could be a very important clue."

But Gracie was already shaking her head. "I can't be involved in this, Nellie. If it's the cartel, they'll go after me and my dad."

"The cartel? What do you know about the cartel?"

Gracie looked at me as though she had just discovered roaches scampering among the freshly baked pastries.

"I didn't mean—"

"Gracie, you said that your dad might have seen things on that boat . . ."

"Well, that doesn't mean it's the cartel." Gracie swallowed hard. "I don't know anything about the cartel."

Her voice was now a whisper and her dark eyes were darting around the deck, seeing shadows maybe? She was about to bolt, but I needed to keep her talking.

"Okay. Then how about your dad? Has he ever mentioned—"

"No . . . I don't know . . . maybe. I really can't be involved."

"Then why did you write that message on my cup?"

"Because I was thinking that maybe I saw something in that trunk that could be important."

"Then you need to talk to Wendy. You can trust her."

"I'm scared, Nellie. People are dying!"

I reached out and gently patted her arm. "I understand, Gracie. But no one needs to know you are talking to Wendy about anything other than her order. We are here all the time, so just sit down with us for a few minutes and tell her what you told me. Nobody will suspect anything."

"No, we can't meet here. I never sit down with guests. It'll be suspicious."

Well, she was sitting with me, but I let that pass.

"Okay, my place then?"

Trevor then appeared at the door with a pained expression. Gracie sighed and stood up.

I stood too.

"Well, Gracie, are we on?"

She started walking away, but turned and said over her shoulder, "I'll think about it."

I had just arrived at the office when Gracie called and agreed to meet with me, Finn, Cilla, and Wendy that evening. In the meantime, we had work to do.

Finn had set up a meeting with Wendy, giving her a quick summary of Cilla's abduction. Wendy also agreed to help us fetch Cilla's car where she had pulled over before she was snatched and stuffed in the trunk.

Now that Wendy was assigned to cold cases, she had more freedom to come and go, although there was always a possibility that she was being watched, maybe by Sylvia to catch her as the leaker.

But, according to Finn, Wendy seemed as fired up, and angry, as Cilla when it came to breaking the case. I guess she was willing to take the risk.

It was late morning when we all met at the cove. The plan was for Cilla to ride with Wendy, giving her directions to where she had parked her car while filling Wendy in on the kidnapping. I hopped into Finn's sports car and we followed, heading south to Otay Mesa, which was just north of the Mexican border.

The area was predominately industrial and there were a lot of heavy trucks plodding along on the freeway.

Less than an hour later, Wendy's turn signal went on and she exited onto a bumpy road intersecting a hodgepodge of warehouses. Up ahead, she slowed down and pulled in behind Cilla's caddy.

Finn pulled in behind Wendy and we all disembarked, with the good detective taking the lead. Then Cilla, right behind her, grabbed Wendy's shoulder.

"Hey, what if they booby-trapped my car?"

After a moment's hesitation, Wendy shook her head as she pointed to the windshield.

"You see that, Cilla? Looks like a ticket. You're lucky that your car wasn't towed. Besides, they didn't expect you to escape, right? Why would they booby-trap your car?"

Cilla nodded. Then she marched over to the windshield and grabbed the ticket as though it were one of her abductors.

"I'm not paying this!"

She furiously tore it to pieces and tossed the scraps into the gutter. A quick inspection of the car, inside and out, didn't turn up any obvious evidence of her abductors. No big surprise, since they had dragged her out of the car after they had knocked her out.

Before Wendy returned to her cold cases, we found a little hole-in-the-wall, no-frills Mexican café and ordered our beverages, then sat down at a table out on the back deck.

"So, Wendy, cops or no cops?" Finn said, getting right to the point.

Wendy was sipping from a bottle of fizzy water and took her time before answering. "You don't wait more than a day to report a botched kidnapping. You do it as soon as you get away and find a phone. You didn't do that, did you?"

She was staring at Cilla.

"Well, no, but—"

"Cilla, how do you think this will look? When Finn called me this morning to set up this meeting, he said he was afraid that Chief Leonard would laugh it off as a cheesy publicity stunt, isn't that what you told me, Finn?"

"Yeah and I still feel that way, Wendy. Is Cilla still in danger? How hard would it be for them to track her down?"

Wendy took another pull on the bottle and shrugged. "Cilla, you got snatched before you ever got to this Overdrive warehouse, right?"

Cilla nodded.

"And you were following this lead because you suspected that this outfit might have been the one that assigned those drivers to the Morrisons' party?"

"Well, that's the name that kept coming up when I was asking around, so I thought it was a place to start."

"Probably still is, Cilla, but you've got nothing to go on, do you? Just a hunch. So what if the drivers were sent by Overdrive? They were making a delivery. Okay, they had no tags, and that's shady. But really, what were you going to do? 'I'm a reporter for the *Coastal Crier*. Were your drivers involved in the heist at the Morrisons' shindig?'"

Cilla rolled her eyes.

"Oh, come on, Wendy, do you think I'm that stupid?"

"No, Cilla, but I don't think you've thought this through. So let me think about it, okay? Meanwhile, just be careful and stay with your friend until we figure this out. Don't go anywhere alone, if you can help it, especially after dark."

Cilla smacked her bottle of guava juice down on the table. "Great, so I don't get to do my job? I need a babysitter?"

We kicked this around for a while and got nowhere, so we regrouped for the ride back to La Joya. Wendy and Finn got in their cars, while I decided to ride along with Cilla and try to calm her down. We would next reconvene at my place that evening, awaiting Gracie.

Cilla and I rustled up some snacks and assorted beverages while Finn and Gracie had fun playing with my kitties, who quickly lost interest when no treats were offered and retreated to the stairway. Wendy was pacing and checking her cell-phone messages, and I felt the tension radiating off of her.

I offered the comfy chair to Gracie; Cilla and I took the settee, while Finn and Wendy straddled a pair of kitchen chairs. Our young guest unzipped her shoulder bag and took out a bottle of water, unscrewed the cap and took a big gulp. No doubt stalling for time, but who could blame her? She was neither a cop nor a reporter. Why wouldn't she feel intimidated?

"Mind if I take some notes, Gracie?" Finn asked, taking out a notebook and pen from his pocket.

Gracie shrugged.

With some gentle prodding from me, Gracie finally began her story about what she had discovered on the Morrisons' boat, speaking hesitatingly and frequently biting her lower lip. When she finished, she sat back in the chair, depleted.

"This is good stuff, Gracie," Finn said, slapping his notebook. "Now, maybe we can take a run at the Morrisons, maybe get Mitzi talking. Right, Wendy?"

The good detective had been taking her own notes and was now biting down hard on her pen while we all waited for her professional appraisal. Finally, Wendy turned to Gracie, who was looking very small and fragile in the big chair.

"We could have a problem here," she said. "Gracie, you let yourself into the Morrisons' cabin uninvited and opened a trunk that had been locked. Correct?"

"But I explained that!" she said, seemingly upset that her behavior was being called into question. "The door wasn't locked, and I had to pee and then the boat got knocked around and I fell against the trunk and, well, it popped open . . ."

Wendy held up her hand like a traffic cop. "Gracie, we know all that and I'm not accusing you of breaking and entering or forcing the trunk's lock. But the Morrisons might. The fact is, you were in a place that was clearly marked private and off-limits and had no permission to disregard the rope, regardless of your intentions. Normally, this would be no big deal. Trespassing is a misdemeanor. But when you discover possible contraband in someone's possession and you don't have a . . ."

I could literally see Gracie's anxiety level rise even before she spoke.

"Shit, do I need a lawyer?"

"Let's not get ahead of ourselves here," Wendy said. "I mean, we don't even know if what you found is contraband.

It was dark, even with your flashlight, so it might have been cheap trinkets for all we know. Maybe things their kids made out of macaroni . . ."

Finn grunted. "Macaroni? What happened, Wendy? Some sea creature swim into your ear when you were surfing and ate your brains? How about the rest of the stuff that Gracie felt in there? They were wrapped tight. Could be pottery, jewelry, made from smuggled wild animal parts?"

"Finn, we don't know what she found. I have to think about this. Maybe the chief—"

Finn almost fell out of his chair. "Lamo? Are you fricking kidding me? He'd tear Gracie apart."

The poor kid was the color of parchment paper and close to tears. "This was a big mistake, coming here," Gracie said, standing up. "I should have kept my mouth shut. That's what my dad always tells me. Could I go to jail?"

Cilla got up and hurried over to her, gave her a hug and led her back to the settee, silently telling me to skedaddle. I took the hint, got up, and plunked myself down in the comfy chair, while Cilla gently eased Gracie into the settee and sat beside her.

"Don't pay any attention to Finn, Gracie," she said, giving him the evil eye. "He's a real drama king."

I looked at Wendy and wondered what was going on with her. Even though she was officially off the case, she had seemed eager enough to join us, under the radar, of course. Maybe we'd crack the case and she could reclaim her career momentum. Was she having second thoughts now? I remembered how she had lectured me on confronting my fears and how it had pissed me off. It occurred to me that Wendy was probably not used to failing. She was humiliated and probably demoralized by her sudden demotion. Wendy had to get her mojo back, and fast.

I decided to put in my two cents, for what it was worth.

"Assuming the stuff is contraband and the Morrisons got busted for having it in their possession, what would keep them from saying it was planted, that they were being framed? I mean, they're wealthy, they travel the world collecting things—presumably legal—but who knows? Maybe they have enemies who want to put them away."

I looked around and realized that my two cents hadn't bought me much.

"What ifs, maybe this, maybe that. Nell, we don't have enough evidence to prove anything," Finn said.

That's when my kitties let out a spine-chilling shriek, scampered down the stairs, and skidded on the hardwood into the kitchen. What now? More monsters? We looked over to the stairs and watched as a figure made her way down in those feathered mules, spreading her arms wide in greeting.

"Cate?" I was on my feet, hands on hips, and ready for combat. "What are you doing here?"

Cate ignored me, strolled over to the comfy chair, elbowed me aside, and settled in, helping herself to a chunk of cheese on the snack tray.

"Make me a martini, will you Nellie? I am parched."

Finn and Cilla were used to my eccentric landlady, but Wendy and Gracie were not and just gawked.

"I don't have any martinis . . ." I sputtered, but Cate cut me off.

"Well, of course you do, Nellie. I put the shaker in your fridge myself. Did you drink it all?"

Cilla started to giggle. Patting Gracie on the shoulder, she got up and headed for the kitchen.

"I'm sure Nellie left a few drops for you, Cate. Be back in a jiffy."

"What were you doing upstairs—again?" I asked.

"Checking to make sure that monster didn't return, what else?"

Gracie had all but curled up in a fetal ball. "Monster? What monster?"

I waved my hand. "A prank, Gracie."

At that point, Cilla came out with the shaker on a silver platter and a glass, and placed it on the coffee table. Cate took the shaker and poured. "Join me?"

Everyone shook their heads, and as much as I needed one, I also declined.

"Suit yourself. More for *moi*." She then hoisted her glass and said, "Cheers!"

I found an empty spot on the rug and eased myself into a lotus position.

"Okay, Cate, what did you hear and, probably a better question, how much do you know?"

Ignoring me, Cate regarded her assembled audience, homing in on two members she had not yet met.

"Detective Nostradamus, I presume?" she said, pointing her blood-red talon at Wendy. "Wanda is it?"

Uh-oh. Here it comes.

"I am Detective Wendy Nakamura and this is a private meeting, Ms. Cavendish—"

"Dame Cavendish, my dear, but you might as well call me Cate, as we're all chums now, no?"

"No, we are not. I am here on police business—not a cocktail party. You'll have to excuse us."

Cate seemed amused by this.

"Actually, Wanda—"

"Wendy, and it's Detective Nakamura—"

"While I let Nellie stay here, with her dreadful felines—" Cate gave the kitties the death stare "—this is my property and I will do as I please. But as you are here on police business, are you not interested in Nellie's question? How much do I know about what was found in the Morrisons' cabin?"

If Cate had a superpower, it was her ears. Eavesdropping didn't even begin to describe it.

Cate then turned her gaze at Gracie, who had wrapped herself in an afghan that had been tossed over the settee and was doing her best to hide.

"You, young lady, made the discovery, am I right? What was your name again?"

"Gracie," she said, just above a whisper.

"Well, Gracie, welcome to my home. Now I have a tale to tell, but this is all strictly hush-hush, do you all understand?"

"No, Cate, I don't understand," Finn said. "We report the news, we don't hush it up."

"And I'm here to solve a crime, maybe more than one, so if you have something to say—" Wendy broke in.

Cate waved her hand at them. "I have deep background to share and I cannot be quoted. Did Nellie explain to you that I am the subject of a blood oath? Well, of course she did." She looked around the room and out the window, as darkness was descending, and shivered. Lowering her voice, Cate added, "They could be out there right now."

She turned to Wendy. "Are you armed, my dear?"

Wendy patted the shoulder bag she had placed at her feet. "Always. Okay, you think someone's out to get you, and yes, Nellie has kept me posted on all the strange happenings around here. If what you say is true and someone is after you, clamming up isn't going to help you."

"An interesting turn of phrase, detective," Cate said, pouring herself another drink. "Clams, fish—sleep with the fishes. You see, that's just what Junior would say, not that I've ever met him, but it would suit him. I do not intend to bed down with fishes—although I must say I regret turning down that role in the black lagoon movie. Anyway, I am certain that my information will prove useful in your investigation and—" she turned to Finn "—in your story. But you must not use my name or even hint at who I am. Agreed?"

We all exchanged looks and nodded.

"Should I get my recorder? Take notes for the memoir?" I asked, and added, "For those who don't know, I'm helping Dame Cavendish write her memoir."

"Please do, so I won't have to repeat myself," she said, and then whispered, "You will then have my own words recorded in the event that I am no longer able to speak at all."

Cate knew how to grab an audience's attention. She began to explain the seedy side of Milt and Mitzi, a couple of grifters, she claimed, that she knew from back in the days when they traveled the carnival circuit.

Cilla's violet eyes popped. "No way, Cate. Milt and Mitzi Morrison, scamsters? They've been La Joya royalty forever."

"Oh, Priscilla, I do adore you, but you can be naïve about the way of the world. Before they were high society, they were lowlifes. This was many years ago, long before you were even born, but we were part of the same social circle back then, when I was a chorus girl on my way to a studio contract. They were on the make too. We all were. The difference with them, however, is that they had no boundaries or scruples. They did what they had to do to get ahead, whatever it took."

Wendy, who had been jotting down notes, stopped. "How do you know this? Are you telling me that they told you about their crimes?"

Cate took another sip. "Well, certainly not Mitzi, but Milty—well, let's just say that his pillow talk was lubricated by quite a few highballs—"

"Wait a minute," Wendy interrupted. "You were sleeping with him, right under Mitzi's nose?"

Cate chuckled. "Back then, Mitzi's nose was so big that Ringling Brothers Circus could have set up under it. That was before she stole enough to have some work done. And yes, Milty and I did enjoy a brief fling, until I tired of him. Not only a sloppy drunk but a bore as well. But they were quite good at ingratiating themselves into café society. Did you know that Mitzi even took voice lessons from an over-the-hill actress to sound highbrow?"

Finn shook his head. "No, Cate, I think it's safe to say none of us knew that."

"You're saying they were carnies?" Wendy asked. "What did they do exactly?"

"They did magic tricks, you know, hokey stuff like pulling rabbits out of hats and cutting Mitzi in half. Card tricks. They did psychic readings too, of people in the audience, who were ringers, of course. It was a very bush-league outfit."

"Wait a minute, Cate," I said. "You started out as a chorus girl, so how do you know about the circus?"

"Well, I have to admit, I did spend a little time as a hootchy-kootchy dancer in the carnie, but that's not anything I'd want to put on my résumé. The Morrisons certainly weren't planning to put their past on their applications to the country clubs either."

"So how did they scam people?" Finn asked.

"The usual. Mitzi would lure a rich married guy into bed, Milty would be hiding somewhere taking photos and she'd make sure the mark had his face in full focus. The marks always paid up and they were not going to the police. They tried other scams, lonely hearts classifieds, things like that, but from what Milty told me, blackmail was the golden goose that launched them into a life of luxury."

Wendy stopped writing again. "They blackmailed and cheated people, and then they were invited into high society?"

Cate poured herself another.

"They didn't stay in the same place, Wanda—uh—Detective. They were always moving around. At one point, they were hosting gambling parties on riverboats down south and, believe me, the house never lost, not with those two in charge."

I raised my hand. "If they were traveling and there wasn't any more pillow talk, how did you get all this intel?"

Cate sipped. "Oh, Milty would call me from time to time, when Mitzi wasn't around, trying to rekindle, I guess. I mean, at that point I had graduated from the chorus and had nailed down a contract, and he would have dropped that cow in a minute if he thought he had a chance with me. He was usually half in the bag when he called and he liked to brag, trying to impress me with how clever he was and how much money he was making from these dimwits. I'm sure he had no idea I was taking notes."

Wendy was losing patience. "Your memoir is going to expose the Morrisons as grifters?"

Cate picked up the shaker, peered in, and frowned. "Did I say that? I don't think I said any such thing, did I, Nellie?""

She sort of did, but I just shrugged.

"Wasn't it awkward to run into those two, both of you knowing about each other's pasts?" Wendy said.

"Not at all," Cate said. "They have no idea I used to be that glamour girl back then."

Wendy just gawked.

"You see, Detective, I am a great actress and a master of reinvention. I have lived many lives and assumed many personas. For years now I have been Dame Catherine Cavendish, patron of the arts and the grande dame of La Joya, mysterious and reclusive. I intend to keep this particular persona. It suits me, and frankly, I'm much too old to reinvent myself again." She looked at each of us. "Do you understand? Hush-hush!"

I glanced over at Gracie, who continued to disappear into her cocoon, no doubt wondering how she got involved with a bunch of wackos.

"Okay, Cate, let's cut to the chase," Wendy said, drumming her pen on her pad. "Can you connect the dots and confirm that the Morrisons are smuggling in contraband?"

We all waited.

Finally, Cate yawned and stood. "That's a very good question, Wanda. I'll have to sleep on it."

"Wendy—"

"Whatever. I'll bid you good night and we'll talk again. For now, I must tend to my flock."

Cate did love her cliffhangers, but Wendy wasn't having it.

"If you've got something to say, please say it. This is a murder investigation, not dinner theater."

Ohhhh, not good.

"I have never stooped to dinner theater!" Cate hissed, as though this were several steps below a hootchy-kootchy dancer. Then the room was filled with the sound of the front door opening and footsteps approaching. A tall, imposing figure appeared in the archway.

"Oh my God! They're here!" Poor Gracie sunk so far down into the settee that she almost disappeared.

"Gracie, everything's fine," I said. "That's only Quigley, Cate's—"

"Aide-de-camp, dear," Cate offered. "Punctual as ever."

"Good evening," Quigley said, his baritone reverberating. He circled around us to the coffee table, gathered up the martini shaker and glass, then followed Cate out to the foyer, where she waved and said, "Sweet dreams everyone!"

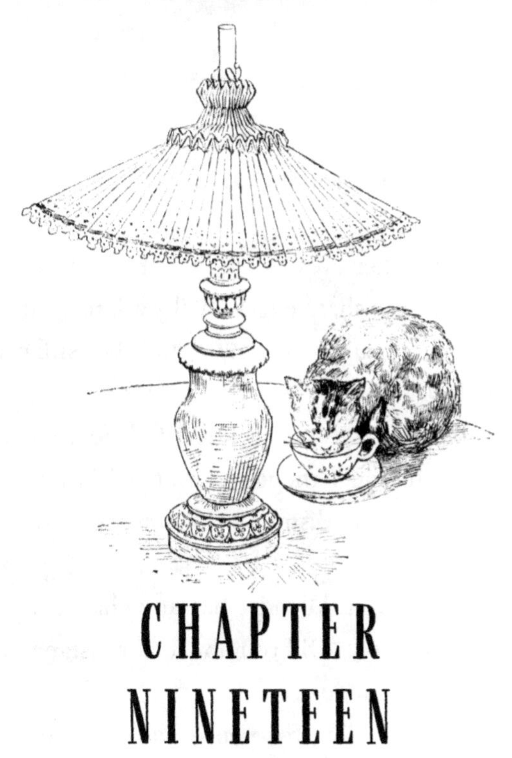

CHAPTER NINETEEN

After they were gone, I locked the door and set the chain, although I don't know why I even bothered. I reclaimed the now empty comfy chair and regarded my guests, who all seemed to be stewing in their own personal juices. Wendy was just plain pissed off.

"What the hell?" she said. "Who does she think she is, the queen of fricking England?"

I thought about that.

"If I recall, she claims to be a duchess, but she's had so many lives, who knows?" I said. "So, what's the plan? Anything we can work with?"

"Our lede's going to be Perreau—not a suicide, a murder, with the same calling card as Milo—the chunk of ivory in his craw," Finn said, then looked over at Wendy. "Any problem with that?"

She shrugged, her eyes cast down at her notepad, where she drew figures with sharp edges. "Why ask me, Finn? I'm off the case. It doesn't really matter now, and they still can't prove I leaked anything."

Maybe, but it made me wonder if she'd been followed. Then, for some reason I thought about Sylvia and her fancy car and the way she had dismissed Wendy from the case. Any connection?

"Not to spook you, Wendy, but any chance you've been followed here?" I asked. "Did you notice, for instance, a cherry-red Ferrari in your rearview?"

Did the hand holding the pen tremble slightly? Maybe I was just imagining it.

"No," she said. "Sure, there was traffic, but I didn't notice anything suspicious. Why did you mention a cherry-red Ferrari?"

Good question.

"I don't know," I said. "I guess I'm trying to make connections to all the loony stuff that's been going on around here. Sylvia was your mentor, right, then she suddenly yanks you off the task force and reassigns you to duties that are guaranteed to keep you far away from the action. Why?"

"What about the car?" she persisted. "What are you getting at?"

I had everyone's attention. "When I was at Starbucks—before my chat with Gracie—Sylvia stomped in and berated me about nosing around in what she called police business. Later, out on the deck, I tried to reason with her, but it didn't end well. She even threatened me with 'mayhem.' No witnesses, though. Then she got up and headed out to her car—a cherry-red Ferrari."

"I know," Wendy said, shrugging. "That's her personal car. I've ridden in it." Wendy looked at each of us for a reaction, I suppose, but we just waited. "What's your point?"

Her defensiveness rattled me.

"Well, the car looked brand new and—"

"Oh, it is, Nellie," Cilla said, still seated next to Gracie. "It's a Ferrari F8 Tributo coupe. Fresh out of Milty's showroom."

"Milty—as in Milton Morrison?"

Cilla nodded, bouncing her red curls. "The very same, Nellie. And the chief—"

"Lamo?" Finn asked.

"He's got a Lamborghini Huracán Evo Spyder. Milty is famous for his luxury rides."

I had no idea how much these cars cost, so Cilla enlightened us before I could even ask.

"The Ferrari goes for more than a quarter of a million and the Lambor—"

"In the same ballpark, give or take a few thou," Finn said.

"No way could Sylvia afford a car like that on her salary," I said. "Same with Lamo. So, what gives? Are they both independently wealthy and toiling away for kicks?"

"Okay, I see your point, Nellie," Cilla said. "I'll poke around some more, but I'm telling you: I do not intend to end up stuffed into another trunk—or anywhere else, for that matter."

It was dawning on me that we were getting in over our heads. Then it hit me.

"Gracie, you didn't tell anyone about what you found on the Morrisons' boat, did you?" I asked. "The other servers? Your dad, maybe?"

Gracie's eyes grew large and she started to twist the afghan into a narrow rope.

"Oh no, I wouldn't do that. I'd never gossip about a thing like that, and no way would I tell my dad. I'm all he has left since my mom died, and he'd be scared that they'd come for me. He'd want to pack me up and disappear."

Wendy wanted to pounce, I could tell from her reaction, but she knew enough not to spook this young woman.

"Who would be coming for you?" Wendy asked, in a surprisingly nurturing tone. "What do you know, Gracie? I can protect you."

I wondered how she intended to do this, given her current status, but kept my mouth shut.

"I just know that my dad keeps saying that I should never mess with 'them' whenever he comes back from some of his charter rides."

"You don't know who hires him?"

"No, I don't. I never ask."

Gracie was getting stressed at all the questions, Cilla could tell, so she stepped in.

"I hear that your dad is a very good fisherman," Cilla said.

Gracie seemed to relax a bit. "You know my dad?"

"Well, we haven't met personally, but I know that he supplies seafood to Mitzi and her pals for their parties, at least for some of them."

"His boat isn't that big, but he knows all the best fishing spots. He gets a lot of work from the party people," Gracie said proudly. The conversation finally wound down and it was time to say our good-byes.

After Wendy and Gracie had left, the three of us were quiet for a while, mulling things over.

So much to digest.

Finn started doodling.

"You think this Sebastian guy is hanging out with the cartel on fishing charters?"

"Hold on, Finnian, I never said her dad was hanging out with the cartel. I said that he crewed for rich guys. Maybe they're stockbrokers and urologists, I don't know."

Finn kept doodling. "Could be," he said. "Anyway, now we know he has a connection to the Morrisons, supplying them with fish. Coincidence?"

I hadn't thought about that and I did not like where this was going.

Cilla grabbed the blanket and tucked it under her chin. "Poor Gracie, she'd be heartbroken if he was involved in anything like that. She idolizes her dad."

Finn stopped doodling.

"Should we trust Gracie?" he asked. "I mean, she seems like a good kid, but I don't really know her outside Starbucks. Do you?"

Cilla picked up a throw pillow and tossed it at him.

"Hey!"

"Gracie is a fine young woman, Finnian, and I do trust her. I have very good instincts about people." Cilla narrowed her violet eyes. "Well, I guess there are exceptions."

"You can't possibly mean me, Cill." Finn gave her that grin that made women melt. "Fine, but how about this? We have another chat with Gracie and ask her if she could set up a meeting with her dad? Deep background. Totally off the record. Couldn't hurt, and who knows? Maybe Papa will be happy to unburden himself. Just a thought, ladies."

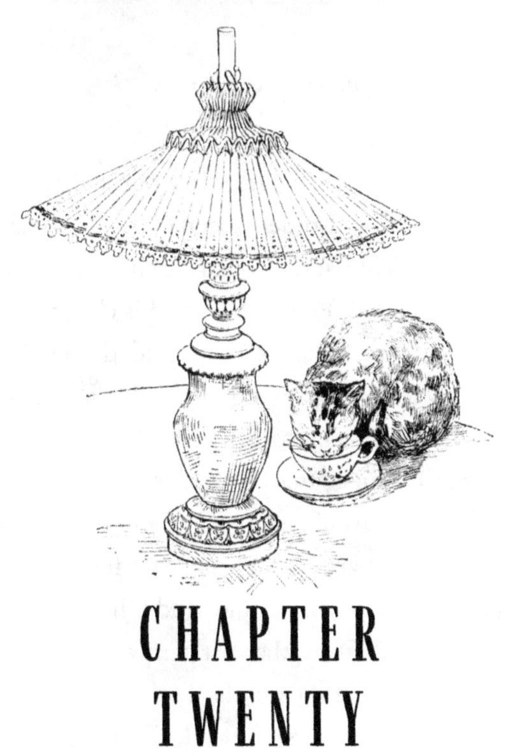

CHAPTER TWENTY

The next day at the *Crier* we huddled around the banquette at the former Jack in the Box that now served as our newsroom. It had been a couple of weeks since Milo's demise, but it felt like a year. We were trying to cobble together the bits and pieces that would become our next page one installment of the story we had dubbed "The Elephant Diaries." Tomorrow was our deadline, and the paper would hit the streets on Friday with the help of a veteran printer named Inky Bob Pitts, an old pal of Cap'n Jack. His operation was far from state of the art, but he did manage to crank out the paper on time. Then he drove around the village, tossing the plastic-wrapped missiles onto La Joyans' well-tended lawns, under their cars and maybe onto their roofs.

Anyway, we had finally agreed on our assignments. Finn would handle the law-and-order aspects of the story, highlighting the similarities of Milo and Perreau's murders. I'd handle the obit elements, including Perreau's work, his charities, survivors, and memorial service, while Cilla would devote her society column to the glitz-and-glamour stuff. We were a good team and, when we put our heads together, we'd manage to grind out a decent story. Of course, this one had more holes than the La Joya Golf Club, but it would have to do for now. We still had the Morrisons' footlocker angle to pursue, but for now, we would have another scoop, one that would send Chief Lamo charging at us like a crazed bull. Okay, that last part was a little disturbing.

Finn seemed to read my mind.

"Lamo's going to go nuts," he said, chortling and smacking his notebook against the table. "Poor Sylvia's going to have her work cut out for her, administering CPR." What we would not be including in the story was Cilla's abduction. We still needed to connect the dots on that one.

Then Cap'n Jack rambled over to what had been the counter where fast-food orders used to be taken. He had built a little office for himself back in the kitchen.

"I'm going out," he said in his growly voice. "You getting anywhere?"

Finn and I gave him the thumbs-up sign and Cilla trilled, "We are a well-oiled machine, Captain!" then saluted.

After we heard the back door bang, Cilla's cell chimed.

It was Gracie.

After a minute Cilla said, "You know that you can trust us. Uh-huh, uh-huh, you bet. Okay, let me check with Finn and Nellie, and I'll call you back."

After she signed off, Cilla had a big smile on her face. Mission accomplished.

"Sebastian said that he'd meet with us, but not on his boat. He suggested we get together around sunset at the gazebo at the cove." Then her smile faded. "But he'll only meet with us—no cops."

Meaning no Wendy. What was he afraid of?

CHAPTER TWENTY-ONE

We had each bought snow cones at a nearby kiosk and were now licking the last of the melting ice, seated on benches covered with matching sea-foam-colored cushions. Gracie joined as soon as she had finished her shift at Starbucks.

She had changed out of her barista uniform into a coral-hued T and black clam diggers, a white cable-knit sweater draped over her shoulders. The sun was starting its descent and the breeze had grown chilly. Autumn was coming, however subtly in this part of the country.

Cilla patted the space next to her.

"Everything good, Gracie?" she asked. "Papa's on his way?"

Our young friend gave us a worried look. "Last I heard, he'll be here."

We waited.

Finn crumpled the snow cone wrapper and looked around for a place to dump it, spotted a trash can outside and set up his shot. Basket! Or whatever the heck they say.

Meanwhile, the sunset was at its peak, a glorious blend of pink, yellow, and purple, but still no Sebastian.

"Spectacular sunset," I said, not wanting to address the obvious fact that Gracie's dad was nowhere to be seen. "Maybe he got a late catch?"

Gracie shook her head. "No, he goes out really early. By now, I'm on my way home and he's getting the grill ready for the fish he caught." She peered out at the sea as the sun continued to make its descent and rubbed her arms, pulling the sweater tightly around her.

We were quiet for a while, listening to the waves and the gulls and watching the sky turning into a dark velvet.

I could sense the anxiety building.

"You should call him, Gracie," I said. "If he's busy, we could reschedule."

Gracie pulled out her phone from a canvas tote embossed with seahorses and made the call. No answer. She disconnected and sat there staring at the phone.

"Maybe he's finishing up on his boat and lost track of time." Cilla patted Gracie's shoulder. "He's probably on his way."

Gracie shook her head. "No, he's always on time. And, like I said, he's very protective of me. We almost always have dinner together, unless I have plans with my friends. There's no messages either."

Gracie abruptly stood. "I'm going home." She started down the short set of steps.

We all stood and followed.

"It's not that far from here, if you want to come," she said, turning back to us. "It won't take long."

We followed Gracie across the lawn, depositing our snow cone wrappers in a trash can and then walking down the wooden stairway to the now cool sand and proceeding up the beach and along the rocks, while the waves made their slow journey to high tide. I hoped that we'd make it to Gracie's cottage before we got drenched. But in only a few minutes, we were climbing up another flight of wooden steps to what looked like a small fishing village dotted by small cottages, weathered by salt and storms, and nothing like the posh seaside beach homes of La Joyan society.

We made our way along a sandy pathway to a white clapboard cottage, trimmed in blue, with a weathervane on the roof shaped like a trident. No light came from inside. Gracie stood at the door, a half-circle of glass embedded in the wood just above a brass knocker. She fished in her bag for keys, but then stopped.

"What's wrong, Gracie?" I said, stepping closer to her, and then understood. That door was slightly ajar.

She pushed it open and peered inside. "Papa?"

Finn stepped forward and gently grabbed her shoulder. "How about I take a look, okay?"

Before Gracie could respond, Cilla put her arm around her while Finn stepped inside, calling, "Mr. Galioto? Sebastian?" No answer. He then flicked on a light switch by the door. The room was empty. Gracie broke loose from Cilla and ran through the small cottage calling for her dad, while the rest of us chased after her. There wasn't much to search. The neat and tidy home included the parlor, a galley-style kitchen, two small bedrooms and a single bathroom with a shower, clawfoot tub and a sink, all authentically vintage.

Gracie then circled back to the parlor and into the galley, where a door led to a small fenced-in backyard and a deck, no doubt handmade by Sebastian, that sported a picnic table, benches and a brick grill. But no papa.

"Where is he?" Gracie walked around the perimeter of the fence and I could sense panic setting in. "He'd never leave the house unlocked. Papa has his prize lures and other stuff he keeps in his room, hidden in his closet. But I checked and it's all still there."

"Does your dad have a car?" Finn asked.

Gracie spun around.

"No. He's always on his boat. I have a car, and if he needs anything in town, I pick it up for him." She was on the move again. "We've got to get to his boat. He's got a slip at the marina. It's not far."

"Fine, Gracie, but lock up first, okay?" Finn said.

Her hand was shaking as she fit the key into the lock. She headed down a narrow, curvy road that fronted the cottages. Lampposts installed along the way, plus the lights that shone from inside the ramshackle homes, lit our way, as the silver waves rolled in below us, splashing against the rocks. We had to sprint to catch up to Gracie, who had the cell to her ear, but I could tell she was not getting an answer.

Shoving the phone back into her tote, she rounded a bend in the road, and up ahead was a small marina where a half dozen fishing boats were tied up, gently rocking in the sea breeze.

Gracie stopped when she arrived at the third slip, where a small open boat with an unusual triangular sail was tied up. There were lampposts here too, and I could make out the name *Graciella* on the side of the boat, which under the light appeared to be painted in shades of green, red, gold, and blue. Gracie was already running up the short plank, calling, "Papa!" We followed her as she climbed onto the deck. Then from out of the darkness, came an unfamiliar voice.

"Gracie? Is that you?"

I felt so relieved, but that emotion quickly faded when I heard Gracie call out, "Stavros? Where is he?"

We turned to the boat tied up next to us and saw a shadowy figure standing on the deck, holding what looked like a pipe, which emitted a pungent odor that mingled with the salt air.

"Sebastian? I don't know; I just got back. What's wrong, Gracie?"

Stavros spoke in accented English, Greek maybe?

"We were supposed to meet, but I can't find him. He's not at the house and he doesn't answer his phone."

"Hmmm. That don't sound like your papa."

"Did you see anything suspicious around here today?" Finn asked.

"Suspicious? Like I told you, I was out on my boat since morning. You a cop?"

"No, we're friends of Gracie. Just trying to catch up with her dad." Finn gave a salute. "Thanks, Skipper. Have a good night."

The shadowy figure returned the salute, turned and went below—at least, he disappeared from view, so I assume that's what he did.

Gracie was pacing around the deck. Like the cottage, there wasn't much to search. Then Gracie abruptly stopped, knelt and picked up something. A rag maybe? We walked over and found her holding what looked to be some sort of cap, but not an ordinary cap. This one had a length of fabric attached to it and appeared to be black or navy blue.

I knelt next to her. "What is it, Gracie?"

When she spoke, it was almost a whisper.

"It's Papa's fishing cap—a Portuguese fishing cap. It's been in our family for generations, all the way back to the old country, he told me. He wears it every day when he's on the boat and he always brings it home with him."

She turned the cap around in her hands and then suddenly dropped it as though she'd been shocked, her breath coming in short, rapid gasps. Cilla leaned down and put her arms around her. I picked up the cap and felt something wet along the crown. A splash of salt water? And then Finn was by my side and leaned in so that the fabric was close to his nose.

"Salt water?" I whispered.

He shook his head. "No, Nellie. It's blood."

CHAPTER TWENTY-TWO

We decided that our best course of action was to call Wendy. She'd be able to tell us whose blood was on that cap. This would be awkward, because we hadn't invited her to our meeting with Sebastian, but she'd probably understand. Some people are skittish around the police. Finn pulled out his cell and called Wendy, who, as luck would have it, had just finished riding the waves and was still at the beach.

Finn filled her in on our disturbing evening and she agreed to meet us at the marina.

After she arrived, Wendy took possession of Sebastian's cap and placed it in one of the evidence bags she kept in her car. Then she canvassed his neighbors on board the other boats but turned up empty.

Gracie paced the dock, furiously punching in her dad's number, but there was no answer.

Cilla and I sat on a bench, watching her, not wanting to violate her space. Finn paced nearby. Finally, Gracie walked back to us.

"He didn't fall over the railing and drown," she said at one point, although none of us had suggested it. "He always wore his life preserver when he was on the boat, even when he was cleaning his fish. He didn't care that he might look dorky, because he's lost a lot of his pals who weren't so careful."

Of course there were other possibilities, but none of us suggested any of them. Tightly wrapped inside her sweater, Gracie fought back tears, and Cilla did her best to soothe her. Then Wendy was heading our way and Gracie leaped up and sprinted to meet her.

We followed.

"Has anyone seen him?" Gracie asked, breathless.

Wendy put her hands on Gracie's shoulders. "Nobody has seen your dad all day, but maybe he had some emergency?"

Gracie stomped her foot, her hands gesturing wildly. "No! He would have called me."

That's when the foghorn sounded on her phone and she looked at the screen and started sobbing, putting the cell to her ear and whispering, "Papa! Where are you? I've been so worried!"

Then she stumbled back to the bench and sank down, listening.

"What? I don't understand, Papa, who called you?"

That's when Wendy stepped forward and put out her hand. "Gracie, let me talk to him, please."

Gracie held up her hand and said into the phone, "Papa, a police detective is with us, she's really nice, and she'd like to talk to you, okay?"

She listened for his response and said, "I know, but you can trust her. I do." Another pause and then she handed the cell over to Wendy.

"Mr. Galioto? I'm Detective Wendy Nakamura," she said. "I'm a friend of Gracie's. Are you okay?"

It would have been good to have Sebastian on speaker, but that probably was not a wise move, given that we were out in the open and voices carried at night. So, we waited while Wendy took a seat next to Gracie and took her notebook and pen out of her shoulder bag and listened to Sebastian on the other end.

From the look on Wendy's face, it must have been one whale of a tale.

Poor Gracie looked bewildered.

Finally, the conversation wound down and Wendy said: "That's quite a story, Mr. Galioto. Okay, Sebastian then. You must be exhausted, so I'll let you go, but why don't I pick you up—Okay, then I'll drive Gracie home, if that's all right with you. Do you want to speak to her again? Okay, I'll tell her. See you soon."

Wendy then returned the phone to Gracie, who seemed to be holding her breath. "Your dad's fine and he's on his way. We'll meet him back at your place."

Gracie looked dazed, but she stood and tucked her phone back inside her tote.

"Hold it, Wendy," Finn said, "What's going on? You can't just leave us hanging."

"I need to get Gracie home," Wendy said. "Sebastian's on his way back. I'll brief you later tonight. See you at the *Crier*, say around nine?"

True to her word, Wendy met us at the *Crier* at the appointed time that night. The village's small commercial district is a virtual ghost town at that hour, with nothing but streetlamps to light up the neighborhood.

It was dark inside and we figured that Cap'n Jack was probably holding forth at O'Toole's, but we all had keys to get in after hours. I had my key out and was trying the lock, which often stuck due to the salt air.

"Hey, Wendy, you want to kick this sucker down?" Finn asked, clearly amused at my clumsy efforts.

Finally, I got the door open, but before I had the chance to flip the light switch, a fierce growl came from inside, followed by a raspy voice warning us, "Down on your knees, ya bastards, or I'll blow yer heads off! I'm warning ya, my pit bull, Spike, will rip ya to shreds!"

I sighed, Finn snorted, Cilla giggled, but Wendy was going for her gun. Cilla put a calming hand on Wendy's shoulder and whispered, "It's okay."

"Jack, it's only us," she cooed. "We came in to work."

The growling stopped, and Jack grunted, "Oh, fer crissakes."

I flipped on the light and we found our boss crouched down behind the old fast-food counter, a spear gun clutched in his hands, but no pooch. Jack doesn't own a poodle, let alone a pit bull, but he had recorded his version of a cheap alarm system. He also doesn't own a firearm, as he is a convicted felon busted by the Coast Guard way back for smuggling weed and hosting floating craps games on his boat, which he ended up forfeiting.

His lawyer, Dapper Dan Dunlevy, a sleazy but talented shyster, did manage to keep him out of jail. But Jack's probation had required him to spend a bunch of weekends scraping guano off the seaside benches.

Apparently, there was nothing that prevented him from packing a spear gun, so here we were.

"Meant to ask, Jack, how come you sounded like a pirate?" Finn asked, headed over to the banquette.

"Why do you think, O'Connor?" he said, smacking his spear gun down on the counter. "It adds to the menace, that and my pooch, Spike, of course."

We collectively rolled our eyes, except for Wendy, who simply looked baffled.

"Who be the young lady?" Jack said, fluffing his bountiful gray beard and smoothing the tufts that grew on either side of his otherwise bald head.

"I be Detective Wendy Nakamura," she said walking up to the counter and offering her hand. "And you be Cap'n Jack, editor in chief of the *Coastal Crier*, am I right?"

He took her hand in his meaty paw and wiggled his bushy brows.

"Guilty as charged, my girl. To what do I owe the presence of the constabulary?" he asked. "And, for the record, I wasn't even in town that day."

That was his go-to alibi for just about everything, I'd learned.

Before Wendy could answer, Cilla glided over to the counter and took Wendy's arm, leading her over to our table.

"How come you're not at O'Toole's?" Finn asked. "They run out of booze already?"

Cap'n Jack picked up the spear gun and chucked it in a space under the counter, ready to use on any marauders.

"You know I don't imbibe the night before I got to do a shitload of newspapering," he said, adding, "You remember you got a deadline tomorrow?"

"We remember," Finn said.

Cap'n Jack looked at Wendy, was probably thinking, and rightly so, where does a cop fit in here?

Well, this was awkward. Even if Wendy was officially off the case, we still didn't want anyone spilling the beans that she had met with us after hours at the paper. But Cap'n Jack seemed sober enough, so maybe we could trust him not to blab. Then it occurred to me, he was an old salt. Maybe he knew something about Sebastian that could be useful.

I huddled with Finn, Cilla, and Wendy, who wasn't happy about the prospect of possibly exposing herself again. Already banished to cold cases, she knew all too well that it could get a lot colder for her. But she also understood that Cap'n Jack might be able to plug some holes, so she agreed to share, with one caveat directed at Jack.

"You have to promise that you will not mention that I met with you here tonight—"

Finn jumped in. "Or anything else about what Wendy tells us, not until we say so, okay, Jack?" he said. "You've got to trust us on this."

Cap'n Jack snorted. "I don't got to do nothing, O'Connor. This is my paper and I call the shots." He sighed and hoisted his considerable girth up on his bar stool behind the counter and rested his shiny head on his folded arms. "This better be good."

Wendy started her story, and at the sound of Sebastian's name, Cap'n Jack's head came up.

"Seb? I had a slip right next to him—well, before that unfortunate misunderstanding with the Coast Guard, those bastards."

"How well did you know him?" Wendy asked.

"Well enough to say hello, you know, what's biting out there, hear there's a storm coming in, like that," he said. "But Seb wasn't much for gabbing, and he never accepted my invites to O'Toole's. I heard that he was a widower with a kid, so I guess he spent a lot of time with her."

Cap'n Jack slid off his stool, hauled some bottles of water out of the mini-fridge, bundled them up in his burly arms, came around the counter, and handed them out to us.

"Here, whet your whistles, folks. Sounds like you got a tale to tell."

Wendy unscrewed the cap on her bottle, took a hefty swallow, then continued her story.

"Sebastian got a call as he was walking to his boat this morning, after Gracie had left for work. He said that he didn't recognize the voice, that it was distorted. Whoever it was told him to go back to the cottage, leave the door unlocked, and leave his fishing cap and his cell phone in the parlor. They said that they had Gracie and if he didn't do what he was told, he'd never see her again. Well, that got his attention and he ran back to his cottage and did as he was told.

"The caller told him to head to the depot downtown and take the train to LA, and gave him instructions on where to go next. After he got there—some abandoned warehouse—he found a written note telling him to go to another location and to destroy the message. He took out his lighter and burned the note. He was terrified, but he had been warned not to call the police, so he followed his instructions. Poor guy, he spent hours roaming around, from one place after another, until it was dark. The final note told him to go home and to destroy any remaining notes. They were watching him, or so they told him."

"Were they really watching him, do you think?" I asked.

Wendy shrugged. "No way to tell, but Sebastian believed it."

He had then hitched a ride from a long hauler and made it back to Union Station in time to catch the last train back to San Diego, Wendy told us. We knew the rest of the story and filled Jack in.

He shook his head. "What the hell's going on?"

Nobody had any answers, only speculation.

"Gracie was afraid he might have seen or heard something he shouldn't have on the charters," I said. "Some customers, she said, seemed sleazy. Maybe he did, they found out, and were sending him a message. Clam up or your daughter is dead."

Cap'n Jack thought about that. "So why not just kill him on the charter and dump his body out to sea? They weren't shy about whacking Perreau and the shoe guy, right? Why not Seb?"

"We have no proof that what happened to Sebastian has anything to do with those murders," Wendy said.

"Any chance Seb has his own enemies?" Finn mused. "Did you ask him about that, Wendy?"

She nodded. "I did, and he said he had no idea who would do this to him. He didn't owe anybody money, he hadn't cheated anybody or flirted with anyone's wife. When he was on a charter, he said, he always kept his head down, did his job, and never asked any questions. He didn't even make eye contact. But I noticed that when he said that, Gracie gave him a look, but she didn't say anything. He could be hiding something."

"So, what happened to his cap? Was that blood on it?" I asked.

"I sent it to the lab, so I have no idea. It smelled like blood, but whether it was human, we'll have to wait and see."

An image of the big-cat heart fished out of Cate's well flashed in my mind.

"How about Alphonso Junior?" I asked. "Cate never met him, but said she knows about his reputation for being a psycho sadist. My mother said the same thing about him. And remember that blood oath? Maybe this is what it's all about. Payback for something. They said that Junior likes to take his time, like a cat playing with a mouse before the kill. So, Junior sent Sebastian on this wild goose chase just to play with his head? Raise the terror level?" I asked.

Well, it seemed to have worked.

"What about Gracie and her dad?" Cilla asked. "They're not going to stay in the cottage, are they?"

Wendy shook her head.

"No, I told them that they needed to lay low for a while and he said he had a cousin who could put them up. I arranged for them to be transported there—I won't say where—and we moved Gracie's car to our impound lot for safekeeping."

It was late and clearly we were all running out of gas. Wendy said her good nights, reminding us to keep her name out of anything we might print. She'd share if and when she could.

After she was gone, Cap'n Jack stretched and yawned.

"Okay, folks, what do we got? You got a scoop or not? Or do I have to fill the space with a photo of some drunken rich jerks living the life of Riley?"

"Not to worry, Skipper," Finn said, closing his notebook. "We've got it covered."

CHAPTER TWENTY-THREE

We spent most of the next day perfecting our "Elephant Diaries" opus and frequently checking our cells and laptops for any breaking news related to our story. We were holding our breaths that nobody would steal our scoop now that the big-media fish were on high alert. Then Wendy called and Finn put her on speaker.

"Sebastian's cap? It was animal blood, but that's all we got," she told us, her voice low. "I've got to go."

"Wait a minute, Wendy," I said. "Who's on the case? Did Sylvia have anything to say about what happened?"

Wendy was quiet for a minute and I thought that maybe she'd already ended the call. Then she said, her voice still low, "Like last time, she told me to get back to cold cases and that she'd handle it. None of my business who she assigns, right?" Then she did end the call.

Wendy's mojo seemed to have deflated again, but I understood that. After all, her former mentor did not trust her anymore. It seemed a bit of a miracle that Wendy still had a job.

We each had our laptop in front of us on the table, where we were about ready to send the story to Cap'n Jack, who regularly popped his head out like a groundhog to check on our progress. While we toiled away, our leader was frittering his time away playing poker with his pals out on the deck.

"Pranks?" I said, sparking a review of current events. "The big-cat heart in the well, the boogeyman at my window—"

"How about the horse glue and the fake engines revving up?" Cilla said. "You all thought you were going to die."

"Getting run off the road was no joke either, Nell," Finn reminded me.

Cilla raised her hand. "Let's not forget about me."

"That was no prank, Cill," Finn said. "You could have been killed. Nellie, too."

"So how does all this tie in with Milo, Perreau, and Junior's inherited blood oath against Cate?" I asked. "Speaking of whom, notice how Cate is the common denominator in all of this? I mean, she was cozy with Milo, 'Philly,' and Junior's dad, who swore vengeance against Cate for betraying him, right?"

"Yeah, but they're all dead, Nell," Finn said. "And Cate claims that she's never met Junior, and I tend to believe her. She seems genuinely spooked by this snake."

The story was filed, the sun was setting and the three of us decided to clear our heads and take in the sunset. We relaxed on the gazebo's padded benches.

"Watching the sunset is good for the soul," Cilla purred, leaning her head back and breathing in the salty air.

So true. As the sun was making its descent, there was something magical—and rejuvenating—about the glorious pink and orange hues painting the sky. I closed my eyes, feeling the balmy breeze waft over me. I was getting drowsy and felt myself drifting off into sleep when a scream pierced my ears.

Cilla was standing on her bench, while Finn grabbed me by my arm and hauled me up next to her, then joined us. The cove, at least the area surrounding the gazebo, was deserted.

"What the hell are you doing?" I said, glaring at Finn, who was pointing his finger outside the gazebo.

"Holy shit, it's a fricking crocodile," Finn whispered. "In San Diego? Can you believe it? Look at that sucker."

In the dim light from a nearby lamppost, I could see its smoldering eyes and powerful jaw, still closed. It kept lazily crawling our way. Then suddenly it hissed, snapping open its mouth and revealing a set of Ginsu knife-sharp teeth. That was enough for Cilla, who turned and jumped through the railing behind us, screaming, "Let's get the hell out of here!"

We joined her, landing on the lawn, running up the slope and onto the boardwalk. Did I recall hearing a slapping sound and wood splintering back there? Fortunately, it didn't take long to get back to the paper, where I fumbled for the keys, all of us looking back to see if that crazy croc was chasing us. They move fast, right? Well, they did in all those old Tarzan movies I used to watch with my mom. We hurried inside and slammed the door shut, locking it behind us and turning on the light switch.

Cap'n Jack wasn't waiting at the counter drawing a bead on us this time. Was he tucked away on his cot back in the storage room, or was he snoozing outside in his hammock, as he likes to do on balmy nights? We needed to check on him. Cilla had the same thought and was already making her way around the counter, past the old drive-through window and over to the storage room.

"Oh shit, Jack's not on his cot," she called to us.

We were right behind her now. Finn shouted, "Hey, Jack, you taking a leak?"

But the porta-potty tucked into a dark corner of the storage room, behind a partition, was empty.

"It's deadline day," I reminded them. "So, he wouldn't be at the tavern, at least not this early."

"He's gotta be out on the deck," Finn said, heading out the back door.

I tugged at his sleeve.

"How fast can crocodiles run?"

Finn broke free and waved me off.

"Do I look like Crocodile Dundee, Nell? How the hell should I know? But we need to get Jack inside just in case. For all we know, the croc had a chauffeur. I don't think he swam here all the way from Australia."

A chauffeur? So, who's the driver? Junior? The smugglers? Was I hallucinating again?

When we reached the deck, Cap'n Jack was in his hammock, swinging in the breeze under a now fog-shrouded moon, snoring, his arm dangling over the side, hovering above an empty bottle of Captain Morgan. I guess he got an early start tonight. There were no croc sightings or hissing sounds and the gate to the deck was padlocked. Jack was sloppy about a lot of things, but he was a stickler for security—in a low-tech-padlock kind of way.

Finn shook Jack awake, deftly avoiding the skipper's fists, which were waving around frantically. Jack tended to go into combat mode when he'd had a snootful and was suddenly jerked from his slumber. Disentangling him from the hammock was even more of a challenge, but Finn managed. He steered Jack inside. Cilla secured the door, while Finn deposited Jack in his captain's chair—a beat-up old La-Z-Boy that he used when he edited our copy, usually resting his laptop on his belly.

"What the devil are you doing?" Jack growled, trying to stand up but instead managing to hit the chair's lever, which sent him crashing down into a reclining position.

"Are you all out of your freaking minds?"

While Cilla was doing her best to calm him, I heard the roar of an engine approaching and walked over to the front window. The fog had rolled in, but I could see headlights in the haze, getting closer. Then the headlights snapped off, and the engine died.

"Finn!"

But he was right there, pulling me away from the window, checking the lock and then shutting the blinds.

"Someone's out there," I whispered. "What are we going to do?"

Jack was now fully alert, his antenna primed and ready for action, while Cilla clutched his arm with what looked like a vice-like grip.

"Hey, Cap, might be a good time to get out your spear gun," Finn said, over his shoulder, while he snapped off the light and checked the deadbolt on the door.

"Some punk wants to mess with me, I'll nail his hide to the wall," Cap'n Jack said, disentangling himself from Cilla and hoisting his spear gun out from under the counter.

We waited in the darkness, holding our collective breaths. No one made a sound.

"Maybe it's just one of the shopkeepers, Finn," but no sooner had I said that than the front door was hit from outside by a powerful blow, followed by a low hissing.

The good news was that Cap'n Jack had replaced the original glass door of the former fast-food eatery with a sturdy door made from scraps he had salvaged and cobbled together. The bad news was that we couldn't see whatever it was that was trying to batter down the door. Was it croc-resistant?

"Finn, this is no prank!" I said, scooting behind the counter, where Cilla had hunkered down next to Cap'n Jack, who was aiming the spear gun at the door.

Whap, whap, whap. I could picture that giant reptile out there whipping its tail against the door, loudly hissing. But where was his chauffeur? The car's engine was powerful and conjured up memories of being run off the road.

Finn just stood there by the door, his hands on his hips.

"I'm calling nine-one-one!" Cilla said. "That stupid door is going to splinter into pieces and then that creature is going to tear us into pieces!"

Cap'n Jack snorted. "That door is solid as they come, Ms. Potter. Genuine hardwood, handcrafted by the best artisan—me."

Whap, whap, whap.

"Hold on, Cilla. Maybe the crocster will wind down," Finn said. "Then, if we're quick, we can find out who drove it here and get some ID for once. But, if whoever's out there hears the sirens, they'll scram and we're back to square one."

I crept around the counter and peeked between the slats in the blinds. I couldn't see a thing but the ghostly glow of the streetlamp.

"If that thing slithers off, we'll never see it, and I don't see any sign of the car or the driver," I said. "How the hell did they manage to wrangle that beast into the car anyway? What did they do, put him in the passenger seat and fasten its seat belt?"

Then everything got quiet and we waited for the sound of the engine, but there was nothing but silence. Until—

Whap, whap, whap!

I was pretty sure that my heart had leaped out of my mouth and was now splattered on the floor. There was a crash. The croc apparently had managed to crash through the gate leading to the deck and was now, no doubt, slithering its way up to the back door, only a few feet from where Cap'n Jack had not long ago been blissfully snoozing. The hisses were fiercer than ever, and it was not winding down.

Whap, whap, whap! It was now battering the back door, only a few feet away from us. This was one pissed-off beast.

"That's it, Finn," Cilla said. "I'm calling nine-one-one!"

She sprinted around the counter and grabbed her bag, which she had tossed on the floor. Digging her phone out, Cilla made the call, while I watched as the back door rattled with every *whap*.

"Jack, please tell me that you built that door too," I said.

Before he had the chance to answer, a massive blow struck the door, splintering the wood, while Cilla was babbling to the 911 dispatcher. "Yes, a crocodile! I am not kidding you and I am not drunk. I am a responsible adult and I am telling you that we are in danger!"

She looked over at the now splintered door, which continued to rattle, and her voice went up several octaves.

"We need help. Now!"

Meanwhile, Finn and I were frantically looking around for ways to barricade the door, but Cap'n Jack's mini-fridge and beat-up footlocker weren't going to do the job.

"How about your cot, Cap?" Finn said. "Maybe we can upend it and put it against the door. Looks solid enough."

Cap'n Jack, hoisting his weapon, walked back to the storage room and nodded.

"Yeah, it's got a steel frame. Let's give it a try."

He handed me the spear gun, not realizing that they had a better chance of surviving the croc than surviving me with a loaded weapon.

Finn and Cap'n Jack hauled the frame over to the door, angling it against the wood, then jumped back as another fierce blow sent a cascade of sharp splinters their way. Then, at long last came the sounds of sirens, and the *whapping* and hissing suddenly stopped.

Finn was brushing splinters off his T-shirt and out of his hair, and Cap'n Jack hollered, "Ya bastard!" while he examined the damage.

I gingerly deposited the spear gun on the counter, and Cilla emerged from the storage room with a first-aid kit.

"Are you guys all right?" she asked. "Anybody bleeding?"

"A few scratches, Nell," Finn said, just as an engine roared and we heard tires squealing.

"Shit, there's goes the croc-mobile," Finn said, heading to the window and opening the blinds. "So much for getting an ID. We got nothing."

I joined him, peering out into the foggy night.

"Nothing?" I said. "What about that door, Finn? Doesn't that prove anything? We were under attack!"

Finn grunted.

"Sure, but by a fricking crocodile? In La Joya? Did we see a crocodile out there?"

"No, but we sure did back at the gazebo. Maybe he left some damage there too."

"No witnesses, Nell, and do you really think that a department run by Lamo and Psycho Sylvia will believe us? Wait till they get a load of our story tomorrow. They'll be telling the whole damn village what nut cases we are, and there goes our credibility."

Cap'n Jack had retreated to his La-Z-Boy and leaned back. "Maybe I shoulda had some cameras installed outside," he mumbled. "But I wasn't expecting a crocodile invasion.

"Woulda, shoulda, Cap," Finn said. "We need a real plan. Fast."

The patrol car turned out to be one of those RSVP vehicles, driven by a retired cop, Dexter Sims, who did his best to keep from peeing in his pants from laughter.

"This your idea of a joke, folks?" he sputtered, trying to get his breathing under control.

While he did examine our splintered door, he found no evidence of a crocodile. No scales or scat or whatever the hell a croc leaves behind after a rampage. But it was dark and foggy and, even with Officer Dex's industrial-sized flashlight, how much could he really detect?

"You should check out the gazebo down at the cove, Officer," I said. "We think the croc might have caused some damage there too."

"Sure, I'll do that, lady."

Stifling more guffaws, Officer Dex duly recorded our names, flipped his notebook shut, and bid us good night.

Meanwhile, Cap'n Jack assessed the damage to the door.

"Looks like I'll have to get my ass over to the dock tomorrow and salvage more wood."

"How about you find some scrap metal and build a steel door, Jack?" Finn was in a foul mood, but so were the rest of us.

I wondered what Dame C's take would be on this latest bizarre event. Well, that would have to keep, as I accepted Cilla's invite to crash at her place, a cozy studio perched above a boutique dress shop a few blocks from the *Crier*. Fortunately, I make it a habit to leave out a good supply of food and water for the felines on deadline days, in case I'm late getting home. The kitties would be fine, unless the googly-eyed monster decided to make a return. Finn headed home to his bachelor bungalow on the beach, while Cap'n Jack had decided to stand guard, or rather, sit guard and sleep in his La-Z-Boy, the spear gun resting by his side.

But our croc caper was a virtual day at the beach compared to the next morning after the *Crier* landed on La Joya's well-manicured lawns. We reconvened at the paper around eight, having stopped for a takeout order at Starbucks. Walking in, I made a point to lock the door behind me. Cap'n Jack was snoozing with his mouth wide open, stretched out in his La-Z-Boy, easy pickings for any croc that dropped by. Nothing looked out of place, and since Jack was still breathing, there seemed to have been no further assaults, either by belly crawlers or two-legged predators.

Suddenly there was a fierce banging on the front door, remarkably unscathed from the night before. But this time it didn't sound like a croc's tail, and there wasn't any hissing. But there was a lot of growling, along with cursing and threats, and a furious rattling of the doorknob.

Cilla peered outside and said, "Oh crap. That's the chief's car out there."

"The Lamborghini?" I asked.

"No, his cop car."

More banging and rattling.

"Let me in, you idiots, this is the law!" spoken in the dulcet tones of a South Bronx expatriate.

Jack snorted and opened his peepers, pulling the lever on the recliner to upright. "What the hell?"

Finn walked to the door, unlocked it, and yanked it open, as a startled Chief Lamo nearly fell forward onto the floor.

"What's the problem, Chief?" Finn said, barely concealing a smirk.

The chief stormed in past Finn, furiously waving a copy of the *Crier* in his meaty paw. "Piece of Pachyderm Pierces Perreau?"

Did Cap'n Jack write our headlines when he was sober or half in the bag? It was hard to tell, but his alliteration was always spot on.

"Are you fricking kidding me?" the chief sputtered, spitting saliva. His face was even redder than it had been at the news conference last week, and Sylvia wasn't around to calm him down this time.

"Yeah, Jack's got a way with words," Finn said. "You got a problem, Chief? Fake news, maybe?"

His eyes bugging out, Chief Lamo swung around, his fist clutching the rolled-up newspaper, but his timing was a tad off and Finn easily managed to duck the blow, while once again our uninvited guest almost took a nosedive, his short, beefy arms flailing for balance. Things were not going well for the chief, but he did possess a badge and a gun, so he technically had the advantage.

"I oughta bust the lot of you," Lamo screamed.

"What are you talking about, Leonard?" Cap'n Jack said, glaring at him from behind the counter. "You ever hear of the First Amendment? You got nothing, so beat it."

"Nothing, my ass. You hacked into our system, somehow, and when we find out how you did it, you'll all be doing hard time. And you," Lamo said, pointing the tightly wound paper at Cap'n Jack, "once a crook, always a crook. You think I don't know about your Coast Guard bust? I'm warning all of youse, I'll be shutting down this rag, and you can take that to the bank!"

"Fine, Chief, you get your evidence and do your worst," Cap'n Jack said, whacking the counter with his open palm. "Meanwhile, get your butt out of here, or I'll be filing a complaint that the police chief of our fair city is harassing the Fourth Estate."

Finn walked over to the open door and grandly gestured for Lamo to leave.

"Maybe I'll file a complaint too, Chief," he said, grinning. "Trying to assault a member of the press is not cool. And I've got witnesses."

He glanced over at Cilla, who had been recording the whole scene on her cell. She giggled and said, "Who, me?"

"Yeah, me too," I added, not wanting to be left out of the action.

Outmatched and no doubt wishing he had brought along Sylvia for backup, Lamo exited, growling, "This isn't over!"

I'll admit he was one scary dude and we were full of false bravado, but I'd call it a draw.

Cilla and I watched the chief as he stomped down the walk, hefted his bulk into his car, slammed the door, and peeled out.

"You think the chief heard about our croc encounter last night?" I mused. "He didn't mention it, and that would have been great ammunition to throw at us. A bunch of cranks, right?"

Finn shrugged. "How do you know that Officer Dex even reported it?"

"Why wouldn't he?" Cilla asked. "The door was splintered, and you and Jack had a few scrapes from the flying splinters. Officer Dex can't laugh that off, can he?"

Finn shook his head. "No, but I think old Dex probably right this minute might be entertaining his pals over at the cop shop about a bunch of crazy reporters who were eating magic mushrooms or smoking loco weed and thought they saw a crocodile down at the cove. Or he thought we'd pissed off somebody, a reader, maybe. Who knows?"

What we did know, after scouring the internet, was that the media, especially the tabloids, were buzzing about our latest scoop. It wasn't long before the *Crier's* landline was ringing away, with reporters from near and far trying to draw a bead on our sources. Then, around noon, we each got emails that the chief of police would be holding a news conference at 4:00 p.m. concerning this latest development.

Cilla had spent the morning tapping into her network and trying to get some intel on how Lamo and Sylvia had managed to acquire two ultra-luxe cars on their salaries. Was it relevant to our story? Maybe. Then, out of the blue, she got a call.

Cilla stared at the screen and called out to us, "It's Wendy."

We watched her as she took the call, her violet eyes growing wider. Then she said into the phone, "Are you sure? I mean, I wouldn't ask you to—I know—well, okay. I'll see you there."

She ended the call.

"What's up?" I asked.

"Wendy wants me to go with her to this warehouse tonight. You know, that place down in Otay Mesa I was heading to when I got grabbed? Overdrive, the one that hires out drivers. Maybe some of them worked Mitzi's party." Cilla closed her eyes and took a deep breath. "I did need to follow up on that, but no way was I going down there again, certainly not alone. Anyway, Wendy said she might have a lead. Now I don't have to go down there alone, so that's good, right?"

Finn stared at her. "You wouldn't have had to go down there alone, anyway," he said. "I would have gone with you."

Cilla shrugged. "Well, maybe I was trying to work up my courage," she said. "This makes it easier for me."

Girl power.

"Fine, Cill, but how about you and Wendy try to find out what else this Overdrive supplies?" Finn said. "You ever hear of a warehouse dispatching drivers? I mean, they're not driving tanks, right?"

We all pondered that and Cilla said, "We'll check it out, Finn."

Then Finn mused, "I wonder what's going on with Wendy these days?" Finn leaned back in his seat, his laptop open on the table. "She's in, she's out." He looked at Cilla. "You sure about this? You trust her?"

"Again with the trust stuff, Finn?" Cilla said in a sharper tone than I normally heard from her. "Anyway, what do I have to lose? Besides, Wendy's still a cop, you know, and she'll be armed."

But Finn wasn't convinced.

"Why did Wendy call you and not the rest of us?" he asked.

Cilla blinked, clearly surprised at his question. "Well, I was the one who got the lead on Overdrive and then got stuffed into a trunk on my way down there. Why *not* me? She probably didn't want a whole caravan. If we're going after hours, we'll have to be stealthy."

Stealthy?

"So, you've made up your mind?" I asked. "You're going?"

She nodded firmly. "Yes, I'm going."

At noon, I took a break and went home to check on the kitties. When I arrived, Cate was puttering in her herb garden, which was decorated with fanciful fairies and gnomes. My attempt to sneak by her was foiled when she called after me, "Good day to you too, Nellie. And no need to thank me for feeding your wretched felines. Do you know they have a taste for truffles? They may be better bred than I imagined."

Truffles? Oh thanks, Cate, for elevating my cats' palate. Good-bye Friskies. I waved but she was already heading my way.

"Tell me, Nellie, how did your run-in with that dreadful crocodile go?"

I stopped and spun around, nearly sending us both to the ground. "How did you hear about that, Cate? Nobody knows about that, except the creep who sicced that creature on us."

"Aren't you forgetting Dex?" Nobody did smug like Cate did smug.

"Dex?"

"Officer Dexter Sims, of course." She sighed. "Do try to keep up, Nellie."

"You know that guy?"

Cate took a step closer, her gardening shears dangling from her gloved hand. "No, not directly, but Freddy does. They go back a long way, when Dex was still on patrol. Let's just say their paths used to cross on occasion."

"Freddy got busted?" I don't know why I said that, but there was something sketchy about the guy.

"No, Nellie, they know each other from the track," she said. "Freddy used to be a jockey, you know, and Dex adores playing the ponies. At least, that's what Freddy told me."

"Cate, this only happened last night. How did you—"

She just waved me off and glided over to my cottage, which was unlocked. Why did I even bother with locks?

"I have more important things to discuss with you," she said, dropping the shears, brushing herself off, and ushering me into my place, and then taking a seat in the comfy chair. I half expected her to retrieve a martini shaker from inside her gardening hat, but none materialized.

I planted myself on the settee, and looked over at the stairs, where Pru and Pat were sleeping off their truffle treats.

"Do you realize how much trouble you might have caused by printing that story about Philly?" She had removed her gloves and had a free finger to wag at me. "Don't you realize that Junior is watching—reading, seeing, and hearing everything?"

Cate actually shuddered.

I took a look around the room and wondered about bugs. "Are you saying that we're under surveillance?"

"No, Quigley already swept for devices at the main house, my craft room and here, of course. But that means nothing, Nellie." She lowered her voice. "He has his ways, you know."

I gulped. "No, Cate, I don't know and neither do you. You never even met him, right?"

She sighed again. "I know things, Nellie. Who do you think planned the attack on you and your friends last night? Do you think that crocodiles are roaming around the village? In La Joya? I tell you, Nellie, that creature was delivered to your door—and the gazebo. By the way, that nasty thing took quite a big chomp out of it, according to Dex. That could have been you and your mouseketeers."

"Musketeers."

"Whatever."

"Wait a minute." I held my hand up. "I got the impression that Officer Dex thought we were a bunch of loonies."

"Oh, he does, dear. Dex doesn't believe that a crocodile vandalized the gazebo, he thinks that you folks were on a drunken rampage. So he just decided not to report it. No doubt despises paperwork. Anyway, it's not important what that ninny thinks. I know the truth and I know that Junior is behind this. You mark my words."

My head was spinning.

"Look, Cate, I've got a news conference to get to and I need to have a quick lunch before I go, so—"

"Chief Leonard will be having you and your friends for lunch, Nellie. As I have said before, loose lips—"

"Sink ships. Yeah, I know, Cate, but I've got a job to do. Maybe we'll manage to flush Junior out."

"The only ones who will be flushed will be you and your comrades, Nellie. Don't be foolish. Just drop this story and go back to your dead beat and my memoir.

That really pissed me off.

"This story is the dead beat, Cate, as in Milo and Philly are dead."

"And if you keep pursuing this, they will have company!" With that, Cate rose imperially, strode to the door and then turned dramatically, pointing that long finger at me again.

"You'll ignore my warnings at your own peril!"

Then she was gone. I locked the door, attached the chain, closed my eyes, and took a deep breath.

I was trapped in a B-movie starring Catherine Carlisle and a fiend named Anaconda, and I was scared shitless.

CHAPTER TWENTY-FOUR

Chief Leonard was already flushed and looking fierce when he stomped up to the podium, a junkyard dog looking for a hunk of red meat to chew on and finding a potential feast sitting right before him. Sylvia stood in the background, looking both protective of her boss and tense.

A motley horde of reporters, including tabloid stars and camera folks, jockeyed for good spots to set up. I craned my neck to look around the room, but didn't spot Wendy. I wasn't surprised. She was lying low.

"Okay, listen up," Lamo said without preamble. "I'll take your questions, but keep your yaps shut until I'm finished. Unnerstand?"

Then he trained his reptilian eyes on us.

"You can blame the clowns in the front row for probably blowing our shot at finding out who offed Milo and the gallery guy—" He rifled through the notes that Sylvia had placed on the podium for him. "Phileep Perro."

The chief clearly was not a linguist. I looked at Sylvia, as she bit her lip, knitted her hands tightly in front of her, and probably wanted to beam herself out of there. But Sylvia was a loyal minion and she would stand by her lord, no matter how much of a fool he made of himself.

"We got a loony on the loose, folks, and whoever it is probably is deep unnerground by now, thanks to the hacks at that rag, the *Coastal Crapper*."

Finn was on his feet.

"The *Coastal Crier*, Chief Leonard, and by the way, our rag publishes news, the kind that our readers need to know about so maybe some of them don't end up hanging from chandeliers."

Lamo looked like a beet that had mated with a fire hydrant, one that was leaking. Sweat poured from his brow and Sylvia hurried up to him, ready with a fresh hanky. The chief tore it from her hand without so much as a thank-you, wiped his brow, and bellowed, "Shut the hell up, O'Connor, or I'll have your ass hauled out of here! Or maybe you'd be more comfy sitting in a cell, which is where you belong!"

Despite his bluster, Lamo had lost control of the news conference and the flood gates opened.

"So Milo and Perreau's murders are linked, Chief?" asked one perfectly coiffed and made-up anchorwoman. "Do you have suspects?"

"Haven't you been listening, honey? We got zip, thanks to those idiots."

"Where did they get the intel, Chief?" asked a dapper-looking Brit, his silky baritone offering a pleasant counterbalance to the Bronx bomber up on the stage. "Do you have leaks?"

"Like a fricking sieve, your highness, and you can take this to the bank. We're turning up every fricking rock and we'll find the bastard or b—"

Before he could finish, Sylvia zoomed to his side, took his arm, and said, "I think that will be enough for now, ladies and gentlemen. We'll notify you if and when we have more information for you."

With that, Sylvia scooped up the notes and hustled her boss off the stage. Lamo grumbled all the way, but he did not resist and was probably relieved to get out of there. I know that I was.

When I got home, I locked the door, set the chain, and was greeted by Pat and Pru, who no doubt expected a serving of truffles in their kitty bowls. Tough luck. I put out the Friskies and fresh water, then trudged up the stairs to my bedroom to make a quick survey, but everything seemed to be in order, and the windows were still locked. No googly-eyed monsters gazing in at me.

I sat on the bed, kicked off my shoes and laid my head on the fluffy pillow. My fatigue hit me big-time and I was down for the count. When my cell meowed me out of sleep, I couldn't be sure if it was the phone or my cats. Time to change the ringtone. I opened my eyes and was surprised to see that the moon was peering out of the clouds and filtering its beams through the slats in my window.

I fumbled for the phone and through bleary eyes noted the ID. Cilla. I checked the time. Midnight. When I answered, the screen was filled with the nightmarish image of my friend inside a cage, curled up against a wall.

"Nellie!" she screamed before the screen went dark.

My brain had to make a decision: give in to hysteria or spring into action. Propelled by sheer adrenaline, I considered my options. Finn had Wendy's cell number and would be able to reach her. That's what I'd do, except I didn't get the chance. My phone went off and when I answered, this time, an image filled the screen of a massive creature, swimming below water, its head barely breaking the surface, and then it struck, its jaws snapping open on its prey, and the terrible squealing—a pig? No, a wild boar. Nora had taught me about the snakes she encountered in the rain forests of the Amazon and their preferred prey. Then came a voice, cold and metallic. "The anaconda is hungry. It is watching you. It is listening. You will deliver Catherine Carlisle to him on Raptor Island within twenty-four hours. She will appreciate the irony, our bird lady. Our dear friend Sebastian Galioto shall guide you."

"Sebastian? I don't even know where he is now!"

A metallic chuckle.

"Oh, but I do, Nellie Bly. Your dear friend, Detective Wendy Nakamura, was kind enough to tell me and I have called him."

It took a while to understand his words and then it hit me like a live wire.

"Wendy? But how—"

"How? Why don't you ask her yourself?"

A video clicked on and there she was, also huddled against a wall in a cage, muted light filtering in. But Wendy didn't speak. Her head was slumped down and her face was shrouded in shadow.

"What did you do to her?" I screamed, sending my cats skittering down the stairs. "If you hurt—"

The picture faded into black and the voice returned.

"No, no, she wasn't harmed, Ms. Bly. You see, a brave woman such as Detective Nakamura would have gladly sacrificed herself and been fed to our serpentine friend, rather than give up Sebastian. Alas, her soft heart prevented her from witnessing your dear friend suffering that fate."

"Cilla?" I remembered her plan to meet up with Wendy that night. The warehouse. Who could have tracked them there? "Let me talk to her!"

"Not just yet," he rasped.

Then I heard another voice, one I knew well: Gracie, breathing hard and clearly terrified.

"Nellie, help!"

Then silence.

"Gracie!"

The metallic voice returned.

"Your friends are well. For the time being, that is, Ms. Bly. But if you fail to follow my instructions or if you go to the police, I will know and they will die a very gruesome death. I'll send you a video of that too. Now I must sign off."

"Wait! How can I reach Sebastian?"

"Sebastian will contact you tonight. You have twenty-four hours, Ms. Bly. These games have been amusing for me, but they are over. Do not disappoint me."

I sat in the moonlight, shivering. I wrapped my arms around my body and rocked back and forth. Then my phone purred again. There was no ID.

"Ms. Bly?" His voice was filled with despair.

"Sebastian? Where are you?"

"I am parked outside your house. We must leave at once."

"They have Gracie and Cilla and Wendy . . ."

"I know, Ms. Bly. They promised me that they won't harm Gracie, or the others, if we do as they say. Now, please, we need to get this Catherine Carlisle."

"What are you suggesting, Sebastian? We kidnap her and deliver her to this monster? We need to call the cops!"

"No!" he shouted. "They will kill my daughter. You don't know these men, but I do. We have no choice. Maybe the son of the snake only wants his money and then he'll let her go."

"The snake? Are you talking about Alphonso Anaconda Junior? He really exists?"

He didn't respond right away, then said, "I'm just a fisherman, Ms. Bly. I work on Junior's boat sometimes, I hear things, I keep my mouth shut."

"You've actually seen him?"

"His men, they wouldn't let the crew anywhere near him. I only saw him from a distance. He always wore hats, sunglasses. I could not describe him or identify him, but we all knew it was Junior."

"What do you know about Raptor Island? What is that, his hideout? Is it even a real place?" More silence.

"It is very real, and I have been there on his boat, with his friends. Evil men, dangerous men, I think. It's a very desolate place, a place of pirates and the cartels. You will not find it on any map. He named it himself. Raptor. We must go now."

"Are you insane? Do you think Cate will just go with us and offer herself up as dinner for God knows what animal he showed me on the video?"

"An anaconda probably."

"Is that real, too?"

"It is Junior's pet and he keeps it well fed. It's maybe twenty-five feet and weighs more than two-hundred pounds. A monster, much like its master. The anaconda, see, it doesn't poison you, it crushes you and then devours you." Sebastian was breathing heavily. "He brought it back from the Amazon—the rain forest."

The rain forest. My mother had just been there and brought home pictures, many of them likely showing the destruction of the land and wildlife caused by Anaconda Jr. and others like him. A dangerous mission, but that was Nora. Fearless. Proud. Relentless. But who was I? Was this my test? As a journalist? As a friend?

"I will come to you now. Please let me in."

Then I heard a noise that sounded like someone tapping on glass and Sebastian seemed to grunt.

I could hear a car door being opened and a thump, then a groan and then another voice came through my phone, a familiar one.

"Well, Nellie, what have you gotten us into this time?"

"Cate?"

"Who else would it be, dear? I have Quigley with me, and he has a shotgun. Your gentleman caller, I'm afraid, has some explaining to do. So do you."

We convened in my sitting room so we wouldn't disturb Cate's aviary. Quigley, looking very much the mercenary soldier that he might once have been, prodded Sebastian in the back with the shotgun, while Cate took her usual position in the comfy chair, and I went to the settee. The cats had retreated to their beds upstairs.

Sebastian looked terrified, his muscular arms raised high, while Cate took her time to take his measure.

"Quigley, you can step down, or whatever it is you fellows say. Please bring this man, whoever he is, a chair from the kitchen, and then we will sort this all out."

I glanced at the antique clock on the wall and it was clicking down the time—twenty-three hours and thirty minutes left to deliver Cate to Junior and his pet anaconda.

Cate, dressed in a verdant green turban and what looked like her crafting attire, smock and all, pointed her finger at Sebastian as he sank into the chair unsteadily, the sweat pouring down his face, although the night was cool. Without a word, Quigley, who was standing guard, shotgun at the ready, removed a crisp white handkerchief from his denim work shirt and handed it to the fisherman.

"Now, sir, tell me who you are, what you are doing on my property, and why you were harassing my boarder."

Before Sebastian could answer, I jumped in.

"Let me explain, Cate. We don't have much time. This is Sebastian Galioto. You met his daughter, Gracie, the other night, sitting right here. She, Detective Nakamura, and Cilla have been kidnapped by, I presume, Junior."

Cate seemed to turn the same shade as her turban and started to tremble. Quigley turned to me and commanded, "Please fetch her some water."

I did and Cate gulped it down, probably wishing for a martini.

Once she had collected herself, Cate barked, "What are you babbling about, Nellie?"

"I'm trying to tell you, Cate. My friends and Sebastian's daughter have been snatched by your stalker, Alphonso Junior, and he's given us twenty-four hours, less than that now, actually, to—"

Cate's face shifted from green to pale white and her eyes took on a look of terror I had never witnessed before, not even in a B-movie.

"Junior?" Her usually vibrant voice was a whisper. She gulped down more water. Then she glared at Sebastian. "Why did you come here, to my home?"

Sebastian gave me a desperate look and I continued.

"Junior sent him here to bring you to a place called Raptor Island in an exchange for Gracie, Cilla, and Wendy."

At that, Quigley grabbed a hunk of Sebastian's thick mane of hair, yanked his head back, and from out of nowhere produced a fishing knife that he pressed against the poor man's throat.

"Quigley! Are you crazy? He's not the enemy. Put that down!" I screamed.

Cate looked stunned by the scene unfolding before her, but she recovered quickly.

"Put that knife down at once." She was in command again. "Where did you get that thing?"

Ever the obedient servant, Quigley released Sebastian's hair and palmed the knife.

"Why don't you ask our guest here, madam?" Quigley said coolly. "He was carrying it. Weren't you?"

Sebastian said nothing. He looked at the clock, his breathing labored.

"Oh, for heaven's sake, Quigley, the man is a fisherman," Cate said. "It's a fishing knife."

Then she downed more water. "The question is, how on earth did you think you were going to convince me to accompany you to this Viper Island?"

"Raptor Island," I said. "It's uncharted, Cate, and seems to be where Junior has been hiding out, that is, when he, or his minions, aren't running around the village killing its denizens. Why? I don't know, but I suspect you might. Anyway, Sebastian has a boat and he was ordered to take both of us there. He seems to believe that Junior only wants to get his father's money back, then he'll let everyone go."

Cate laughed harshly. "This is not about money, Nellie, and you know it."

"Yes, Cate, I know. Lives are at stake." I glanced at the clock again.

"Yes, mine or that of the hostages. How many lives am I worth?" For a moment it seemed she was flattered by the fact that Junior held three people just to get to her.

But then Sebastian started to sob, his strong, calloused hands covering his face. "She's all I got in this world. She has her whole life in front of her, Miss Carlisle, while you are not so innocent, no? You steal from him?"

Cate's glass froze halfway to her lips.

"Carlisle? Where did you get that name?"

"Where do you think?" I said. "Isn't that the name Senior Snake knew you by?" My patience was running thin. "Look, Cate, Junior is a psycho, and he's going to feed these women to his pet, a twenty-five-foot, two-hundred-pound-plus anaconda, according to Sebastian. We need a plan fast."

"And that plan is to offer me up as a human sacrifice to save the damsels in distress? Do I have that right?"

They were all looking at me now, so I had to think fast, but I kept seeing the images of Gracie, Cilla, and Wendy in that cage. I had to get my head straight and think like Nora, dammit.

"We'll have backup, Cate."

"No, no, Ms. Bly, they'll kill Gracie if you call the cops!"

"I'm not talking about cops, Sebastian," I said. "Here's the plan. Cate, Sebastian, and I will sail to the island, as ordered, while Finn, Quigley, and Cap'n Jack will follow."

"Cap'n Jack? Jack Cobb, you mean?" Sebastian said. "The Coast Guard took his boat."

I waved my hand.

"I know, but Jack has lots of pals in the marine community. I'm sure he can borrow a boat." I had no clue if this was true.

"You have weapons, Nellie?" Cate looked doubtful. "Do your friends?"

Cap'n Jack had a spear gun and I had a sharp tongue. Maybe Finn?

"We'll figure it out," I said. "We need to get moving now."

Then the front door opened and another visitor stepped in.

"What's going on, Catie?" Freddy asked. "I've been waiting for you guys in the craft room." He looked at Sebastian. "Who the hell is he?"

Cate stood. "I'm so sorry, Freddy, we were delayed, as you can see, but you couldn't have come at a better time."

Freddy looked confused.

"How would you like to be a musketeer?" she purred.

"What?" he removed his yellow jockey cap and scratched his head. "I can't sing or dance."

Cate sighed. "Oh, Freddy, dear, do try to keep up. A musketeer, not a mouseketeer. We need backup on a rescue mission to a place called Raptor Island."

Freddy blinked and nodded. "Why didn't you say so? Let's go."

I looked at the clock. We had little time left to assemble the team, secure a boat, and work out the logistics. Fortunately, Freddy would be an excellent communications officer, as it turned out. Just in case the rest of our cell phones were compromised, Freddy had a burner, assuming we had decent reception out there.

That was probably the least of our worries.

I was able to reach Finn right away, but the most important recruit, Cap'n Jack, had turned his phone off and was no doubt sleeping off another toot.

Not good.

We needed a sober captain and, most critical, we needed a boat. Finn drove over to the *Crier* and found Cap'n Jack asleep in the La-Z-Boy, woke him up, again ducking his fists, briefed him, and together, they went into action. One of Cap'n Jack's drinking buddies, a fellow named Barnacle Bill, lent him a boat that would be fueled and ready to go. As for weapons, Cap'n Jack arranged that too, but none of us needed to know how. He must have had a few chits to call in.

At my end, Sebastian had driven back to the harbor, while Cate and Quigley had returned to the main house to suit up. I had to keep tamping down a rising panic, stay in the moment, and ignore all the noise, as my mom would say. Well, actually I could only imagine what she'd say or do if she knew that I was about to go into battle with Junior.

I went to my bedroom and quickly dressed in jeans, a sweatshirt, sensible boat shoes and my all-weather hooded coat. I then put extra food and water in the cat bowls, made sure all the doors and windows were locked and headed out to the driveway to meet Cate, Quigley, and Freddy.

Off we went to the dock where we would meet up with the rest of the crew.

Cate, Sebastian, and I were in the lead boat, the *Graciella*, while Finn, Quigley, and Freddy rode in the backup boat with Cap'n Jack at the wheel. As it turned out, Quigley was a seasoned sailor, something that the skipper was going to need given the heavy fog that had rolled in, reducing our visibility to zero. Sebastian seemed to have transformed from desperate dad to stoic sailor, prepared for whatever lay ahead—or so I hoped.

As for firepower, we had an array of weaponry. Quigley came armed with his shotgun and a scary-looking rifle, and Cap'n Jack had a couple of handguns, plus his trusty spear gun. Finn had a .38, while Freddy—who knew? He seemed to be a man of many talents.

Sebastian had retrieved his fishing knife from a reluctant Quigley, who still didn't trust him and had demanded that he turn over his cell phone.

As for me, before we left the harbor, Finn had handed me a Glock. "Aim and shoot and don't be a wuss." Glocks, he also told me, had no safety setting, so there was a good chance that if I didn't shoot my boat mates, I might blow a hole in the hull and send us all to Davy Jones's locker.

Cate was dressed in yachting attire better suited for a regatta, her head wrapped in a Jackie O-style kerchief, her feet shod in knee-high snakeskin boots. The irony was not lost on me. But was she armed? When I asked, she just smiled and purred, "Don't you know, dear, that I'm a maneater?" Maybe she had a stiletto tucked in her boot, and maybe it had been designed by Milo.

None of this would make any difference if Junior employed a cadre of cutthroats, who'd have us all in their crosshairs as soon as we were in sight of the island. But what choice did we have?

The wind was fierce, and I was cold. Our boat had no cabin, so Cate and I were huddled against a bulkhead. Sebastian had tossed us a couple of life jackets, which we put on. I remembered telling Wendy, at our first meeting, about my childhood swimming trauma and how she had told me to face my fears. Now I was on my way to rescue her.

I looked at Cate, who was folded into her navy-blue fleece coat and appeared to be napping. This I found odd, considering that she was the main dish on the anaconda's menu. Did she trust us that much to save her from Junior?

"I do hope you have a good memory, Nellie, as you clearly won't be able to take notes or record our visit to the island."

I jumped at the sound of her voice. Her eyes were still closed.

"Oh, I don't think you have to worry that I'll forget anything, Cate. This should be quite the capper for your memoir."

Cate opened her eyes and snorted. "Or my obituary."

"I'm not writing your obit, Cate. Knock it off. I'm not in the mood for your sardonic wit right now."

Cate let out a deep sigh. "Oh please, Nellie, I've dealt with much worse than this, as you will find out during our next sessions."

I hugged myself against the chill wind. "You are a lady of many moods, Cate. One moment you are terrified at the thought of Junior coming after you, and the next moment you are as cool as a—"

"Cucumber? I will abide no clichés in my memoir, Nellie. Make a mental note of that, will you? Yes, I am a woman of many faces and that's what made me a great actress—even if no one else seemed to notice. In any event, I've been meditating, something that I learned from a guru during my travels. It was a long climb up that mountain, I tell you, but it was well worth it. I am at peace."

If bravado was the way she wanted to play it, fine with me. I looked behind us and couldn't see or hear a thing. Were Cap'n Jack, Finn, and Freddy still following us? The wind and the fog disoriented me, and the waves that rocked our boat were making my stomach churn. I had lost track of time. All I could do was hope that we'd make landfall while it was still dark and we had some cover.

CHAPTER TWENTY-FIVE

Despite my nerves and heaving belly, I dozed off. When I woke up, the sky was still dark and we were still swathed in heavy fog. Our boat seemed to change course and I strained to see what lay ahead. I felt foolish asking, "Are we there yet?" but damn it, I was tired of guessing.

"Sebastian," I hollered over the wind and waves. "How much longer?"

In response, Sebastian turned, gave me a ferocious look, and put his finger to his lips. In other words, shut the bleep up. Did that mean we were getting near enough for us to be heard? Our skipper made another turn and up ahead, through the haze, I could make out a dark mass. He made yet another turn and we were sailing around this mass and I could hear a faint slapping sound, maybe waves splashing on the shore? I felt a tug on my arm and looked down at Cate, who was wide awake now and smiling.

"Well, Nellie, dear, I do believe we are ready for our entrance." She sat up and adjusted her kerchief, which she had knotted tightly under her chin. "Showtime."

"How can you be so calm?" I whispered. "Meditation? Really?"

"Well, yes, that too. Also, I've been spending this quiet time reexamining my life—you know, employing flashbacks, a useful convention in films. I've come to the conclusion that fate has called me here and I'd better face it and stop hiding like wounded prey. If this is my destiny, so be it."

There were no words, but I still found a few.

"Your fate? Your destiny? What about everyone else on this mission? What about Cilla and Wendy and Gracie? What's the matter with you? Do you actually believe that this is all part of a grand cosmic script written to showcase the great Catherine Carlisle?"

Moonlight was now filtering through the haze, softly illuminating Cate's timeless face. Her eyes glistened. I almost felt sorry for her. Almost. But the time for soul searching had ended, as Sebastian held up his hand, beckoning me. Every bone and muscle ached, but I managed to crawl over to him, fearful that I'd fall overboard.

"There is a stretch of land where pines grow. I will tie up there and then we will make our plan."

Sebastian kept his voice low and I took his lead.

"What about Jack's boat? Can you tell if they were able to follow us?"

Sebastian shrugged. "We will know soon enough."

We drifted toward the stand of pines as Sebastian deftly maneuvered around the rocks that dotted the shore. Then we were still, and he motioned for us to be silent. For several minutes we listened, but all I could hear were the waves lapping the shore. Where the hell were Cap'n Jack and the gang? Shouldn't they be here by now?

Then, like a ghost ship, they appeared in the mist and Sebastian let out a long breath, as though he'd been holding it throughout the entire trip.

The skippers proceeded to tie up their boats, while the rest of us tried to get our land legs back in working order. Running might turn out to be our best option. From our position, I had no idea what sort of terrain we were dealing with, or how far we'd have to walk to case Junior's lodge. We stood leaning against some pines, the needles covering the otherwise barren ground.

"The lodge is maybe a quarter mile up that hill," Sebastian told us, gesturing.

"Does the lodge have a second floor, a lookout?" Finn asked.

"No, just a roof. Flat, but high enough to spot boats in daylight, when the skies are clear."

"But not in this fog?" I asked.

Sebastian shrugged again. "Maybe, maybe not. But if they see us, they would be on us now, no?"

Cate sighed. "Are you forgetting how much Junior enjoys toying with us? For all we know, he might be watching us now as we scamper around and then—bam!—he'll spring his trap."

"Hey, Catie, maybe you should keep it down, huh?" Freddy was pacing like a skittish lawn gnome.

Everyone checked their weapons. It was time to go.

"Mr. Galioto, might I suggest that you lead the way?" Quigley said, very much in command mode. "However, I must advise you that if you try to warn them—"

"You'll shoot me? Do you think I am stupid? I want my Gracie back. Don't insult me."

Sebastian took the lead, Cap'n Jack stayed in the middle, while Quigley brought up the rear, as they were the ones with the major firepower. This was all too real. We were heading into combat and we had no idea what we were up against.

The night was grimly quiet, with only the faint sounds of waves, the breeze rustling trees and bushes, and the occasional gull gliding by.

The Glock felt heavy in my right coat pocket and I kept my hand over it for fear that I'd jostle the trigger and shoot poor Freddy in the fanny. That was probably why Cate had opted to walk behind me.

It was rough going, especially in the dark, and I was careful about stumbling over the thick roots that crisscrossed the hard ground.

Moonlight played hide-and-seek with us, peering in and out of the pine trees. Fortunately, the fog had lifted enough for us to see a reasonable distance ahead. Of course, on the downside, the bad guys might be able to see us coming.

Then, way off in the distance, came a blood-curdling howl. What predators were likely to be lurking on this strange uncharted island? Sebastian raised his hand, and we managed an abrupt stop without knocking into each other.

"What the hell was that?" I whispered.

"There are things out here—wild things," Sebastian said.

"I know you worked on Junior's boat," Finn said. "But have you ever actually been on the island?"

Sebastian nodded.

"One time, very quick, because only Junior's men are allowed on the island. But the crew was asleep and Junior and his friends had gone back to the lodge. I took a chance. I was curious." He shrugged. "But then I hear them coming back and I ran back to the boat. They'd didn't see me."

Finn smirked. "Says who?"

Sebastian raised his palms. "I'm still here, am I not?"

"Okay, so did you see enough to figure out a back way into this place?" Finn asked.

Sebastian nodded. "I see enough. I read maps, I read the stars, I can always get my bearings, no matter where I am."

"Hey, can we get moving, folks, while the snake's still snoozing?" Freddy urged.

We reassembled and continued to walk, single file, up the hill, as the sky began to get a shade lighter.

Sebastian raised his hand again and we all stopped our ascent.

"We are almost in sight of the lodge, but we must stay low and be silent," he said. "Watch and listen."

"And check your weapons, please," Quigley whispered.

Sebastian led us the rest of the way up the hill and then lowered himself down on his belly, while the rest of us followed his lead. With Quigley's help, Cate arranged herself next to me and whispered, "Kate Hepburn would have killed for a part like this!"

Again I heard the brutish growl, but it was closer now. Were we being hunted by a four-legged predator too?

Our view was partly obscured by underbrush and rocks, but with the moonlight filtering through the mist I could make out the outline of a building. I didn't see any lights, nor did I see anyone on the roof watching for us. If they were, no doubt they'd be just as stealthy as we were being, and probably a whole lot more experienced in guerrilla warfare. I glanced over at Quigley and figured that he might be our best bet if it came to that.

I heard something else too. A faint splashing sound was coming from the same location as the building.

"Did you hear that splash?" I asked Finn, who was on my other side.

He nodded, staring down the hill.

"I may have forgotten to mention that there's a moat around the building," Sebastian mentioned with a smirk.

"A moat?" I screeched. "And what's in it?"

Sebastian shushed me.

"I think I know," Finn whispered, patting the pocket that held his gun. "Wonder if you can kill an anaconda with a thirty-eight? Maybe Cap'n Jack will have better luck with his spear gun."

I swallowed hard and forced myself to keep my eye on the prize. "Where do you think Junior is keeping them? Do houses on islands have basements, or underwater vaults?"

"I don't know," he said. "If we get lucky and take out whoever is down there, we need to figure out how to find them. It's a big island, from what I can see."

I remembered TV shows where kidnap victims had been buried alive underground, their oxygen supply slowly running out. That would be Junior's style. Then my fevered brain did another flip. What had Finn just said to me?

"Did you just say 'take out whoever is down there'?" I whispered. "You mean shoot them?"

"How do you think this is likely to go down, Nell?"

"Well, aren't you the cool one. You ever shoot anyone?"

He was quiet for a while and then said, "Yes."

Before I could respond, we heard furious splashing below us, mixed with a chilling squeal, and then, up on the roof, we could barely see a shadowy figure emerge.

"Oh shit," I said. "What the hell was that?"

"And *who* the hell is that?" Finn said, pointing to the roof.

I let out a deep breath and observed, "What's going on?"

"I'd say it's feeding time for Andy," Finn said.

"Who?" I asked.

"The anaconda."

"Would you two shuddup?" Cap'n Jack said in a harsh whisper.

We obeyed and watched silently until the shadowy figure below disappeared. I glanced over at Cate, who was tops on Andy's menu. She must have been thinking this too, when she quipped, "Well, at least he has a full belly for now."

Then Sebastian started crawling backward, belly down, and the rest of us followed, keeping low. He stopped, rolled over and sat up, while we gathered around him, as the splashing from the moat abruptly stopped.

"What was making those squealing sounds?" I said in a low voice.

"A wild boar, I'd guess," Sebastian said.

Quigley nodded, saying, "Yes, that would be my opinion too."

"What now, Sebastian?" I asked. "At least, now we know there's at least one person down there."

He nodded. "We cannot risk going over the hill. We must circle around it to get another view."

"We need to figure out where Junior is most likely to have stashed our friends and I'm thinking it's not going to be at the lodge," Finn said. "I'm guessing the ladies are being kept much farther back on the island."

Quigley again checked his weapons.

"Perhaps, but we need to move before first light." Quigley turned to Sebastian. "I agree, we should go around the hill, so please lead us."

We again fell in behind Sebastian, only this time it was much harder to keep our footing, as we were moving crablike and trying not to fall down the hill. It was still dark and foggy, and the moon was in hiding at the moment. The ground was covered with brush, roots, and God knows what else, and I was afraid of grabbing hold of something slithery, slimy, or sharp-toothed. We kept moving, our ears on high alert. Then came that growl again, a bit louder this time, joined by other feral sounds.

"What kind of wild kingdom is this?" I asked of nobody in particular.

Finally, Sebastian held up his hand. "We will climb to the top and wait and watch and listen, then we will climb down."

Well, that made sense, and I was pretty sure the bad guys were also waiting and watching and listening, and they probably could hear my heart banging around in my chest too. We climbed up to the top on our bellies and peered down through the mist. There were no visible lights on at the lodge, although I did see a shimmer of moonlight reflecting off the moat. No sign of Andy, who might have been sleeping off his meal.

Then Sebastian raised his fist, started his descent, and we followed. Climbing down the hill wasn't any easier than climbing up, and I struggled to keep my footing, grabbing onto roots and rocks and wishing that I had worn sturdier shoes. Was anybody watching us? Were we in someone's crosshairs? If so, which one of us would be the first to go?

We kept moving, dodging the rocks and debris that tore loose from under our feet, and finally we made it to the bottom. Again we waited and watched and listened. More wild sounds, only louder now. Sebastian gestured for us to stay low in the underbrush.

Then came a new sound. Not a growl, not a squeal, but a full-throated bellow that could only have come from a massive trumpet, or—

"Was that an elephant?" I whispered.

"Sure sounded like one," Cap'n Jack said.

Then other discordant sounds joined in.

Cap'n Jack plucked his spear gun off of his shoulder and sighted toward the sounds, and Quigley was ready with his shotgun.

"Will you two please put those things down," Cate commanded. "You're going to get us all killed. I'd rather take my chances with a rogue elephant than you two cowboys."

Finn pointed up ahead.

"Let's follow the noise, guys, because that's where the action's going to be."

Sebastian nodded. "He's right. We need to go in that direction and quickly. We have little time, I think."

Still crouching low to the ground, Sebastian led us to a nearby stand of pines and then stood. My knees crunched as loudly as my heart was beating, but it was a relief to stretch out. The moon was again playing hide-and-seek with the fog, but it was the only light we had. We kept walking toward the ruckus. A few minutes later, we were climbing up another hill, this one smaller, and the growls and the squeals and the bellows seemed very near.

Then we were at the top of the rise, looking down, and there they were—a menagerie of wildlife secured in enclosures that spread out in an open field. In the center of it all was a single-story structure that looked to be made of concrete, with a single door, but no windows, at least none that we could see.

"Dammit, why didn't I think to bring my spyglass?" Cap'n Jack muttered. "What do you think is down there?"

In the darkness, even with the intermittent moonlight, it was hard to make out the animals that were pacing in their cages, with the exception of the elephant, whose leg seemed to be anchored to the ground in one of the larger pens. He, or she, didn't sound happy, and perhaps sensing our presence, let out another loud bellow.

"I'll bet those are big cats down there," Finn said, squinting. "Lions, tigers, leopards? I'm guessing crocs too, maybe?"

That would explain our intruder at the gazebo.

"And maybe rhinos?" I whispered. "Didn't Wendy tell us how valuable they are to smugglers?"

Then it hit me. We had landed at ground zero of the criminal caper that had finished off Milo and Perreau and who knew how many others. Was it our turn now?

"I guess your mom was right, Nell," Finn said, his .38 now in his hand. "Junior must be the smuggler. I'll bet Milo and Philly were up to their ascots in poached skins and ivory, and somewhere along the way, they crossed Junior. Just like Cate crossed his daddy."

I held up my hands. "Wait a minute. Wendy schooled us on the smuggling of endangered animal parts, but I don't recall that she said anything about smuggling in an entire menagerie."

Cate snorted. "Well, dear, you must remember that nothing Junior does makes any sense to a sane person. He's quite mad, you know. And, there were the rumors about his—proclivities."

"What the hell does that mean?" Finn asked.

"It means that he liked to use rather unconventional ways to rid himself of enemies."

"Like that freaking snake?" Freddy asked.

"Indeed," she said. "Wild boar too. I hear they rather like the taste of human flesh, and this way—"

"The snake eats the boar that ate the human," Cap'n Jack said. "Like one of those Russian nesting dolls, right?"

"You must admit, it is an efficient way to dispose of remains," Cate said.

"And I suspect that Junior found legal ways to transport his wildlife," I said.

I looked up at the sky and tried to calculate the time.

"Okay, folks, so what's the plan?" Cap'n Jack said, his spear gun at the ready.

Sebastian breathed in deeply. "Maybe I have one."

We waited.

"They're expecting me, no? I go down there, knock on the door, they come out, and you be ready to fight."

Quigley did not like the sound of that. "That won't do, Sebastian, although you are a brave fellow to make the offer. But we have no idea what we're dealing with here. It could be a suicide mission for all of us."

What I suspected Quigley was actually saying was, "You're going to betray us. You're one of them!"

Freddy did not look happy either.

"Hey, I didn't sign up for no suicide mission, and no one said nothing about marauding elephants and psycho snakes. I'm outta here."

When he turned to go, Cate stuck out a snakeskin boot and tripped him, and if Finn hadn't grabbed his arm, Freddy would have rolled back down the hill. He yelped and Finn clapped a hand over Freddy's mouth.

"Shut up," he whispered.

Cate looked down at her little buddy and shook her finger at him.

"You signed on for this mission, Freddy Fiedler, and you're going to keep your word, or—"

"Yeah, yeah, I know, Catie," he said, settling back down on the ground. "But I'm not gonna be paying off that debt forever, ya know."

There was a story here, but no time to hear it now.

"We need to get closer to that building down there to see if that's where they're being held. And find out if there's a back way in," Finn said. "Sebastian, is there a way we could loop around the pens without raising a ruckus?"

Sebastian considered the landscape and nodded. "Maybe. But what if the back door is locked?" he said. "What you going to do then?"

Good question.

"Well, we can't just sit here until daylight," I said. "We'll be sitting ducks."

Cate nodded.

"I agree, Nellie, and I know just the fellow who could do reconnaissance." Cate smiled and turned her eyes on Freddy, who was already shaking his head furiously. "Freddy is not only quite agile, but he was an excellent second-story man back in his day, weren't you dear?"

Freddy was still shaking his head. "Whadda ya talking about, Catie? That building's only got one story. You don't need a second-story man."

"Beside the point, Freddy. You're a furtive little weasel and you could make it down there, unseen, in no time. Then do your magic, get in there, and report back to us." Cate gave us a wink. "Freddy's also quite talented at breaking and entering."

He let out a long breath. He knew when he was beat. What did she have on him?

"Okay, Catie, but I'm not going down there without heat."

Fair enough. I handed him the Glock, more than happy to be rid of it. Finn gave me a look.

"Thanks." He tucked it in his belt and peered down at the building and penned animals, who had quieted down some.

But would that last once they got Freddy's scent, which was quite pungent after all the exertion?

"Here goes nothin'."

Quigley grabbed Freddy's arm. "If you run into trouble, fire a warning shot and we'll come running."

Freddy tugged his arm away and snorted. "If I run into trouble, Mr. Q, you'll hear plenty of shots, but not mine. Or maybe I'll just get eaten. You might hear a scream. That would be me."

Then he turned and started to crawl down the hill.

I turned to Cate. "Are you sure about this?"

Cate watched Freddy as he made his descent. "No, but if anyone can get down there and make it inside, it's Freddy."

"Yeah? What's he going to do if he runs into armed guards?" Finn asked, his eyes also fixed on Freddy as he disappeared into the shadows below. "Is he going to start a shootout?"

Cate glanced over at Finn. "Oh, I wouldn't fret. Freddy has many survival skills."

CHAPTER TWENTY-SIX

We were all staring down into the darkness, with no sign of Freddy, who by now must have disappeared into the brush, no doubt trying to stay as far away from the critters as possible, while not losing sight of the building. How long would it take him to get there, and what were the odds that he'd be able to get inside? Was there even a way inside?

Then, movement down below. A figure emerged from the back of the building, but I could tell by the stride and the stature that it wasn't little Freddy. Another figure followed, shorter, but bulky. Again, not like the jockey.

"Who are they?" I whispered. "Is that Junior down there?"

"They're carrying something, I think, buckets maybe?" Sebastian said, staring down at the figures that were still cloaked in shadows. "Junior, he don't carry nothing. He has servants for that."

The bulky figure started flinging something into an enclosure and from what I could hear, a feeding frenzy ensued. Where the hell was Freddy? The other figure set down what looked like another bucket, water maybe? While the bulky one took over that duty, the taller one walked over to the pen where the elephant was tethered and knelt down. The elephant snorted and stomped over to the fence and the kneeling figure reached through an opening and started stroking its trunk. Then, he or she stood and walked over to the bulky one and they exchanged words. I couldn't make out any of them, with the wind whipping the trees.

"What the hell's going on?" Cap'n Jack said

Then the tall figure turned and strode back over to the elephant enclosure, and I could hear a vague sound. Clinking? Yes, they were keys, and whoever was down there was unlocking and then sliding the door to the fence open. That figure walked through, proceeded to untether the pachyderm, and appeared to be giving the animal commands, both spoken and through gestures. Dumbo went down on its knees and the figure gracefully climbed onto its neck and reached back and gripped something, maybe a rope that had been tied around the elephant? Then the beast stood and, apparently after a command, stomped through the fence opening and headed toward the back of the building.

"Holy shit!" Finn said. "They're on a collision course with Freddy."

Cate started to rise, but Quigley grabbed her arm. "No, madam, we cannot give up our position."

She yanked her arm away. "What about Freddy? That beast will crush him! We've got to do something. Dammit, Quigley, go down there this minute and shoot that creature!"

Then things got really crazy.

We could no longer see Dumbo, but we could sure hear his trumpet blaring and feel the earth shake beneath us. He was in attack mode, from what we were hearing, which consisted of high-pitched screams—from Freddy. And there, in the distance, coming around the bend were the silhouettes of Dumbo rampaging toward our little friend, who seemed to be running as fast as his thoroughbred used to, his arms pumping fiercely, and was bellowing, "Do something, you bastards!"

Easier said than done, as the bulky figure below had suddenly acquired what looked to be a long weapon and was aiming it right at us.

"Get down!" Quigley commanded, and he didn't have to tell us twice. An explosion of gunfire and then rocks, shrubbery, and tree branches were raining down around us, as we scrambled for cover. Freddy was still screaming and cursing, so we knew he was alive. For now, anyway.

"He's got an assault rifle," Finn said. "You think we're a match for that?"

Sebastian stayed low, peering out from behind a bush.

"There were weapons on Junior's boat," he said. "I seen them. Big, powerful, like this one. Once, I see Junior and his friends shooting at a dolphin. They were all drunk."

Nobody was bothering to whisper anymore.

"Guns aren't our only problem," Cap'n Jack said. "Let's not forget about those cats, if that's what's down there. If he unlocks that pen, we're all goners. They'll be up here in seconds."

"Yeah, they just got fed, and we'll be the seconds," Finn said.

"We've got to get down there and save Freddy!" Cate said, and then screamed, "Use your gun, you idiot!"

"You think that Glock he has is going to stop a rampaging elephant?" Finn said. "And even if he manages to take out Rama of the Jungle, or whoever that is riding him, you think Dumbo's going to turn around and go back to his pen?"

Another spray of bullets, more rocks, bushes, and branches coming down on us as we ducked and covered. What I no longer heard were Freddy's screams or the trumpets and thundering feet that had shaken the ground. Not good.

Then there seemed to be a cease-fire, and a voice called out to us.

"We got your little buddy, folks, so you might as well come down, while you still have the chance. My kitties here are still hungry."

Well, that answered two questions: Yes, they were indeed big cats down there and, yes, they were still hungry.

As if on cue, they started prowling and growling in their cage.

"I cannot believe this!" Cate said breathlessly.

"Chill, he's just bluffing," Finn said, although he didn't sound convinced.

"No, not that," she whispered. "I know that voice."

"What the hell are you—"

"It's Milty."

"Milty?" I said. "As in Milt and Mitzi Morrison?"

"The very same, dear," Cate said.

"You mean that drunk I played poker with at their party?" Finn asked.

I had a quick flashback of chatting with Mitzi in the study, listening to her tell me about the elephant that she and Milt had arranged to have transported to the zoo. Kubwa? I also recalled the tawdry tales that Cate had shared with us about the Morrisons being carnies back in the day. Then, there was Gracie's story about finding the footlocker, stuffed with suspicious items, in their bedroom.

"Well, folks, what will it be?" Milt said. "My cats got a big appetite. Maybe I'll serve them an appetizer while we're waiting on you. We've got four prime specimens down here now, well, that little runt is hardly prime, but my kitties aren't picky eaters."

Oddly, those words filled me with relief, because it told me that Cilla, Wendy, and Gracie were still alive.

"Milton Morrison, you fool, how dare you threaten us!" Cate stood with hands on hips, before anyone could stop her. "Put down that rifle and stop this nonsense at once."

Quigley sprang to her side.

"Cate, is that you, you crazy old broad?" Milt had a very nasty laugh. "Good of you to accept our invite."

"Dame Cavendish to you, you third-rate grifter. Where's that harlot of a wife of yours? Oh, don't tell me, Milt, let me guess. She's down there playing Sheena of the Jungle. My goodness, she has many talents, doesn't she? But you know, dear, you can take the girl out of the carnie, but you can't take the carnie out of the girl, can you?"

Milt chuckled again. "You should know, Cate. You parade around like royalty, but you're still nothing but a hootchy-kootchy dancer to me, although we did have some good times."

Sebastian had no idea what they were talking about and didn't seem to care, because he leaped up and roared, "You give me my Gracie back, or I will kill you with my bare hands!"

Cap'n Jack and Finn were now on their feet, grabbing him by each arm before he could scramble down the hill and either be riddled with bullets or be eaten by the big cats.

"My, my, that's quite an entourage you got up there, Cate," Milt said. "I don't think that Junior will be happy about this." He then pointed his rifle at us. "Sebastian, didn't you understand your orders? Cate and Ms. Bly were supposed to be the only guests at this party, correct? Otherwise, the ladies would be treated to a relaxing soak in the spa. Well, it's more of a moat, but I'm betting that you already saw it, right? Maybe you got a glimpse of Junior's pet too? Talk about a big appetite. And now she'll get an extra course, with that little guy you brought along. He sure can run, I'll give him that."

Then another figure, tall and graceful, came into view, taking long strides and carrying a rifle. Mitzi.

"He's an agile little fellow too," she said. "You should have seen him shimmy up that pine tree. He's still up there, far as I know."

"Where is that beast of yours, Mitzi?" Cate hollered down. "The four-legged one, I mean?"

"Hi, Cate." Mitzi waved. "Oh, Kandula's keeping your buddy company. That little guy was wrapped around one of the higher branches, and I'm not sure how much longer he can hold on. But not to worry. My big boy won't shake him down until I give him the signal."

She snapped her fingers as though she were giving commands to Kandula. "Now it's time for you all to come down so we can have a nice little chat before we take you to see Junior."

What choice did we have? We could hardly engage them in a firefight, especially not knowing what kind of backup they had tucked away in the shadows. Were we in someone's crosshairs at this moment? All we knew was that they had Freddy, Wendy, Cilla, and Gracie. And now they had us.

Cate had put herself at center stage and she was not eager to relinquish the spotlight. "Very well, Mitzi, let's get on with this so we can get off this dreadful island," she said, straightening her kerchief. She then turned to us. "Let's go, musketeers."

Of course, there was no way that the Morrisons—or Junior—were going to let us leave the island alive, and I'm pretty sure that we all knew that, even Cate. But she was in character, channeling Miss Hepburn.

"Oh Cate, just one more thing," Mitzi said, lifting her rifle and putting us in the crosshairs. Milt followed suit. "Please tell your entourage to throw their weapons down the hill. Safeties on, please. We don't want any ricocheting, do we?"

I thought about the Glock that had no safety option and had been in the possession of Freddy, who probably was still clinging to that pine tree where Kandula stood guard. Could he take out an elephant with a Glock? Would he even try? A wounded beast would be dangerous, right? Maybe he'd dropped it when he scampered up the tree. While I was ruminating, the others tossed their weapons down—or did they? There was a clattering of the big guns, followed by the pistols, but did Sebastian toss down his fishing knife? I couldn't tell.

We made our way down, kicking dirt and rocks as we went, and I took another look at the night sky, which was still cloaked by clouds and the intermittent moonlight. But the day was dawning. I wasn't sure at this point what would give us a better advantage, darkness or daylight.

"Okay, then, folks, hands up and walk our way until I say stop," Milt said, with a geniality that made me feel that he was welcoming me on board his boat.

When we were about ten feet away, he held up his hand.

"Now, down on your bellies, hands behind you, while I frisk you."

We complied. If Sebastian still had his knife, I sure hoped he had a good hiding place for it.

Again I remembered the old movies I used to watch with my mother, the sort where the leading lady always carried a hairpin or some other homey item that could be transformed into a deadly weapon.

Unfortunately, pin curls were long out of fashion, so I had nothing. Even my nails were short. Mitzi had us in the crosshairs as Milt patted each of us down.

Then he got to Finn and grabbed him by his hair, pulling his neck back. That must have hurt, but Finn clenched his teeth and stayed cool.

"You? You're that jerk who tried to cheat us out of our money at that poker game. It's payback time, buddy."

He then slammed Finn's face back in the dirt and moved on. When he got to Cate, she said coolly, "If you try to take liberties with me, Milton, you will regret it."

Again, the nasty laugh.

"You should be so lucky."

Then it was Sebastian's turn and I held my breath, but no fishing knife was found.

"Well, Sebastian," Milt said, "Junior tells me that you crewed for him a few times, that right?"

How close was Sebastian to a meltdown that could get us all killed? But all he did was nod.

"Too bad you couldn't follow orders, but you'll have to sort that out with him. I sure don't envy you. That man's got a fierce temper."

Milt stood and turned to Mitzi. "Honey, you keep them covered and I'll grab the guns."

Milt was wearing a canvas jacket with lots of pockets, and he was no doubt stuffing them with the handguns and shouldering the big guns, not that I could see him. I peered up at Mitzi, who was waving her rifle back and forth at us, obviously having the time of her life.

Where was Junior? Back at the lodge or in this building, and where were Cilla, Gracie, and Wendy?

When he returned, Milt walked over to the big cat pen and slid the guns through the bars. Good luck getting them back. Then he dug into a large pocket and retrieved what looked to be plastic ties and reminded us not to try anything stupid. I didn't need reminding.

One by one, he came down the line and fastened our wrists, making sure the plastic straps were good and tight. Then he ordered us to get on our feet, not an easy task without the use of hands. I managed to get up on my sore knees and then eased one leg up and tried to get to a standing position without toppling over. Milt was getting impatient, walked over and hauled me up, nearly dislocating my shoulder. As old as Cate must have been, she was agile and stood with the grace of a ballerina.

Milt herded us around the pens, where the big cats, including a tiger, a leopard, and panther-looking creature, paced and made low growls. There didn't seem to be any other critters in the immediate vicinity, but who could tell on an island this size? Milt and Mitzi made us walk single file to the back of the building, and that's when I saw poor little Freddy off in the distance, looking very much like a koala clinging to a high branch on the tree. Kandula stood at the base, still as a statue. If Freddy could see us, he knew better than to make any noise.

"Mitzi, dear, could you please put that beast back in its pen and get Freddy down from there?" Cate said. "He's quite harmless. Does odd jobs for me."

"Oh, I have no doubt that anyone who works for you does odd jobs, Cate, but all in due time."

As we were herded through the back door, I was instantly struck by odors, pungent and dank, and I wanted to cover my nose, but that was not an option. The light was dim, and it took my eyes a while to adjust as we moved along over what felt like a concrete floor. The space felt more like an above-ground bunker than a barn. The light source, I now could see, was a series of battery-powered low-watt lanterns hung on pegs along the bare walls. Then Milt hollered for us to stop, while Mitzi kept us covered from the rear. He walked past us, the rifle slung over his shoulder, until he stopped and fished out from one of his deep pockets a set of metal keys. I strained to see what lay ahead, but the light was too dim where we stood. I heard a click and then watched as he opened what sounded like a metal door that scraped over the concrete floor. He then waved for us to keep coming.

Even before I was close enough to see, I knew what we'd find in there.

Mitzi prodded us. "Go on now. I'm sure the girls will be happy to see you."

Milt had retrieved a couple of lanterns from out of the shadows and turned them on, exposing doors with metal bars and, inside, a room about the size of my parlor. But instead of a comfy setting, there was a row of cages lined up against the far wall and three sets of eyes staring out at us, belonging to Cilla, Wendy, and Gracie. At the sight of his daughter, Sebastian hollered, "Gracie!" and seemed to go into a seizure, hyperventilating and shaking. Then, before anyone could react, he leaped forward and rammed Milt with what sounded like the power of a Mack truck, before either he or Mitzi could react. Milt crashed to the floor and his rifle skittered over the hard surface. Sebastian had the fishing knife in his hand now, a plastic tie dangling from his wrist. Had he hidden the knife in his shirt sleeve? Gracie was rattling the bars of her cage, screaming.

"Papa! Don't—"

But it didn't take long for Milt to recover and retrieve his weapon, and as Sebastian charged him again, Milt swung the barrel against Sebastian's chest, knocking the wind out of him and the knife out of his hand, while Gracie screamed, "Don't you hurt my father, you monster!"

Sebastian was bent over, sucking in the foul air, and I was sure that Milt would finish him off with a blow to his head. Instead, he kicked the knife out of reach, turned the rifle and aimed at the cages, singling out poor Gracie.

"You see that, Sebastian, I've got your little girl in my crosshairs. You want to try messing with me again?"

Sebastian slowly straightened up and shook his head.

"Good." Milt lowered his rifle and ordered us to sit on the floor. We complied. While Mitzi covered us, Milt fished another plastic tie out of his pocket and secured Sebastian's wrists. "If we knew you all were coming, we'd have set up more cages in there, but once Junior gets here, we probably won't have to bother with that. You've got nothing to trade anymore."

Then came another voice from inside one of the cages, raspy but still strong.

"I am Detective Wendy Nakamura and I am arresting you for kidnapping and false imprisonment. You have the right to remain—"

"Oh shut up, dragon lady, you aren't arresting anyone today," Milt said. "In fact, Mitzi and I are making a citizen's arrest, as we've come under attack by these folks here."

Then Cate, who was sitting cross-legged, heaved a sigh.

"Oh please, Milton, you sound like a third-rate B-movie villain, and I should know. I'm the one Junior wants, so why don't you let my friends go, and Junior and I can have a nice little chat. If this is all about the money and the cocaine that I appropriated from his daddy—"

"Like I said, honey, you've got nothing to trade," Milt said. "And I can guarantee you, your offer will be dead on arrival."

The nasty laugh again.

"Oh Milton, I always did admire your sophisticated wit," Cate said. "You can't possibly think you can get away with this. Executing a police detective? Are you mad?"

"As a hatter, Cate," Cilla said, somehow still managing to look glamorous, as disheveled as she was, locked in that cage.

"You know, we left word where we were going," Finn said with as much conviction as he could muster.

"Sure you did, pal," Milt said, cupping a hand to his ear. "I think I can hear the choppers overhead."

Then Mitzi pointed at me. "I know you."

I just nodded and smiled. "How's Kubwa doing?"

She came closer to me. "You were at our party. I caught you snooping around in the study. You said you were a server. Should have known you were a spy."

I shook my head. "Just doing my job, Mitzi."

"You were all spies!"

Milt snorted. "You got that right, honey," he said. "We know Cilla here, the gossip lady from that rag. This fellow, O'Connor, was at the party too, trying to cheat us out of our dough. Now, you add this lady, the so-called server, to the bunch, and what have we got?"

Cap'n Jack, who had been uncharacteristically quiet, had an answer. "Ace reporters who are going to serve up your ass to the cops, that's what you got, ya bum."

And then another voice boomed from behind us. "Hey, Cobb, you're right! The cops are here. No copters though."

I looked up at Wendy and saw the relief wash over her.

"Chief Leonard? What are you doing here? How did you find—" But the relief quickly turned to confusion. "They're armed, Chief," Wendy warned him.

But Milt and Mitzi weren't raising their rifles. They seemed to be standing at attention.

"We were just going to—"

"Shuddup, Morrison, we got work to do."

"Yes, Junior, sir!"

Junior?

Cate craned her neck as she watched the pit bull approaching, her face a mixture of disbelief and terror. Lamo was Junior; Junior was Lamo. She had nowhere to run, and Quigley, her longtime protector, wouldn't be able to save her this time. Lamo swaggered over to her, spookily backlit by the lanterns.

"You know where I keep my father's blood oath, Miss Catherine Carlisle?" He patted a pocket over his heart. "Right here. Did you think I wouldn't hunt you down, you thieving, conniving bitch?"

Cate looked up at him; her chin was trembling, but her voice was strong. "You waged all this madness for money? If you're the Alphonso Anaconda Junior I've been hearing about all these years, you must be worth a fortune, what with your very successful smuggling racket."

He grinned like a wolf, his white teeth flashing in the dim light. "You know what they say about revenge best being served cold, right? I'm shivering all over."

"Is that how it went down with Milo and Philly too, Junior?" she asked. "Were they part of a blood oath as well?"

He leaned down closer, his face only a few inches from hers. "Nobody cheats an Anaconda. Nobody."

"Just curious," Finn asked, "but how did you manage to transform yourself from a murdering mob boss to the police chief of a major city?"

"Oh, it was easy." Another voice. Another one we all knew too well. Sylvia Sheldon.

Junior straightened up and seemed to glow. "Hey, sis, you got things ready?"

Sis? Holy, shit. This was a family affair?

Sylvia surveyed the scene and frowned. "Jeez, Junior, I didn't plan for all these folks. Guess we'll have to improvise."

"How about an answer first?" Finn asked. "I'm impressed. How'd you do it?"

Sylvia walked over to us and stood beside her brother. She was dressed in a black jumpsuit with high, expensive-looking black boots.

"Well, if you must know, O'Connor, we've lived undercover since we were kids, growing up in the Bronx," she said. "The heat was on, but our Uncle Vinny wanted us to have a normal childhood. Except he never let us forget our father's blood oath, and that one day, we would have to honor it."

"So you both became cops?" Cap'n Jack said. "And worked your way up in the ranks? No offense, but, from what I've seen, neither of you could detect yourselves out of an outhouse if it had three doors."

I expected either Lamo or Sylvia to stomp Jack into dust for that bit of candor, but Junior surprised me.

"It helps to know people. Our uncle was well connected," Lamo said.

"And nobody knew who you were?" I asked.

"No," Sylvia said. "We were orphans in the storm—Lamont Leonard and Sylvia Sheldon, raised separately. Our uncle hired a couple of ladies he knew and set them up in a nice duplex. No one knew that we were really brother and sister. You see, I was a love child, and back then, in the Anaconda family, that would have been a scandal."

"Tell me, Sylvia, who was your mother?" Cate asked. "Perhaps I knew her. Your father and I did travel in the same circle for a while."

"I don't know," Sylvia said. "Nobody ever told me, and I never asked. Who needed her, anyway?" Then she took a few steps closer to Cate. "Was it you? Did daddy knock you up? Did you give me away?"

"No, dear, I have no progeny," Cate said, genuinely horrified at the very thought. "I had to watch my figure, you know." Then she added, "To be honest, I much prefer to nurture birds. Less messy."

"Enough of that chitchat." Lamo broke back into the conversation. "As cops we could run the business under the radar, no questions asked. Worked like a charm."

Finn smirked. "Until we showed up, you mean?"

Way to go, Finnian, poke the lion in his den.

"Don't flatter yourself," Lamo said. "You and your loser pals were nothing but flies buzzing around us." He smiled. "You wanna see our fly swatter? Time to boogie."

Apparently, the dialoging was over, although Quigley gave it a shot.

"You are making a very big mistake, sir."

Unfortunately, that's all he had.

The next few moments were a blur as Milt released Cilla, Wendy, and Gracie from their cages and fastened their hands behind their backs, shoving them out with the rest of us. With all the time they had spent cramped in their pens, they moved stiffly. Our keepers then herded their hostages into a single file and marched us out the back door. I glanced over at poor Freddy, who was still hanging on to the high branch, Kandula waiting patiently beneath him, no doubt awaiting his mistress's command.

The sky was brightening now, not that it mattered. No one would be coming to rescue us.

"Mind if I ask what's the plan, Chief?" Finn asked. "A firing squad?"

Junior, who was walking next to him, roared. "You should be so lucky, O'Connor. No, I got something a lot more fun planned. Well, fun for me and Sylvie, not so much for youse guys."

"You really intend to feed us all to that moat monster?" Cate asked. "That snake cannot possibly have that big an appetite."

Sylvia laughed.

"That's the best part. You'll all have ringside seats and can watch as your friends get crushed and consumed. Of course, it will take a while, but we've got all the time in the world, don't we, Junior?"

"You bet, sis. Who wants to go first?"

Sylvia giggled. "Oh, I've taken care of that, too. You'll see."

"What about Freddy?" Cate asked. "Are you saving him for dessert?"

Sylvia giggled again. "Sure, we'll save the runt for last."

We were getting nearer to the lodge and the moat and the monster. I was sure my legs would buckle. This could not be happening. I kept expecting to wake up in a cold sweat, Cate banging at my door. Then I thought about my friends and wondered what they were thinking and feeling. I looked back and my eyes connected with my old pal, Cilla, sweet and silly and now so strong. She smiled and winked, and then she mouthed, "We're not dead yet, Nellie."

And then I felt a tremor coming from the ground. Was I shaking that badly? It was mild at first, but then it felt like an earthquake—an earthquake that didn't rumble, but—trumpeted? We all turned at once and out of the early morning mist came Kandula charging us, and he wasn't alone. Freddy was in classic jockey pose, hunched down on the beast's neck, holding on to the rope that was tied around him, heading our way. Mitzi broke away from us and started running directly into his path, screaming commands and making frantic hand gestures. But Kandula kept coming, causing his mistress to leap out of the way and crash onto the hard ground with a sickening thud.

"Do something!" Junior hollered at Milt, who stood in stunned silence. "Shoot that thing!"

When Milt didn't move, Junior backhanded him, and Milt sprang into action, like a good soldier. He advanced toward the rampaging elephant, pointed his rifle, took aim and shot. Unfortunately for Milt, the bullet only seemed to piss Kandula off—a lot. The elephant howled and reared up. Milt started running for cover, but Kandula reversed course and pursued him, no doubt under Freddy's control. Junior screamed at his sister, "Get Mitzi's rifle! Shoot that thing!"

Sylvia grabbed the rifle off the ground, turned and took aim, thought better of it, threw the rifle down and started running. At that point, Milt sprinted toward Mitzi, who was now standing, stunned, and grabbed her arm. Off they went, following Sylvia, who was heading back to the dungeon where their hostages had been caged.

Junior roared, "Get back here, you—" but one look back at the beast bearing down on him shut him up and he, too, started sprinting on his stumpy legs, trying hard to catch up as his minions desperately tried to reach the shelter before Kandula stomped them into the dust. Freddy seemed to be in control, reining the massive creature in until it gradually came to a stop.

"Did he just herd four people into the dungeon?" I said to nobody in particular.

"Sure looks like it," Finn said. "Freddy's got some skills. Who knew?"

"Oh, I knew," Cate said, winking at Quigley. "I told you he'd save the day."

Our wrists still bound behind us, we gingerly walked over to Kandula, keeping a safe distance just in case Freddy didn't have as much control over him as I thought. But I was close enough to hear Freddy coo, "Ya done good, Kandy." Freddy was hunched down and was whispering in Kandula's ear, stroking his hide.

"Kandy, is it?" I said.

Freddy straightened up, looking embarrassed.

"How the hell did you do that, Freddy?" Finn asked.

Freddy shrugged. "We had a lot of time to bond, you know? You ask me, I don't think he had much use for Mitzi. She didn't treat him right, I'm thinking."

"Are you telling me you're an elephant whisperer?" I said.

Freddy shrugged again. "Elephants, horses—same difference. We speak the same language."

Cate beamed up at him.

"Well, no time to rest on your laurels, Freddy. Why don't you mosey on over to the dungeon and make sure our hosts are contained, while we gather up the weapons that they so carelessly tossed on the ground back there."

"How you gonna do that, Catie? You're all trussed up. All I got is this peashooter."

"Too bad I don't have my knife," Sebastian said. "Maybe Freddy could fetch it."

"No need, my dear," Cate said, sticking out her leg like a Rockette. "Seeing as how dexterous you were back there with that knife trick of yours, perhaps you can manage to extract the knife that is attached to my very posh snakeskin boot. It is an attractive accessory, isn't it? Looks like jewelry. I must say Milo does—did—excellent custom work."

Well, I called that one.

Sebastian was dexterous enough indeed. He extracted the knife from Cate's boot, cut the ties on his wrists and then freed the rest of us. After we gathered the weapons that had been dropped during the stampede, we joined Freddy and Kandula, and then entered the dungeon, where our captors were hunkered down inside the cages, the barred doors shut.

Detective Nakamura had assumed authority over Operation Raptors, and used Freddy's burner to call in the troops. Then she, Quigley, and Finn cuffed our captors with plastic ties dug out of Milt's pocket. Sebastian stood near the entrance, his arm protectively around Gracie, as they kept Freddy and Kandula company.

All the while, the Morrisons were trying to cut a deal, promising Wendy that they'd happily give up Lamo and his sister and show her where they had stashed their ill-gotten loot—quite a treasure trove, they promised.

As for Chief Leonard and Deputy Chief Sheldon, they sat stoically in their cages, staring straight ahead and saying nothing.

Cate strolled over to Wendy and whispered something that I couldn't hear. Wendy didn't respond right away but finally nodded.

Cate continued whispering something else, gesturing over to me, and again, Wendy nodded.

Suddenly Wendy turned and waved me closer, then took Cate and me to Junior's cage and left, giving us space, as it were. For what, I had no idea.

"Nellie, dear, I know that you don't have your notebook or recorder, but do keep your ears open while Junior and I have a little tête-à-tête? Assuming, of course, he is in a tête-ing mood."

She turned back to Junior, who was sitting against the concrete wall, hands tied behind him, eyes still staring straight ahead. His bluster and bravado had vanished. He resembled a deflated helium balloon.

"Well, Junior, here we are at long last," she said crisply. "How sad that it had to end this way."

Cate waited for some kind of reaction, I suppose, but I figured it was a waste of time. Like so many times since I'd encountered Cate and her world, I was wrong. Junior slowly looked up at Cate, his eyes wet and his voice tinged with sadness.

"You broke his heart, you know that?"

Cate seemed at a loss for words. As long as I had known her, and it hadn't been long, this had never happened before. But then she rallied, glaring down at him.

"Your father didn't have a heart."

Junior shook his head. "No, you're wrong, Cate. He did have a heart and he was crazy about you. He used to talk about you all the time. Sure, he wanted you to suffer for betraying him, but he never got over you." Junior sighed deeply. "You had to pay, you unnerstand?"

He dipped his chin. "This is where I keep his blood oath, like I told you. Right here in this pocket over my heart. You should read it sometime, Cate. Then maybe you'll see."

Cate didn't speak for a while. Then she nodded. "Yes, Junior, maybe I'll do that some time."

EPILOGUE

Sylvia hadn't been kidding when she told Junior that she had everything set for their moat monster's banquet. A subsequent visit to the moat revealed that she had set out camp chairs for the victims, and had even included a box filled with numbers, from which we would draw lots to determine the order in which we'd be consumed. She'd also set up a camera on a tripod to record all the action. I wondered how many of these films she and Junior had tucked away over the years.

The authorities, including the Fish and Wildlife folks, had a lot of evidence to comb through, but the gist of it was that Junior was indeed the boss of a ring that plundered all sorts of endangered animals and distributed them to unscrupulous dealers worldwide, including to our jewel by the sea, La Joya.

The Morrisons might have started out dabbling in the business for kicks, who knew? But it became clear that their growing taste for the high life sucked them in deeper and deeper. And once you threw in with Junior, there was only one way out, as Milo and Perreau had discovered. As it turned out, those two were double-dealing and skimming off a large chunk of Junior's profits. Nobody cheats an Anaconda. Nobody.

Milt and Mitzi took a plea deal and were awaiting sentencing. Mostly, they confessed to receiving stolen goods, which they had stashed in various tax havens, liquidated, and laundered. The heist at the Morrisons' auction had been faked, with the help of the Overdrive crew, and the loot that Gracie had discovered in their stateroom was awaiting transport to one of their hidey-holes. As it happened, the Overdrive warehouse, along with a fleet of unmarked delivery trucks, had a vast and hidden collection of smuggled parts from endangered wildlife. Unfortunately, the warehouse crew were just hired help and were told only as much as they needed to know, which was not much.

What the Morrisons would not cop to was the abduction of Cilla or the later kidnapping of her and Wendy, who had been on their way to the Overdrive warehouse when they were snatched. The Morrisons claimed that they had nothing to do with any of that and had no idea what Junior had planned for their captives on Raptor Island. That was bs of course, but the prosecutors had Junior and his sister, the big fish, and they also had the potential victims, including a police detective, as eye witnesses to what Junior and Sylvia had told us about their crimes. What would happen to those two had yet to be determined as their trials loomed in the future.

How much of an impact any of this would have on the global plunder of endangered wildlife was anyone's guess. But it had at least a small impact and that meant something.

As for Detective Wendy Nakamura, she was back on her career track, although she wasn't being considered for Chief Lamo's replacement, nor had she expected to be. That decision had yet to be made, although I was fairly certain that Officer Dexter Sims was not in the running.

Freddy received a police commendation for his bravery, while Kandula was treated for a bullet graze and was doing fine. He, the big cats, and Andy, the anaconda, along with the rest of the menagerie, were transferred to the zoo.

Gracie returned to school and her side gig as a barista, while Papa Sebastian retrieved his prized fishing hat and got on his boat and went back to business.

As for Nora, my brave and globe-trotting mother, she had a very large meltdown when she heard about my encounter with "the Snake." I knew she'd get over it. I also knew that she had a newfound admiration for her daughter, and that meant a lot to me. Perhaps I'd be worthy to fill her shoes after all.

Cate and Quigley resumed their life at the estate and enjoyed basking in the spotlight, as Dame C, aka Catherine Carlisle, spun her tale to the media. Old Hollywood, lust, betrayal, mobsters and blood oaths! Not to mention a couple of psychos heading up the police department. Cate was already preparing for a bidding war on the film rights.

The *Coastal Crier* gang rode the wave of fame, if not fortune, for our full fifteen minutes and then settled back into our routines. Cilla convinced Cap'n Jack to give me a byline and photo, which added a bit of panache to the dead beat.

My side gig as Boswell to Cate's Samuel Johnson continued to plod along, as she still had a limitless supply of anecdotes to entertain me with. I had the feeling that her memoir would never be finished. Okay with me. I had come to relish my time with her, and who knew I would develop such a taste for martinis? Cate made a genuine effort to bond with my kitties, adding caviar to the truffles she occasionally slipped into their bowls. Unfortunately, Patience and Prudence developed champagne tastes while I was still very much on a beer budget.

"Nellie!"

Boswell never sleeps. Not even at 2:00 a.m. on a weekend.

"I've got the cocktails, now get your tape recorder. I've got a juicy story to share."

"What? Now?"

"Oh, for heaven's sake, Nellie, do try to keep up."

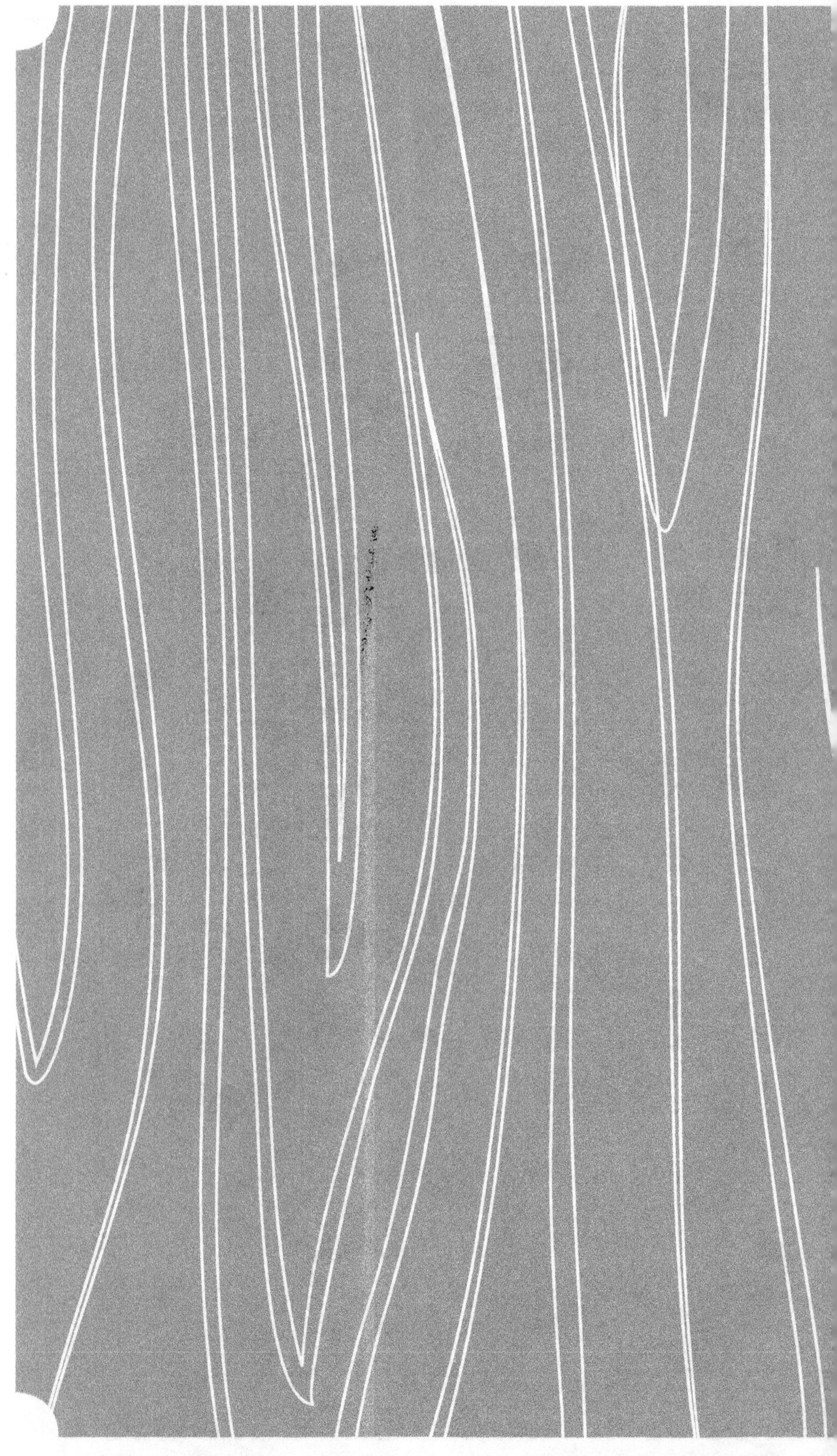

ABOUT THE AUTHOR

Author Patricia Broderick's long career as an award-winning journalist started in college at the University of New Hampshire, where she was news editor of the school paper. Using the byline Pat Broderick, she has since worked for newspapers, magazines and public television, as an anchor, producer and documentary maker in her native New Hampshire as well as Florida and California. *Dead on My Feet* is her debut novel.

The mother of two grown daughters, she lives in San Diego with her husband, Ray Huard, a journalist.

FOR FURTHER DISCUSSION

1. Nellie wants to be a 'real' journalist. What does that mean, in her opinion? And in yours?

2. Some of the main characters are facing career and personal crises. How does the story they are chasing help them deal with their issues?

3. Dame Cavendish is eccentric and self-absorbed, but there seems to be more to her than what we see on the surface. What do you think is motivating her?

4. Finn is a bit of a mystery. Who do you think he really is? Is he a trustworthy character? Why (not)?

5. La Joya is full of recognizable eccentric character types. Do you know such quirky characters in your home town? How are they the same/different from the characters in *Dead on My Feet*?

6. The *Coastal Crier* is a local newspaper trying to survive in an ever-changing media landscape. Does your town have such a paper? Do you read it? Why (not)?

7. Do you think a free press is essential to American life?

8. Should endangered wildlife be protected? Why?

9. How do you feel about products using materials made from animals, such as leather, fur, silk, pearls, wool and feathers?

10. If this were a movie, who should play Dame Cavendish? And the other characters?

ACKNOWLEDGMENTS

Special thanks to my friends and family for their support, notably, Ray, Jess, Bre, Jean, Dennis, Karen, Raven, and younger daughter, Becky, who in particular helped me navigate the world of social media and all things technical; editor John Cannon, who guided me through the first draft of this novel with a keen eye and humor most wry; and to the wonderful staff at CamCat, especially Helga Schier, who inspired me throughout this fascinating journey. A shout-out to photographer Nancee Lewis for her wizardry.

If you've enjoyed
Patricia Broderick's *Dead on My Feet*,
you'll enjoy
***Jove Brand Is Near Death* by J. A. Crawford**

The world loves Jove Brand, and Ken Allen almost killed him. Ken played the famous superspy in *Near Death*, one of the worst movies ever made. When his celebrated successor is killed in the same gruesome fashion he used to dispatch the villain in *Near Death*, Ken's only chance to prove his innocence is to go full method and play the part of Jove Brand for real.

CHAPTER ONE

I was waiting in the wings, staring out at a live studio audience with seven million viewers behind them, and like everything that had ever happened to me worth mentioning, it was because of *Near Death*.

I looked good for my age, trim in my salmon blazer over a blue button-down and brushed-watercolor tie. Vintage Ken Allen, on the bare fringe of pop culture I occupied. For all intents and purposes, I was born in this outfit and had no doubt I would be buried in it. At least the jacket hid the wet patches under my arms.

"We might not even need you."

The executive producer was hoping for the best, but you didn't keep *Beautiful Downtown Burbank* running every Friday night for thirty years without preparing for the worst. Which was why they dug me up. If there was one thing I was good at, it was taking the hit. If the scene needed saving, I would make the perfect sacrifice.

"Keep an eye on the monitors. Come back when the house band wraps up."

It wasn't the most tactful way of telling me to get lost, but the guy had a lot on his mind.

"Just happy to be here," I told him. I'd been living a lie for eighteen years, why not keep it going?

I turned away from the stage that didn't want me and wandered around behind the scenes, following the pre-show progress on the countless monitors mounted in the halls and cramped dressing rooms, both dreading and praying they would need me.

On the far side of an open dressing-room door, a drop-dead gorgeous woman was doing her own makeup. I didn't mean to stare, but it was hard not to, with her making those getting-ready faces that, for whatever reason, I had always found hotter than anything a woman did after getting ready. She was glamorous in an evening gown that had Brand Beauty written all over it.

She caught me reflecting. "Yeah?"

"Sorry. Just killing time until someone tells me to go home."

"What are you here for? Like, who are you?"

I wasn't offended. All those fuses were blown long ago. I wasn't surprised either. *Beautiful Downtown Burbank* was known for its young cast.

"I'm nobody," I said. "But once upon a time, I was Jove Brand."

"No you weren't." She looked up to think, ticking off the timeline on her fingers. "First it was the mean guy— so hot— then the prissy guy, before Sir Collin."

"I was between the prissy guy and Sir Collin."

She didn't reply, but her face said it all. Claiming you were Jove Brand was too big of a lie. You'd be better off pretending you were an astronaut or had invented touch screens. I took my phone off airplane mode and typed *Ken Allen Near Death*. It knew what I wanted when I got to the N in *Near Death*.

The first image result was me, eighteen years ago, pointing a pistol at the camera. I was trying for tough but came off looking confused about how this lemon tasted.

Pretend Brand Beauty—though I suppose they were all pretend—snatched my phone and swiped through the sequence of images that all too accurately told my life story. She stopped on the one of me holding up a container of Kick-A-Noodles.

"Nice."

"A week's worth of sodium in one little can." It was one of the ten or so responses I had ready for one-time exchanges. Meet a hundred thousand people sometime and you'll develop a list too.

Brand Beauty handed my phone back with an appraising tilt of the head, trying to decide if she liked what she saw. She stroked the front of my salmon blazer. "This isn't from props."

"I brought my own."

"You got the look, kid," she said, giving my cheek a squeeze.

My blessing and my curse. "You can't get by on looks alone."

I stepped aside to let her pass. She turned back, just out of arm's reach. That was when I caught the act. Until then her performance had been flawless.

"I'm just screwing with you, Ken. Everyone is so hyped you made it. *Near Death* is such a piece of shit. I love it."

I didn't step on her exit. That girl was going places. I hoped they would be good ones. On the monitors, the cold open was crashing hard. The tension in the air said it all—Jove Brand was in the building, and the audience was restless for his entrance.

I reminded myself to breathe on the path back to stage right. Jove Brand almost ran me over, but I stepped aside in time. He walked onstage ready for action, the king of his jungle.

Bone dry under glaring, thousand-degree spotlights and 14 million eyeballs, Collin Prestor—sorry, *Sir* Collin Prestor—made a tuxedo look like casual wear. There was acting and there was acting and then there was being able to control when you sweat. Whether it came with British blood or was the product of a Shakespearean theater pedigree I would never know. Lawndale, California, wasn't exactly London, England.

The audience went wild. The world's most famous fictional superspy stood before them. Women wanted him. Men wanted to be him. And Jove Brand was about to announce his chosen successor to the waiting world.

That successor now stepped from the shadows to stand beside me in the wings, waiting for his grand entrance. Niles Endsworth would be the next Jove Brand. He bore the same label as his predecessor, but of modern vintage, with a body sculpted by a strict regimen designed to produce a physique like a special effect. I couldn't fault Niles. He was just giving today's audience what they demanded in a hero.

Despite everything Niles had on his mind, I rated a second glance. He had been expecting the Ken Allen of eighteen years past, an image imprisoned in cinematic infamy.

The kid was a good actor. He was almost able to mask his disappointment. When his cue came, Niles snapped to the present and rushed to join his predecessor on stage. The merest sheen of perspiration betrayed the junior man's anxiety. His calculated display won the audience over. They'd be freaking out too, if they had been chosen to be the next Jove Brand. But the next Jove Brand would also have the nerve to mask it.

The two Brands, old and new, discussed the perks of playing an icon of fiction. You wore tailored clothes while driving luxury vehicles to exclusive locales. You could kill anyone who annoyed you. You always got the girl, who either conveniently died or disappeared between escapades. They played their roles to the hilt, master and apprentice. The production assistants could have ditched their cue cards and snagged a sandwich for all the good they were doing.

The problem was no one laughed. The part of Jove Brand had never been cast based on comedic chops. Fault for the only farcical portrayal of the character landed squarely on me and no one was looking to repeat that mistake. Sir Collin and Niles were gifted the perfunctory chuckles any incredibly attractive person with half a sense of humor scores, but the audience rapidly cooled as the initial rush of watching two Jove Brands together faded.

Beautiful Downtown Burbank's executive producer white-knuckled his headset, waving me toward the stage like it was a live grenade in need of a warm body. *This is what you're here for, isn't it?*

Yes, yes it was.

A life lesson: Go at whatever you're dreading full tilt. Sprint right into it. The worst thing that could happen was the entire world got to witness the train wreck for time eternal. That your epic failure would become an object lesson studied—literally—in college courses. That you became a walking punch line.

It really wasn't so bad.

I exploded onto the stage with a butterfly twist, transitioning into a flurry of fancy kicks, battling through a horde of unseen foes toward Sir Collin and Niles. I kept the phantom attacks wide and slow to ensure the audience could follow along. This was all on me. I'd choreographed the sequence myself, drawing from an arsenal of techniques made instinctual through decades of dogged repetition. If you had enough tenacity, you could fool people into believing it was talent.

I hit my mark an arm's length from the two Brands. Right on the bull's-eye. My surprise appearance had shocked the audience into complete silence. A small section of the crowd hooted, then the hoots built to applause and my heart started up again. Some of them were ringers but the rest sounded like my demographic—hipsters in the know.

I stretched the moment, resting my hands on my thighs as if I had come a long way. Pretending to catch my breath let me avoid eye contact not only with the audience but also with the two men who were arguably my contemporaries.

Sir Collin and Niles turned to face the interloper who had fought his way into their conversation. The consummate pro, Sir Collin held his expression through the cheers, freezing the scene for as long as it had legs. Meanwhile, my stomach explored heretofore unknown depths. When the crowd quieted, the time had come for me to deliver my first line.

"Sorry, my good men," I panted. "Bike broke down. Asian imports, you know?"

It was a good thing I was supposed to sound breathless. My American-cum-British accent was atrocious. I could have done better, but who wanted that?

It didn't get a huge laugh, but the audience members in on the joke lost their minds. No one wrote for the audience anymore, anyway. They wrote for the internet, for the bloggers, the tweeters, and the streamers. They let the fans explain the references in postmortem. There was nothing like free labor, and no one worked as hard as someone made to feel smart.

"How *did* you get in here?" Sir Collin asked. Stressing the *did*, not the *you*, kept the question at the appropriate level of condescending. Considering the audience's reaction to my appearance, it was the right choice.

"Who is he?" Niles asked.

Sir Collin moved to block the younger man's view. "No one worth remembering. Now, as I was saying, a gentleman shoots only once, and never first."

I stepped out from behind Sir Collin to add, "But he chops as many throats as required."

Don't ask me why, but that's when I ad-libbed. Not a line, not on live television—I'm not a monster. I offered an unplanned hand to Niles, who furtively extended his own in return. As we were about to touch, I turned my shake into a knife-hand aimed at his Adam's apple. Niles hopped back, genuinely shocked. I threw him a wink and a nod, my eyes a little crazy.

The big screens facing the audience had been playing a *Near Death* highlight montage from the moment I crashed the sketch. Now that everyone was in on the joke that was Ken Allen, the entire studio erupted in laughter at my action and Niles's reaction. It was a dizzying level of hot onstage. I reminded myself to not lock my knees.

Sir Collin moved between us again, precise in rhythm and position. The stage was his native turf, the sacred ground he retreated to when he wasn't playing a super-spy. He was fighting for Niles's attention now.

"He always looks his foe in the eyes." The strain in Sir Collin's voice projected concern his successor was learning all the wrong lessons.

"Then gouges them!" I interrupted, darting my fingers at Niles like a striking snake. I mimed a second, goofier gouge as Sir Collin put an arm around my shoulders. He turned our backs to Niles for a confidential moment as we switched cameras, me and Sir Collin and the millions watching at home.

"Ken, old boy, I'm trying to impart some wisdom on the lad," Sir Collin said. "You understand, don't you?"

Trust me, I did. Sir Collin had starred in six Jove Brand movies over fifteen years, each more successful than the last. If anyone could speak with authority on how to play Brand, it was him. He was so authentic, so genuine, it made me want to leave. But that wasn't the scene.

I hoped my attempt at a wide-eyed, thoughtful nod conveyed understanding. "Oooh. Sorry about that, Sir Collin." I forgot to use my crappy British accent, but breaking character fortuitously worked for the scene. The audience roared at every beat. Opening monologues were tough pitches to hit, and the writers had knocked this one out of the park.

"There's a good man." Sir Collin gave me a pat I liked a little too much before turning to again address Niles. "Now, when a lady demurs—"

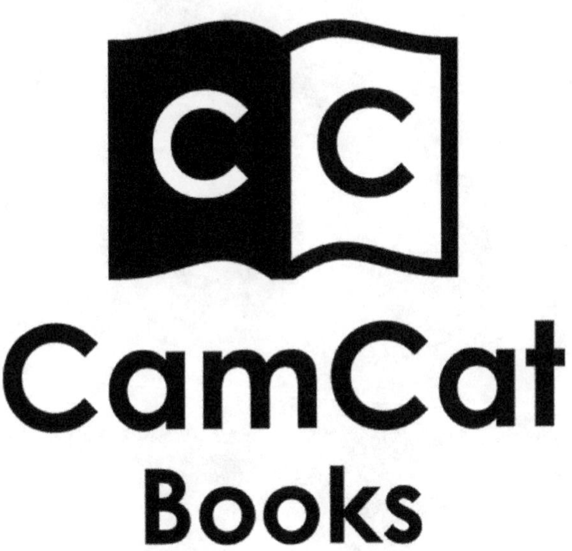
CC
CamCat
Books

CPSIA information can be obtained
at www.ICGtesting.com
Printed in the USA
LVHW111512020621
689150LV00008B/596/J